RAVE REVIEWS FOR KINSEY MILLHONE
AND *E IS FOR EVIDENCE*

"The best detective fiction I have read in years. . . . The plot is just fine and does what a plot ought to in a good detective novel: it keeps us turning pages and serves as a vehicle for the *really* interesting stuff, an unveiling of the characters' foibles by the worldly-wise but uncorrupt private eye. And this is where Sue Grafton shines. She has endowed Kinsey with that most important attribute of a fictional private eye, a distinct voice. . . . Her observations on the surrounding society are right on the money without being condescending. . . . Lord, how I like this Kinsey Millhone. May her practice flourish."
—Vincent Patrick, *The New York Times Book Review*

"A delectable detective. . . . Grafton is a funny writer; her movements are crisp, her dialogue snappy, and (though Kinsey denies it) her heroine has class."
—*Newsweek*

"Kinsey, as always, is a delight. . . . Sharp, sassy, and straight-forward."
—*Christian Science Monitor*

"Grafton has an accurate, wicked eye for California lifestyle and wisecracking Kinsey is an appealing, nonhackneyed female detective. . . . Readers will be glad that further letters of the alphabet await Grafton's imagination."
—*Publishers Weekly*

"An unflagging pace, skilled buildup of tension, lively characters, and Kinsey's offbeat charm make this yet another of the author's first-class entertainments."
—*Kirkus Reviews*

"Exceptionally strong . . . A crackling good story."
—*The Drood Review of Mystery*

"*E* is also for excellent. . . . Grafton is an extremely clever plotter and Kinsey Millhone is a witty and gritty private eye. It will be a pleasure to read her from A to Z."
—*Cincinnati Post*

Also by Sue Grafton

*A Is for Alibi

*B Is for Burglar

*C Is for Corpse

*D Is for Deadbeat

*E Is for Evidence

*F Is for Fugitive

G Is for Gumshoe

H Is for Homicide

I Is for Innocent

J Is for Judgment

K Is for Killer

L Is for Lawless

M Is for Malice

N Is for Noose

O Is for Outlaw

P Is for Peril

Q Is for Quarry

R Is for Ricochet

Coming soon:

S Is for Silence

*From St. Martin's Griffin

E **Is** for Evidence

A Kinsey Millhone Mystery

SUE GRAFTON

St. Martin's Griffin ⚜ New York

www.stmartins.com

Library of Congress Catalog Card Number: 87-28100

ISBN 0-312-35380-4
EAN 978-0-312-35380-3

First published in the United States by Henry Holt and Company

First St. Martin's Griffin Edition: December 2005

10 9 8 7 6 5 4 3 2 1

For my two mothers, past and present:
Viv and Lillian

The author wishes to acknowledge the invaluable assistance of the following people: Steven Humphrey; Jim Hetherington, President, and Dorcas Lube, Office Manager, Hetherington, Inc.; Bruce Boller, First Vice President, Institutional Services, Robert W. Baird, Inc.; Joyce Mackewich and Kim Nelson of Montgomery, Fansler & Carlson Insurance; Dennis W. Leski; William Pasich; Robert Snowball; Caroline Ware, Santa Barbara Travel; Elisa Moran, Santa Barbara County Registrar of Voters; Kathleen Hotchkiss, Culinary Alliance and Bartenders Local 498; Anne Reid; Frank and Florence Clark; Lynn Herold, Ph.D., Senior Criminalist, Department of Chief Medical Examiner-Coroner, Los Angeles County; George Donner, A-1 Tri-Counties Investigations; Detective Robert J. Lowry, Investigative Division, Santa Barbara Police Department; and Deputy Juan Tejeda, Santa Barbara County Sheriff's Department.

1

It was Monday, December 27, and I was sitting in my office, trying to get a fix on the mood I was in, which was bad, bad, bad, comprised of equal parts irritation and uneasiness. The irritation was generated by a bank notice I'd just received, one of those windowed numbers with a yellow carbon showing through. At first, I assumed I was overdrawn, but what I pulled out was a slip, dated Friday, December 24, showing a five-thousand-dollar deposit to my checking account.

"What the hell is this?" I said.

The account number was correct, but the deposit wasn't mine. In my experience, banks are the least helpful institutions on earth, and the notion of having to stop what I was doing to straighten out an error was nearly more than I could bear. I tossed the notice aside, trying to reclaim my concentration. I was getting ready to write up the preliminary report on an insurance case I'd been asked to look into, and Darcy, the secretary at California Fidelity, had just buzzed to say that Mac wanted the file on his desk right away. Mentally, I'd come up with a tart suggestion about what she could do with herself, but I'd kept my mouth shut, showing (I thought) admirable restraint.

I turned back to my portable Smith-Corona, inserting the proper form for a property-insurance-loss register. My nimble fingers were poised to type while I reviewed my notes. That's where I was stuck. Something was off and I couldn't figure out what it was. I glanced at the bank notice again.

Almost with an eye toward the comic relief, I called the bank, hoping the diversion would help me focus on what was bothering me about the situation at Wood/Warren, a local company manufacturing hydrogen furnaces for industrial use. They'd had a fire out there on December 19 that had destroyed a warehouse.

"Mrs. Brunswick, Customer Service. May I help you?"

"Well, I hope so," I said. "I just received a notice saying I put five thousand dollars in my checking account last Friday and I didn't do that. Is there any way you can straighten it out?"

"May I have your name and account number, please?"

"Kinsey Millhone," I said, supplying my account number in slow, measured tones.

She put me on hold briefly while she called up the records on her computer terminal. Meanwhile, I listened to the bank's rendition of "Good King Wenceslas," which I've personally never understood. What's the Feast of Stephen?

Mrs. Brunswick clicked back in. "Miss Millhone, I'm not certain what the problem is, but we do show a cash deposit to this account number. Apparently, it was left in the night-deposit slot and posted over the weekend."

"You still have one of those night-deposit slots?" I asked with amazement.

"At our downtown branch, yes," she said.

"Well, there's some kind of mistake here. I've never even seen the night-deposit slot. I use my twenty-four-hour instant teller card if I need to transact bank business after hours. What do we do now?"

"I can track down a copy of the deposit slip," she said skeptically.

"Would you do that, please? Because I didn't make a deposit of any kind last Friday and certainly not five thousand dollars' worth. Maybe somebody transposed some numbers on the deposit slip or something, but the money sure doesn't belong to me."

She took my telephone number and said she'd get back to me. I could tell I was in for countless phone calls before the correction could be made. Suppose somebody was merrily writing checks against that five grand?

I went back to the task at hand, wishing I felt more enlightened than I did. My mind kept jumping around. The file on the fire claim at Wood/Warren had actually come into my hands four days before, late Thursday, the 23rd. I'd been scheduled to have a farewell drink with my landlord, Henry Pitts, at four, and then take him out to the airport and put him on a plane. He was flying back to Michigan to spend the holidays with his family, some of whom are edging into their nineties with their vigor and good spirits still in evidence. Henry's pushing eighty-two, a mere kid, and he was about as excited as one at the prospect of the trip.

I was still at the office that afternoon with my paperwork caught up and some time to kill. I went out onto my second-floor balcony, peering off to my right at the V of Pacific Ocean visible at the foot of State Street, ten blocks down. This is Santa Teresa, California, ninety-five miles north of Los Angeles. Winter here is a grand affair, full of sunshine and mild temperatures, vibrant magenta bougainvillea, gentle winds, and palm trees waving fronds at the sea gulls as they wheel overhead.

The only signs of Christmas, two days away, were the garlands of tinsel strung along the main streets.

The stores, of course, were packed with shoppers, and there was a trio of Salvation Army horn players tooting away at "Deck the Halls." In the interests of feeling jolly, I thought I'd better work out my strategy for the next two days.

Anyone who knows me will tell you that I cherish my unmarried state. I'm female, twice divorced, no kids, and no close family ties. I'm a private detective by trade. Usually I'm perfectly content to do what I do. There are times when I work long hours on a case and times when I'm on the road and times when I hole up in my tiny apartment and read books for days. When the holidays come around, however, I find that I have to exercise a certain cunning lest the absence of loved ones generate unruly depression. Thanksgiving had been a breeze. I spent the day with Henry and some pals of his, who'd cooked and sipped champagne and laughed and told tales about days long past, making me wish I were their age instead of my own, which is thirty-two.

Now Henry was leaving town, and even Rosie, who runs the dingy neighborhood tavern where I often eat, was closing down until January 2, refusing to tell a soul what she meant to do with herself. Rosie is sixty-six, Hungarian, short, top-heavy, bossy, and often rude, so it wasn't as though I was worried I'd miss any touching heart-to-heart chats. The fact that she

was closing her eatery was simply one more uncomfortable reminder that I was out there in the world all
by myself and had best find a way to look after me.

At any rate, I'd glanced at my watch and decided I
might as well head on home. I switched on the answering machine, grabbed my jacket and handbag,
and was just locking up when Darcy Pascoe, the receptionist from the insurance company next door,
popped her head in. I had worked for California Fidelity full time at one point, doing investigations on
fire and wrongful death claims. Now the arrangement
is informal. I'm more or less on call, doing a certain
number of investigations for them, as needed, in exchange for downtown office space I couldn't otherwise afford.

"Oh, wow. I'm glad I caught you," Darcy said.
"Mac told me to give you this."

She handed me a file, which I glanced at automatically. The blank form inside indicated that I was being asked to do a fire-scene inspection, the first in
months.

"Mac did?" Mac is the CFI vice-president. I
couldn't imagine him handling routine paperwork.

"Well, actually, Mac gave it to Andy and Andy said
I should give it to you."

There was a memo attached to the file cover, dated
three days before and marked RUSH. Darcy caught my
look and her cheeks tinted faintly.

"It was stuck under a big pile of stuff on my desk or I'd have gotten it to you sooner," she said. Darcy's in her late twenties and something of a flake. I crossed to my desk, tossing the file on top of some others I was working on. I'd catch it first thing in the morning. Darcy lingered in the doorway, guessing my intent.

"Is there any way you can get to that today? I know he's anxious to get somebody out there. Jewel was supposed to handle it, but she's taking two weeks off, so Mac said maybe you could do it instead."

"What's the claim?"

"A big warehouse fire out in Colgate. You probably heard it on the news."

I shook my head. "I've been down in L.A."

"Well, the newspaper clippings are in there, too. I guess they want someone out there superquick."

I was annoyed at the pressure, but I opened the manila folder again and checked the property-loss notice, which was posted on top. "Wood/Warren?" I said.

"You know the company?"

"I know the Woods. I went to high school with the youngest girl. We were in the same homeroom."

She looked relieved, as if I'd just solved a problem for her. "That's great. I'll tell Mac maybe you can get out there this afternoon."

"Darcy, would you knock that off? I've got to take

somebody to the airport," I said. "Trust me. I'll make an appointment for the earliest possible moment."

"Oh. Well, I'll make a note then so they'll know you're taking care of it," she said. "I have to get back to the phones. Let me know when you have the report and I'll come pick it up."

"Terrific," I said. She must have decided she had pushed me far enough because she excused herself and disappeared in haste.

As soon as she left, just to get it over with, I put a call through to Wood/Warren and arranged to meet with the company president, Lance Wood, at 9:00 the next morning, Christmas Eve day.

Meanwhile, as it was 3:45, I tucked the file in my handbag, locked up, and headed down the back stairs to the lot where my VW was parked. I was home ten minutes later.

During our little pre-Christmas celebration, Henry gave me a new Len Deighton novel and I gave him a periwinkle-blue mohair muffler, which I had crocheted myself—a little-known talent of mine. We sat in his kitchen and ate half a pan of his homemade cinnamon rolls, drinking champagne out of the matching crystal flutes I'd given him the year before.

He took out his plane ticket and checked the departure time again, his cheeks flushed with anticipation. "I wish you'd come with me," he said. He had the muffler wrapped around his neck, the color setting off his eyes. His white hair was soft and brushed to one side, his lean face tanned from California sun.

"I wish I could, but I just picked up some work that'll get my rent paid," I said. "You can take lots of pictures and show 'em to me when you get back."

"What about Christmas Day? You're not going to be by yourself, I hope."

"Henry, would you quit worrying? I've got lots of friends." I'd probably spend the day alone, but I didn't want him to fret.

He raised a finger. "Hold on. I almost forgot. I have another little present for you." He crossed to the counter by the kitchen sink and picked up a clump of greenery in a little pot. He set it down in front of me, laughing when he saw the expression on my face. It looked like a fern and smelled like feet.

"It's an air fern," he said. "It just lives on air. You don't even have to water it."

I stared at the lacy fronds, which were a nearly luminous green and looked like something that might thrive in outer space. "No plant food?"

He shook his head. "Just let it sit."

"I don't have to worry about diffuse sunlight or pinching back?" I asked, tossing around some plant terms as if I knew what they meant. I'm notoriously bad with plants, and for years I've resisted any urge whatever to own one.

"Nothing. It's to keep you company. Put it on your desk. It'll jazz the place up a bit."

I held the little pot up and inspected the fern from all sides, experiencing this worrisome spark of possessiveness. I must be in worse shape than I thought, I thought.

Henry fished a set of keys out of his pocket and passed them over to me. "In case you need to get into my place," he said.

"Great. I'll bring in your mail and the papers. Is there anything else you need done while you're gone? I can mow the grass."

"You don't need to do that. I've left you the number where I can be reached if the Big One hits. I can't think of anything else." The Big One he referred to was the major earthquake we'd all been expecting any day now since the last one in 1925.

He checked his watch. "We better get a move on. The airport is mobbed this time of year." His plane wasn't leaving until 7:00, which left us only an hour and a half to make the twenty-minute trip to the airport, but there wasn't any point in arguing. Sweet man. If he had to wait, he might as well do it out there, happily chatting with his fellow travelers.

I put on my jacket while Henry made a circuit of

the house, taking a few seconds to turn the heat down, making sure the windows and doors were secured. He picked up his coat and his suitcase and we were on our way.

I was home again by 6:15, still feeling a bit of a lump in my throat. I hate to say goodbye to folks and I hate being left behind. It was getting dark by then and the air had a bite to it. I let myself into my place. My studio apartment was formerly Henry's single-car garage. It's approximately fifteen feet on a side, with a narrow extension on the right that serves as my kitchenette. I have laundry facilities and a compact bathroom. The space has been cleverly designed and apportioned to suggest the illusion of living room, dining room, and bedroom once I open my sofa bed. I have more than adequate storage space for the few things I possess.

Surveying my tiny kingdom usually fills me with satisfaction, but I was still battling a whisper of Yuletide depression, and the place seemed claustrophobic and bleak. I turned on some lights. I put the air fern on my desk. Ever hopeful, I checked my answering machine for messages, but there were none. The quiet was making me feel restless. I turned on the radio—Bing Crosby singing about a white Christmas just like the ones he used to know. I've never actually seen a white Christmas, but I got the gist. I turned the radio off.

I sat on a kitchen stool and monitored my vital signs. I was hungry. One thing about living alone . . . you can eat any time you want. For dinner that night I made myself a sandwich of olive-pimento cheese on whole-wheat bread. It's a source of comfort to me that the brand of olive-pimento cheese I buy has tasted exactly the same since the first time I remembered eating it at the age of three and a half. Resolutely I veered off *that* subject, since it connected to my parents, who were killed when I was five. I cut the sandwich into four fingers, as I always did, poured myself a glass of white wine, and took my plate over to the couch, where I opened the book Henry had given me for Christmas. I checked the clock.

It was 7:00 P.M. This was going to be a very long two weeks.

2

The next morning, December 24, I jogged three miles, showered, ate a bowl of cereal, packed a canvas tote with supplies, and was heading toward Colgate by 8:45, a quick ten-mile drive. I'd reviewed the file over breakfast, and I was already puzzled about what the big rush was. The newspaper account indicated that the warehouse was gutted, but there was no telltale closing line about arson, investigations pending, or any speculation that the nature of the blaze was suspect. The fire-department report was included, and I'd read that twice. It all looked routine. Apparently the origin of the fire was a malfunction in the electrical system, which had simultaneously shorted out the sprinklers. Since the materials stored in the two-story structure were largely paper goods, the 2:00 A.M. fire had spread rapidly. According to the fire inspector at the scene, there was no sign of firetraps, no gasoline or other flammables, and no sign of obstacles placed so as to impede the work of the firemen. There was no indication that doors or windows had been left open to create favorable drafts and no other physical evidence of incendiary origin. I'd read dozens of reports just like this one. So what was the big deal here? I wondered. Maybe I was missing a crucial piece of information, but as far as I could see, this was a standard claim. I had to guess that somebody at Wood/Warren was putting the squeeze on California Fidelity for a speedy settlement, which might explain Andy's panic. He's a nail-biter by inclination, anxious for approval, worried about censure, in the middle of marital problems, from what I'd heard. He was probably the source of the little note of hysteria that had crept into the case. Maybe Mac was leaning on him, too.

Colgate is the bedroom community that adjoins Santa Teresa, providing affordable housing for average working folk. While new construction in Santa Teresa is closely regulated by the Architectural Board of Review, building in Colgate has proceeded according to no known plan, though it leans toward the nondescript. There is one major street lined with donut shops, hardware stores, fast-food establishments, beauty salons, and furniture stores that feature veneer and laminate, velour and Naugahyde. From the main thoroughfare, tract homes stretch out

in all directions, housing styles appearing like con-
centric rings on a tree stump, spiraling out decade by
decade until the new neighborhoods peter out into
raw countryside, or what's left of it. In isolated
patches there are still signs of the old citrus groves
that once flourished there.

Wood/Warren was located on a side street that angled back toward an abandoned drive-in theater that
functions as a permanent location for weekend swap
sales. The lawns of the neighboring manufacturing
plants were a close-clipped green, and the shrubs
were trimmed into perfect rectangles. I found a parking place out front and locked up. The building was a
compact story and a half of stucco and fieldstone.
The address of the warehouse itself was two blocks
away. I'd inspect the fire scene after I talked to Lance
Wood.

The reception area was small and plain, furnished
with a desk, a bookcase, and an enlarged photograph
of the FIFA 5000 Hydrogen/Vacuum Furnace, the
mainstay of the company fortunes. It looked like an
oversized unit for an efficiency kitchen, complete with
stainless-steel counter and built-in microwave. According to the data neatly framed nearby, the front-
loading FIFA 5000 provided five thousand cubic
inches of uniform hot zone for hydrogen or vacuum
brazing, for metallizing ceramics, or manufacturing
ceramic-to-metal seals. I should have guessed.

Behind me, the receptionist was returning to her desk with a fresh cup of coffee and a Styrofoam container that smelled of sausage and eggs. The laminated plastic sign on her desk indicated that her name was Heather. She was in her twenties and apparently hadn't yet heard about the hazards of cholesterol and fat. She would find the latter on her fanny one day soon.

"May I help you?" Her smile was quick, exposing braces on her teeth. Her complexion was still ruddy from last night's application of an acne cure that so far hadn't had much effect.

"I have an appointment with Lance Wood at nine," I said. "I'm with California Fidelity Insurance."

Her smile faded slightly. "You're the arson investigator?"

"Well, I'm here on the fire claim," I said, wondering if she mistakenly assumed that "arson" and "fire" were interchangeable terms.

"Oh. Mr. Wood isn't in yet, but he should be here momentarily," she said. The braces infused her speech with a sibilance that amused her when she heard herself. "Can I get you some coffee while you wait?"

I shook my head. There was one chair available and I took a seat, amusing myself by leafing through a brochure on the molybdenum work rack designed specifically for metallizing alumina at 1450°C. in a bell-style hydrogen furnace. These people had about as many laughs as I do at home, where a prime source of entertainment is a textbook on practical aspects of ballistics, firearms, and forensic techniques.

Through a doorway to my left, I could see some of the office staff, casually dressed and busy, but glum. I didn't pick up any sense of camaraderie among them, but maybe hydrogen furnace-making doesn't generate the kind of good-natured bantering I'm accustomed to with California Fidelity. Two desks were unoccupied, bare of equipment or accouterments.

Some attempt had been made to decorate for Christmas. There was an artificial tree across the room from me, tall and skeletal, hung with multicolored ornaments. There didn't seem to be any lights strung on the tree, which gave it a lifeless air and only pointed up the uniformity of the detachable limbs stuck into pre-bored holes in the aluminum shaft. The effect was dispiriting. From the information I'd been given, Wood/Warren grossed close to fifteen million bucks a year, and I wondered why they wouldn't pop for a live pine.

Heather gave me a self-conscious smile and began to eat. Behind her was a bulletin board decorated with garlands of tinsel and covered with snapshots of the family and staff. H-A-P-P-Y H-O-L-I-D-A-Y-S was spelled out in jaunty store-bought silver letters.

"Mind if I look at that?" I asked, indicating the collage.

By then, she had a mouth full of breakfast crois-
sant, but she managed assent, holding a hand in front
of her mouth to spare me the sight of her masticated
food. "Help yourself."

Most of the photographs were of company employees, some of whom I'd seen on the premises.
Heather was featured in one, her fair hair much
shorter, her face still framed in baby fat. The braces
on her teeth probably represented the last vestige of
her teens. Wood/Warren must have hired her right
out of high school. In one photograph, four guys in
company coveralls stood in a relaxed group on the
front doorstep. Some of the shots were stiffly posed,
but for the most part they seemed to capture an aura
of goodwill I wasn't picking up on currently. The
founder of the company, Linden "Woody" Wood,
had died two years before, and I wondered if some of
the joy had gone out of the place with his demise.

The Woods themselves formed the centerpiece in
a studio portrait that looked like it was taken at the
family home. Mrs. Wood was seated in a French
Provincial chair. Linden stood with his hand resting
on his wife's shoulder. The five grown children were
ranged around their parents. Lance I'd never met before, but I knew Ash because I'd gone to high school
with her. Olive, older by a year, had attended Santa
Teresa High briefly, but had been sent off to a boarding school in her senior year. There was probably a

minor scandal attached to that, but I wasn't sure what it was. The oldest of the five was Ebony, who by now must be nearly forty. I remembered hearing that she'd married some rich playboy and was living in France. The youngest was a son named Bass, not quite thirty, reckless, irresponsible, a failed actor and no-talent musician, living in New York City, the last I'd heard. I had met him briefly eight years before through my ex-husband, Daniel, a jazz pianist. Bass was the black sheep of the family. I wasn't sure what the story was on Lance.

Seated across his desk from him sixty-six minutes later, I began to pick up a few hints. Lance had breezed in at 9:30. The receptionist indicated who I was. He introduced himself and we shook hands. He said he had a quick phone call to make and then he'd be right with me. I said "Fine" and that was the last I saw of him until 10:06. By then, he'd shed his suit coat and loosened his tie along with the top button of his dress shirt. He was sitting with his feet up on the desk, his face oily-looking under the fluorescent lights. He must have been in his late thirties, but he wasn't aging well. Some combination of temper and discontent had etched lines near his mouth and spoiled the clear brown of his eyes, leaving an impression of a man beleaguered by the Fates. His hair was light brown, thinning on top, and combed straight back from his face. I thought the business about the phone call was bullshit. He struck me as the sort of man who pumped up his own sense of importance by making people wait. His smile was self-satisfied, and the energy he radiated was charged with tension.

"Sorry for the delay," he said. "What can I do for you?" He was tipped back in his swivel chair, his thighs splayed.

"I understand you filed a claim for a recent fire loss."

"That's right, and I hope you're not going to give me any static over that. Believe me, I'm not asking for anything I'm not entitled to."

I made a noncommittal murmur of some sort, hoping to conceal the fact that I'd gone on "fraud alert." Every insurance piker I'd ever met said just that, right down to the pious little toss of the head. I took out my tape recorder, flicked it on, and set it on the desk. "The company requires that I tape the interview," I said.

"That's fine."

I directed my next few remarks to the recorder, establishing my name, the fact that I worked for California Fidelity, the date and time of the interview, and the fact that I was speaking to Lance Wood in his capacity as president and CEO of Wood/Warren, the address of the company, and the nature of the loss.

"Mr. Wood, you do understand that this is being taped," I said for the benefit of the record.

"Yes."

"And do I have your permission to make this recording of the conversation we're about to have?"

"Yes, yes," he said, making that little rolling hand gesture that means "Let's get on with it."

I glanced down at the file. "Can you tell me the circumstances of the fire that occurred at the Wood/ Warren warehouse at 606 Fairweather on December nineteenth of this year?"

He shifted impatiently. "Actually, I was out of town, but from what I'm told . . ." The telephone intercom buzzed and he snatched up the receiver, barking at it like a dog. "Yes?"

There was a pause. "Well, goddamn it, put her through." He gave me a quick look. "No, wait a minute, I'll take it out there." He put the phone down, excused himself brusquely, and left the room. I clicked off the recorder, mentally assessing the brief impression I'd had of him as he passed. He was getting heavy in the waist and his gabardine pants rode up unbecomingly, his shirt sticking to the center of his back. He smelled harshly of sweat—not that clean animal scent that comes from a hard workout, but the pungent, faintly repellant odor of stress. His complexion was sallow and he looked vaguely unhealthy.

I waited for fifteen minutes and then tiptoed to the door. The reception area was deserted. No sign of Lance Wood. No sign of Heather. I moved over to the door leading into the inner office. I caught a glimpse of someone passing into the rear of the building who looked very much like Ebony, but I couldn't be sure. A woman looked up at me. The name plate on her desk indicated that she was Ava Daugherty, the office manager. She was in her late forties, with a small, dusky face and a nose that looked as if it had been surgically tampered with. Her hair was short and black, with the glossy patina of hair spray. She was unhappy about something, possibly the fact that she'd just cracked one of her bright-red acrylic fingernails.

"I'm supposed to be meeting with Lance Wood, but he's disappeared. Do you know where he went?"

"He left the plant." She was licking the cracked nail experimentally, as if the chemistry of her saliva might serve as adhesive.

"He left?"

"That's what I said."

"Did he say how soon he'd be back?"

"Mr. Wood doesn't consult with me," she said snappishly. "If you'd like to leave your name, I'm sure he'll get back to you."

A voice cut in. "Something wrong?"

We both looked up to find a dark-haired man standing in the doorway behind me. Ava Daugherty's manner became somewhat less antagonistic. "This is the company vice-president," she said to me. And to him, "She's supposed to be in a meeting with Lance, but he left the plant."

"Terry Kohler," he said to me, holding out his hand. "I'm Lance Wood's brother-in-law."

"Kinsey Millhone, from California Fidelity," I said, shaking hands with him. "Nice to meet you." His grip was hard and hot. He was wiry, with a dark moustache and large, dark eyes that were full of intelligence. He must have been in his early forties. I wondered which sister he was married to.

"What's the problem? Something I can help you with?"

I told him briefly what I was doing there and the fact that Lance Wood had abandoned me without a word of explanation.

"Why don't I show you the warehouse?" he said. "At least you can go ahead and inspect the fire scene, which I'm assuming is one of your responsibilities."

"I'd appreciate that. Is anybody else out here authorized to give me the information I need?"

Terry Kohler and Ava Daugherty exchanged a look I couldn't decipher.

"You better wait for Lance," he said. "Hold on and

I'll see if I can find out where he went." He moved toward the outer office.

Ava and I avoided small talk. She opened her top right-hand drawer and took out a tube of Krazy Glue, ignoring me pointedly as she snipped off the tip and squeezed one clear drop on the cracked fingernail. She frowned. A long dark hair was caught in the glue and I watched her struggle to extract it.

Idly I tuned into the conversation behind me, three engineers in a languid discussion about the problem before them.

"Now maybe the calculation is off, but I don't think so," one was saying.

"We'll find out," someone interjected. All three men laughed.

"The question came up . . . oh, this has occurred to me many times . . . What would it take to convert this to a pulse power supply for the main hot cell?"

"Depends on what your pulsing frequency is."

"About ten hertz."

"Whoa."

"Anything that would allow you to modulate a signal away that was being influenced by the juice going through the susceptors. You know, power on for nine-tenths of a second, off for a tenth. Take measurements . . ."

"Um-hum. On for a half a second, off for a tenth of a second. You can't really do it easily, can you?"

"The PID controller could send the output that fast. I'm not sure what that would do to the NCRs. To the VRT setup itself, whether that would follow it . . ."

I tuned them out again. They could have been plotting the end of the world for all I knew.

It was another ten minutes before Terry Kohler reappeared. He was shaking his head in apparent exasperation.

"I don't know what's going on around here," he said. "Lance had to go out on some emergency and Heather's still away from her desk." He held up a key ring. "I'll take you over to the warehouse. Tell Heather I've got these if she shows up."

"I should get my camera," I said. "It's with my handbag."

He tagged along patiently while I moved back to Lance Wood's office, where I retrieved the camera, tucked my wallet in my tote, and left my handbag where it was.

Together we retraced a path through the reception room and the offices beyond. Nobody actually looked up as we passed, but curious gazes followed us in silence, like those portraits where the eyes seem to move.

The assembly work was done in a large, well-ventilated area in the back half of the building with walls of corrugated metal and a floor of concrete.

We paused only once while Terry introduced me to a man named John Salkowitz. "John's a chemical engineer and consulting associate," Terry said. "He's been with us since 'sixty-six. You have any questions about high-temperature processing, he's the man you want to ask."

Offhand, I couldn't think of one—except maybe about that pulse power supply for the main hot cell. That was a poser.

Terry was moving toward the rear door, and I trotted after him.

To the right, there was a double-wide rolling steel door that could be raised to accommodate incoming shipments or to load finished units ready for delivery. We went out into the alleyway, cutting through to the street beyond.

"Which of the Wood sisters are you married to?" I asked. "I went to high school with Ash."

"Olive," he said with a smile. "What's your name again?"

I told him and we chatted idly for the remainder of the short walk, dropping into silence only when the charred skeleton of the warehouse loomed into view.

3

It took me three hours to examine the fire scene. Terry went through the motions of unlocking the front door, though the gesture seemed ludicrous given the wreckage the fire had left. Most of the outer shell of the building remained upright, but the second story had collapsed into the first, leaving a nearly impenetrable mass of blackened rubble. The glass in the first-floor windows had been blown out by the heat. Metal pipes were exposed, many twisted by the weight of the walls tumbling inward. Whatever recognizable objects remained were reduced to their abstract shapes, robbed of color and detail.

When it became apparent that I was going to be there for a while, Terry excused himself and went back to the plant. Wood/Warren was closing early that day as it was Christmas Eve. He said if I was finished soon enough, I was welcome to stop by and have some punch and Christmas cookies. I had already taken out my measuring tape, notebook, sketch pad, and pencils, mentally laying out the order in which I intended to proceed. I thanked him, scarcely aware of his departure.

I circled the perimeter of the building, noting the areas of severest burning, checking the window frames on the first floor for signs of forced entry. I wasn't sure how quickly the salvage crew would be coming in, and since there was no apparent evidence of arson, I didn't feel California Fidelity could insist on a delay. Monday morning, I would do a background check on Lance Wood's financial situation just to make sure there wasn't any hidden profit motive for the fire itself . . . a mere formality in this case, since the fire chief had already ruled out arson in his report. Since this was probably the only chance we'd have to survey the premises, I photographed everything, taking two rolls of film, twenty-four exposures each.

As nearly as I could tell, the probable point of origin of the fire was somewhere in the north wall, which seemed consistent with the theory of an electrical malfunction. I'd have to check the wiring diagram from the original blueprints, but I suspected the fire chief had done just that in coming up with his analysis. The surface of charred wood bore the typical pattern of crevices known as "alligatoring," the deepest charring and the smallest check in the pattern localized in this rear portion of the building. Since hot gases rise and fire normally sweeps upward, it's usually possible to track the course of the flames, which will tend to rise until an obstacle is encountered, then project horizontally, seeking other vertical outlets.

Much of the interior had been reduced to ashes. The load-bearing walls remained, as black and brittle as cinder. Gingerly, I picked my way through the char-broiled junk, making a detailed map of the ruins, noting the degree of burning, general appearance, and carbonization of burned objects. Every surface I encountered had been painted with the black and ashen pallor of extreme heat. The stench was familiar: scorched wood, soot, the sodden odor of drenched insulation, the lingering chemical aroma of ordinary materials reduced to their elements. There was some other odor as well, which I noted, but couldn't identify. It was probably connected to materials stored there. When I'd called Lance Wood the day before, I'd requested a copy of the inventory sheets. I'd review those to see if I could pinpoint the source of the smell. I wasn't crazy about having to inspect the fire scene before I'd had a chance to interview him, but I didn't seem to have much choice, now that he'd disappeared. Maybe he'd be back for the office Christmas party and I could pin him down then about an appointment first thing Monday morning.

At 2:00 P.M., I packed my sketch pad away and brushed off my jeans. My tennis shoes were nearly white with ash, and I suspected that my face was smudged. Still, I was reasonably content with the job I'd done. Wood/Warren was going to have to get several contractors' estimates, and those would be submitted to CFI along with my recommendation regarding payment of the claim. Using the standard rule, I was guessing five hundred thousand dollars replacement cost, with additional payment for the inventory loss.

The Christmas party was indeed in progress. The festivities were centered in the inner offices where a punch bowl had been set up on a drafting table. Desks had been cleared and were covered with platters of cold cuts, cheeses, and crackers, along with slices of fruitcake and homemade cookies. The company employees numbered about sixty, so the noise level was substantial, the general atmosphere getting looser and livelier as the champagne punch went down. Some sort of Reggae version of Christmas carols was being blasted through the intercom system.

There was still no sign of Lance Wood, but I spotted Heather on the far side of the room, her cheeks rosy with wassail. Terry Kohler caught my eye and shouldered his way in my direction. When he reached me, he leaned down close to my ear.

"We better get your handbag before this gets out of control," he said. I nodded vigorously and inched my way behind him through the reception area to Lance's office. The door was standing open and his desk was being used as a bar. Liquor bottles, ice, and plastic glasses were arranged across the surface, with several people helping themselves to both the booze and the comfort of the boss's furniture. My handbag had been tucked into a narrow slot between a file cabinet and a bookcase jammed with technical manuals. I put away my camera and sketch pad, hefting the bag onto my right shoulder. Terry offered to fetch me some punch, and after a moment of hesitation, I agreed. Hey, why not?

My first impulse was to leave as soon as I could gracefully extricate myself. I don't generally do well in group situations, and in this instance I didn't know a soul. What kept me was the sure knowledge that I had nowhere else to go. This might be the extent of my holiday celebration, and I thought I might as well enjoy it. I accepted some punch, helped myself to cheese and crackers, ate some cookies with pink and green sugar on top, smiled pleasantly, and generally made myself amenable to anyone within range. By 3:00, when the party was really getting under way, I excused myself and headed out the door. I had just reached the curb when I heard someone call my name. I turned. Heather was moving down the walk behind me, holding out an envelope embossed with the Wood/Warren logo.

"I'm glad I caught you," she said. "I think Mr. Wood wanted you to have this before you left. He was called away unexpectedly. This was in my out box."

"Thanks." I opened the flap and peered at the contents: inventory sheets. "Oh great," I said, amazed that he'd remembered in the midst of his vanishing act. "I'll call on Monday and set up a time to talk to him."

"Sorry about today," she said. "Merry Christmas!" She waved and then moved back to the party. The door was now propped open, cigarette smoke and noise spilling out in equal parts. Ava Daugherty was watching us, her gaze fixed with curiosity on the envelope Heather'd given me, which I was just tucking into my handbag. I returned to my car and drove back into town.

When I stopped by the office, I passed the darkened glass doors of California Fidelity. Like many other businesses, CFI had shut down early for Christmas Eve. I unlocked my door, tossed the file on my desk, and checked for messages. I put a call through to the fire chief for a quick verification of the information I had, but he, too, was gone. I left my number and was told he probably wouldn't return the call until Monday.

By 4:00, I was back in my apartment with the drawbridge pulled up. And that's where I stayed for the entire weekend.

Christmas Day I spent alone, but not unhappily.

The day after that was Sunday. I tidied my apartment, shopped for groceries, made pots of hot tea, and read.

Monday, December 27, I was back in harness again, sitting at my desk in a poinky mood, trying to wrestle the fire-scene inspection into a coherent narrative.

The phone rang. I was hoping it was Mrs. Brunswick at the bank, calling back to tell me the five-thousand-dollar snafu had been cleared up. "Millhone Investigations," I said.

"Oh hi, Kinsey. This is Darcy, next door. I just wondered when I could pop over and pick up that file."

"Darcy, it's only ten-fifteen! I'm working on it, okay?" Please note: I did not use the "F" word, as I know she takes offense.

"Well, you don't have to take that tone," she said. "I told Mac the report wouldn't be ready yet, but he says he wants to review the file first anyway."

"Review the file before what?"

"I don't know, Kinsey. How am I supposed to know? I called because there's a note in the action file on my desk."

"Oh, your 'action' file. You should have said so before. Come pick the damn thing up."

Ill temper and intuition are not a good mix. Whatever inconsistency was nagging at me, I could hardly get a fix on it with Darcy breathing down my neck. My first act that morning had been to fill out a form for the Insurance Crime Prevention Unit, asking for a computer check on Lance Wood. Maybe at some point in the past I'd come across a previous fire claim and that's what was bugging me. The computer check wouldn't come back for ten days, but at least I'd have covered my bases. I adjusted the tabs on my machine, typed in the name of the insured, the location, date, and time of loss.

When Darcy arrived to pick up the file, I spoke without looking up. "I dropped the film off at Speedee-Foto on my way in. They'll have prints for me by noon. I haven't had a chance to talk to Lance Wood or the fire chief yet."

"I'll tell Mac," she said, her tone cool.

Oh well, I thought. She's never been a pal of mine anyway.

As there was no slot or box where unspecified hunches could be typed in, I kept my report completely neutral. When I finished, I rolled it out of the machine, signed it, dated it, and set it aside. I had an hour before I could pick up the photographs, so I cleaned up the sketch of the warehouse layout and attached that to the report with a paper clip.

The phone rang. This time it was Andy. "Could you step into Mac's office for a few minutes?"

I quelled my irritation, thinking it best not to sass the CFI claims manager. "Sure, but I won't have the pictures for another hour yet."

"We understand that. Just bring what you've got."

I hung up, gathered up the report and the sketch, locked the office behind me, and went next door. What's this "we" shit? I thought.

The minute I stepped into Mac's office, I knew something was wrong. I've known Maclin Voorhies since I started working for California Fidelity nearly ten years ago. He's in his sixties now, with a lean, dour face. He has sparse gray hair that stands out around his head like dandelion fuzz, big ears with drooping lobes, a bulbous nose, and small black eyes under unruly white brows. His body seems misshapen: long legs, short waist, narrow shoulders, arms too long for the average sleeve length. He's smart, capable, stingy with praise, humorless, and devoutly Catholic, which translates out to a thirty-five-year marriage and eight kids, all grown. I've never seen him smoke a cigar, but he's usually chewing on a stub, the resultant tobacco stains tarnishing his teeth to the color of old toilet bowls.

I took my cue not so much from his expression, which was no darker than usual, but from Andy's, standing just to his left. Andy and I don't get along that well under the best of circumstances. At forty-two, he's an ass-kisser, always trying to maneuver situations so that he can look good. He has a moon-shaped face and his collar looks too tight and everything else about him annoys me, too. Some people just affect me that way. At that moment he seemed both restless and smug, studiously avoiding eye contact.

Mac was leafing through the file. He glanced over at Andy with impatience. "Don't you have some work to do?"

"What? Oh sure. I thought you wanted me in this meeting."

"I'll take care of it. I'm sure you're overloaded as it is."

Andy murmured something that made it sound like leaving was his big idea. Mac shook his head and sighed slightly as the door closed. I watched him roll the cigar stub from one corner of his mouth to the other. He looked up with surprise, as if he'd just realized I was standing there. "You want to fill me in on this?"

I told him what had transpired to date, sidestepping the fact that the file had sat on Darcy's desk for three days before it came to me. I wasn't necessarily protecting her. In business, it's smarter not to badmouth the help. I told him I had two rolls of film coming in, that there weren't any estimates yet, but the claim looked routine as far as I could see. I debated mention of my uneasiness, but discarded the idea even as I was speaking. I hadn't identified what was bothering me and I felt it was wiser to stick to the facts.

The frown on Mac's face formed about thirty seconds into my recital, but what alarmed me was the silence that fell when I was done. Mac is a man who fires questions. Mac gives pop quizzes. He seldom sits and stares as he was doing in this case.

"You want to tell me what this is about?" I asked.

"Did you see the note attached to the front of this file?"

"What note? There wasn't any note," I said.

He held out a California Fidelity memo form, maybe three inches by five, covered with Jewel's curlicue script. "Kinsey . . . this one looks like a stinker. Sorry I don't have time to fill you in, but the fire chief's report spells it out. He said to call if he can give you any help. J."

"This wasn't attached to the file when it came to me."

"What about the fire department report? Wasn't that in there?"

"Of course it was. That's the first thing I read."

Mac's expression was aggrieved. He handed me the file, open to the fire-department report. I looked down at the familiar STFD form. The incidental information was just as I remembered. The narrative account I'd never seen before. The fire chief, John Dudley, had summed up his investigation with a no-nonsense statement of suspected arson. The newspaper clipping now attached to the file ended with a line to the same effect.

I could feel my face heat, the icy itch of fear beginning to assert itself. I said, "This isn't the report I saw." My voice had dropped into a range I scarcely recognized. He held his hand out and I returned the file.

"I got a phone call this morning," he said. "Somebody says you're on the take."

I stared. "What?"

"You got anything to say?"

"That's absurd. Who called?"

"Let's not worry about that for the moment."

"Mac, come on. Somebody's accusing me of a criminal act and I want to know who it is."

He said nothing, but his face shut down in that stubborn way of his.

"All right, skip that," I said, yielding the point. I

thought it was better to get the story out before I worried about the characters. "What did this unidentified caller say?"

He leaned back in his chair, studying the cold coin of ash on the end of his cigar. "Somebody saw you accept an envelope from Lance Wood's secretary," he said.

"Bullshit. When?"

"Last Friday."

I had a quick flash of Heather calling to me as I left the plant. "Those were inventory sheets. I asked Lance Wood to have them ready for me and he left 'em in his out box."

"What inventory sheets?"

"Right there in the file."

He shook his head, leafing through. From where I stood, I could see there were only two or three loose papers clipped in on one side. There was nothing resembling the inventory sheets I'd punched and inserted. He looked up at me. "What about the interview with Wood?"

"I haven't done that yet. An emergency came up and he disappeared. I'm supposed to set up an appointment with him for today."

"What time?"

"Well, I don't know. I haven't called him yet. I was trying to get the report typed up first." I couldn't seem to avoid the defensiveness in my tone.

"This the envelope?" Mac was holding the familiar envelope with the Wood/Warren logo, only now there was a message jotted on the front. "Hope this will suffice for now. Balance to follow as agreed."

"Goddamn it, Mac. You can't be serious! If I were taking a payoff, why would I leave that in the file?"

No answer. I tried again. "You really think Lance Wood paid me off?"

"I don't think anything except we better look into it. For your sake as well as ours . . ."

"If I took money, where'd it go?"

"I don't know, Kinsey. You tell me. If it was cash, it wouldn't be that hard to conceal."

"I'd have to be a fool! I'd have to be an idiot and so would he. If he's going to bribe me, do you think he'd be stupid enough to put the cash in an envelope and write a note to that effect! Mac, this whole thing has frame-up written all over it!"

"Why would anyone do that?" At this point, his manner wasn't accusatory. He seemed genuinely puzzled at the very idea. "Who would go to such lengths?"

"How do I know? Maybe I just got caught in the loop. Maybe Lance Wood is the target. You know I'd never do such a thing. I'll bring you my bank statements. You can scrutinize my accounts. Check under my mattress, for God's sake. . . ." I broke off in confusion.

I saw his mouth move, but I didn't hear the rest of what he said. I could feel the trap close and something suddenly made sense. In the morning mail, I'd gotten notice about five thousand dollars credited to my account. I think I knew now what that was about.

4

I packed up my personal belongings and my current
files. California Fidelity had suspended our relationship until the Wood/Warren matter could be
"straightened out," whatever that meant. I had until
noon to clear the premises. I called the telephone
company and asked to have calls forwarded to my
home until further notice. I unplugged the answering
machine and placed it on top of the last cardboard
box, which I toted down the back steps to my car. I
had been asked to turn in my office keys before I left,
but I ignored the request. I had no intention of giving
up access to five years' worth of business files. I didn't
think Mac would press the point and I didn't think
anyone would bother to have the locks changed.
Screw 'em. I know how to pick most locks, anyway.

In the meantime, I was already analyzing the sequence of events. The Wood/Warren folder had

been sitting on my desk the entire weekend so the fire department reports could have been switched at any point. I'd worked from notes that morning without reference to the file itself, so I had no way of knowing if the inventory sheets were in the file or not. I might not have registered the loss had I looked. My office door and the French doors opening out onto the balcony showed no signs of forced entry, but my handbag, along with my keys, had sat in Lance Wood's office for three hours on Friday. Anybody could have gotten into that bag and had duplicate keys made. My checkbook was there, too, and it didn't take a wizard to figure out how somebody could have lifted a deposit slip, filled it out, stuck it in an envelope with five grand, and put the whole of it in the night-deposit slot at my bank. Obviously my instant-teller card couldn't be used because my code number wasn't written down anyplace.

I drove out to Wood/Warren, my brain clicking away, fired by adrenaline. The moment I'd understood what was going on, the anger had passed and a chill of curiosity had settled in. I'd felt my emotions disconnect and my mind had cleared like a radio suddenly tuned to the right frequency. Someone had gone to a lot of trouble to discredit me. Insurance fraud is serious damn shit, punishable by two, three, or four years in the state prison. That wasn't going to happen to me, folks.

Heather stared at me, startled, as I moved through the Wood/Warren reception area, scarcely slowing my pace. "Is he in?"

She looked down at the appointment book with confusion. "Do you have an appointment this morning?"

"Now I do," I said. I knocked on the door once and went in. Lance was meeting with John Salkowitz, the chemical engineer I had been introduced to on my earlier visit. The two men were bending over a set of specs for an item that looked like a giant diaper pin.

"We need to talk," I said.

Lance took one look at my face and then flicked a signal to Salkowitz, indicating that they'd continue some other time.

I waited until the door closed and then leaned on Lance's desk. "Somebody's trying to shove one up our collective rear end," I said. I detailed the situation to him, citing chapter and verse in a way that left no room for argument. He got the point. Some of the color left his face.

He sank into his swivel chair. "Jesus," he said. "I don't believe it." I could see him computing possibilities the same way I had.

I drew up a chair and sat down. "What was the emergency that pulled you out of here so fast Friday afternoon?" I asked. "It has to be connected, doesn't it?"

"How so?"

"Because if I'd questioned you as I intended to, you probably would have mentioned arson, and then I'd have known the fire-department report was counterfeit."

"My housekeeper called. I'm in the middle of a nasty divorce and Gretchen showed up at the house with two burly guys and a moving van. By the time I got home, she'd cleared out the living room and was working on the den."

"Does she have the wherewithal to set up a deal like this?"

"Why would she do that? It's in her best interest to keep me alive and well and earning money hand over fist. Right now, she's collecting over six grand a month in temporary support. Insurance fraud is the last thing she'd want to stick me with. Besides, she's been in Tulsa since March of this year."

"Or so she claims," I said.

"The woman is a twit. If you knew her, you wouldn't suspect her of anything except licking a pencil point every time she has to write her name."

"Well, somebody sure wanted to blacken your name," I said.

"What makes you think it's me they're after? Why couldn't it be you?"

"Because no one could be sure I'd be called in on this. These fire claims are assigned almost randomly, according to who's free. If it's me they want, they'd have to go about it differently. They're not going to burn down your warehouse on the off-chance that I'll be called to investigate."

"I suppose not," he said.

"What about you? What's going on in your life, aside from the divorce?"

He picked up a pencil and began to loop it through his fingers, end over end, like a tiny baton. He watched its progress and then shot me an enigmatic look. "I have a sister who moved back here from Paris three months ago. Rumor has it she wants control of the plant."

"Is this Ebony?"

He seemed surprised. "You know her?"

"Not well, but I know who she is."

"She disapproves of the way I run things."

"Enough to do this?"

He stared at me for a moment and then reached for the phone. "I'd better call my attorney."

"You and me both," I said.

I left and headed back into town.

As far as I knew, the D.A.'s office hadn't been notified, and no charges had been filed. A valid arrest warrant has to be based on a complaint supported by facts showing, first of all, that a crime has been committed, and second, that the informer or his information is reliable. At this point, all Mac had was an anonymous telephone call and some circumstantial evidence. He'd have to take action. If the accusation was correct, then CFI had to be protected. My guess was that he'd go back through my workload, case by case, to see if there was any whisper of misconduct on my part. He might also hire a private detective to look into the affairs of Wood/Warren, Lance Wood, and possibly me—a novel idea. I wondered how my life would hold up if it were subjected to professional scrutiny. The five grand would certainly come to light. I wasn't sure what to do about that. The deposit was damning in itself, but if I tried to move the money, it would look even worse.

I remember the rest of the day in fragments. I talked to Lonnie Kingman, a criminal attorney I'd done some work for in the past. He's in his early forties, with a face like a boxer; beetle-browed, broken nose. His hair is shaggy and his suits usually look too tight across the shoulder blades. He's about five foot four and probably weighs two hundred and five. He lifts weights at the same gym I do and I see him in there doing squats with three hundred pounds of plates wobbling on either end of the bar like water buckets. He graduated summa cum laude from Stanford Law School and he wears silk shirts with his monogram on the cuff.

Attorneys are the people who can say things in the mildest of tones that make you want to shriek and rend your clothes. Like doctors, they seem to feel obliged to acquaint you with the full extent of the horror you could face, given the current path your life is on. When I told him what was happening, he tossed out two possible additions to the allegation of insurance fraud: that I'd be named with Lance Wood as coconspirator, and charged as an aider and abettor to arson after the fact. And *that* was just what he came up with off the top of his head.

I could feel myself pale. "I don't want to hear this shit," I said.

He shrugged. "Well, it's what I'd go for if I were D.A.," he said offhandedly. "I could probably add a few counts once I had all the facts."

"Facts, my ass. I never saw Lance Wood before in my life."

"Sure, but can you prove it?"

"Of course not! How would I do that?"

Lonnie sighed like he was going to hate to see me in a shapeless prison dress.

"Goddamn it, Lonnie, how come the law always helps the other guy? I swear to God, every time I turn around, the bad guys win and the little guys bite the Big Wienie. What am I supposed to do?"

He smiled. "It's not as bad as all that," he said. "My advice is to keep away from Lance Wood."

"How? I can't just sit back and see what happens next. I want to know who set me up."

"I never said you couldn't look into it. You're an investigator. Go investigate. But I'd be careful if I were you. Insurance fraud is bad enough. You don't want to take the rap for something worse."

I was afraid to ask him what he meant.

I went home and unloaded the boxes full of office files. I took a few minutes to reword the message on my answering machine at home. I put a call through to Jonah Robb in Missing Persons at the Santa Teresa Police Department. As a lady in distress, I don't ordinarily call on men. I've been schooled in the notion that a woman, these days, saves herself, which I was willing to do if I could just figure out where to start.

I'd met Jonah six months before while I was working on a case. Our paths had crossed more than once, most recently in my bed. He's thirty-nine, blunt, nurturing, funny, confused, a tormented man with blue eyes, black hair, and a wife named Camilla who stalks out intermittently with his two little girls, whose names I repress. I had ignored the chemistry between us for as long as I could, too wise (said I) to get pulled into a dalliance with a married gent. And then one rainy night I'd run into him on my way home from a depressing interview with a hostile subject. Jonah and I started drinking margaritas in a bar near the beach. We danced to old Johnny Mathis tunes, talked, danced again, and ordered more drinks. Somewhere around "The Twelfth of Never," I lost track of my resolve and took him home with me. I never could resist the lyrics on that one.

We were currently at that stage in a new relationship where both parties are tentative, reluctant to presume, quick to feel injured, eager to know and be known as long as the true frailties of character are concealed. The risking felt good, and as a consequence the chemistry felt good, too. I smiled a lot when I thought of him and sometimes I laughed aloud, but the warmth was undercut by a curious pain. I've been married twice, done in more times than I care to admit. I'm not as trusting as I used to be and with good reason. Meanwhile, Jonah was in a constant state of upheaval according to the fluctuations in Camilla's moods. Her most recent claim was that she wanted an "open" marriage, his guess being that the sexual liberties were intended more for her than for him.

"Missing Persons. Sergeant Schiffman."

For an instant my mind went absolutely blank. "Rudy? This is Kinsey. Where's Jonah?"

"Oh, hi, Kinsey. He's out of town. Took his family skiing for the holidays. It came up kind of sudden, but I thought he said he'd let you know. He never called?"

"I guess not," I said. "Do you know when he's expected back?"

"Just a minute. Let me check." He put me on hold and I listened to the Norman Luboff Choir singing "Hark, the Herald Angels Sing." Christmas was over. Hadn't anybody heard? Rudy clicked back in. "Looks like January third. You want to leave a message?"

"Tell him I hung myself," I said and rang off.

I have to confess that in the privacy of my own home, I burst into tears and wept with frustration for six minutes flat. Then I went to work.

The only line of attack I could think of was through Ash Wood. I hadn't spoken to her since high school, nearly fourteen years. I tried the directory. Her mother, Helen Wood, was listed and so was Lance, but there was no sign of Ash, which probably meant that she'd moved away or married. I tried the main house. A woman answered. I identified myself and told her I was trying to locate Ash. Often I tell lies in a situation like this, but the truth seemed expedient.

"Kinsey, is that really you? This is Ash. How are you?" she said. All the Wood girls have voices that sound the same; husky and low, underlaid with an accent nearly Southern in its tone. The inflection was distinct, not a drawl, but an indolence. Their mother was from Alabama, if my memory hadn't failed me.

"I can't believe my luck," I said. "How are you?"

"Well, darlin', we are in a world of hurt," she replied, "which is why I'm so glad to hear from you. Lance mentioned that he'd seen you at the plant last Friday. What's happening?"

"That's what I called to ask you."

"Oh Lord. I'd love to bring you up-to-date. Are you free for lunch by any chance?"

"For you . . . anything," I said.

She suggested the Edgewater Hotel at 12:30, which suited me. I'd have to change clothes first. My standard outfit consists of boots or tennis shoes, form-fitting jeans, and a tank top or a turtleneck, depending on the season. Sometimes I wear a windbreaker or a denim vest, and I've always got a large leather shoulder bag, which sometimes (but not often) contains my little .32. I was relatively certain Ashley wouldn't appear in public like this. I hauled out my all-purpose dress, panty hose, and low heels. One day soon, I gotta get myself something else to wear.

5

The Edgewater Hotel sits on twenty-three acres of ocean-front property, with lawns sweeping down to the sea. An access road cuts through, not ten feet from the surf, with a sea wall constructed of local sandstone. The architecture of the main building is Spanish, with massive white stucco walls, arched doorways, and deeply recessed windows. Horizontal lines of red tile define the roof. A glass-walled dining patio juts out in front, white umbrella tables sheltering the patrons from sunlight and buffeting sea winds. The grounds are landscaped with juniper and palm, hibiscus, bottle brush and fern, flower beds filled year round with gaudy annuals in hot pink, purple, and gold. The day was chill, the sky icy white and overcast. The drab olive-green surf was churned up by the outer fringes of a storm system that had passed us to the north.

The valet parking attendant was far too discreet to remark, even with a look, the battered state of my ancient car. I moved into the hotel lobby and down a wide corridor furnished with a series of overstuffed couches, interspersed with rubber plants. The ceiling overhead was wood-beamed, the walls tiled halfway up, sounds muffled by a runner of thick carpet patterned with flowers the size of dinner plates.

Ash had reserved a table in the main dining room. She was already seated, her face turned expectantly toward me as I approached. She looked much as she had in high school; pale-red hair, blue eyes set in a wide, friendly face mottled with freckles. Her teeth were very white and straight and her smile was engaging. I had forgotten how casually she dressed. She was wearing a blue wool jumpsuit with a military cut, and over it a bulky white sheepskin vest. I thought, with regret, of my jeans and turtleneck.

She was still maybe twenty pounds overweight, and she moved with all the enthusiasm of an ungainly pup, leaping up to hug me when I arrived at the table. There had always been a guileless quality about her. Despite the fact she came from money, she had never been snobbish or affected. Where Olive had seemed reserved, and Ebony intimidating, Ash seemed utterly unselfconscious, one of those girls everybody liked. In our sophomore year, we had ended up sitting in adjoining homeroom seats and we'd often chatted companionably before classes began. Neither of us was a cheerleader, an honor student, or a candidate for prom queen. The friendship that sprang up between us, though genuine, was short-lived. I met her family. She met my aunt. I went to her house and thereafter neatly bypassed her coming to mine. While the Woods were always gracious to me, it was obvious that Ash functioned at the top of the social heap and I at the bottom. Eventually the disparity made me so uncomfortable that I let the contact lapse. If Ash was injured by the rejection, she did a good job of covering it. I felt guilty about her anyway and was relieved the next year when she sat somewhere else.

"Kinsey, you look great. I'm so glad you called. I ordered us a bottle of Chardonnay. I hope that's okay."

"Fine," I said, smiling. "You look just the same."

"Big rump, you mean," she said with a laugh. "You're just as thin as you always were, only I half expected you to show up in jeans. I don't believe I ever saw you in a dress."

"I thought I'd act like I had some class," I said. "How are you? When I didn't find you listed in the phone book, I thought you'd probably gotten married or left town."

"Actually, I've been gone for ten years and just got back. What about you? I can't believe you're a private detective. I always figured you'd end up in jail. You were such a rebel back then."

I laughed. I was a misfit in high school and hung out with guys known as "low-wallers" because they loitered along a low wall at the far end of the school grounds. "You remember Donan, the boy with the gold tooth who sat right in front of you in homeroom? He's an Ob-Gyn in town. Got his teeth fixed and went to med school."

Ash groaned, laughing. "God, that's one way to get your hand up a girl's skirt. What about the little swarthy one who sat next to you? He was funny. I liked him."

"He's still around. Bald now and overweight. He runs a liquor store up on the Bluffs. Who was that girlfriend of yours who used to shoplift? Francesca something."

"Palmer. She's living with a fellow in Santa Fe who designs furniture. I saw her about a year ago when I was passing through. God, she's still a klepto. Are you married?"

"Was." I held up two fingers to indicate the number of husbands who had come and gone.

"Children?" she asked.

"Oh God, no. Not me. You have any?"

"Sometimes I wish I did." Ash was watching me

with shining eyes and somehow I knew anything I said would be fine with her.

"When did we see each other last? It's been years, hasn't it?" I asked.

She nodded. "Bass's twenty-first birthday party at the country club. You were with the most beautiful boy I ever saw in my life."

"Daniel," I said. "He was husband number two."

"What about number one? What was he like?"

"I better drink some first."

The waiter appeared with the wine, presenting the label for her inspection before he opened it. She waved aside the ritual of the sniffing of the cork and let him go ahead and pour for both of us. I noticed that the waiter was smiling to himself, probably charmed as most people are by Ash's breezy manner and her impatience with formality. He was tall and slim, maybe twenty-six years old, and he told us about the specials as if we might want to take notes. "The sea bass is being served today with a green chili *beurre blanc*, gently poached first with fresh tomatoes, cilantro, lemon, and white wine, garnished with jalapeños and accompanied by a pine-nut rice pilau. We're also offering a fillet of coho salmon . . ." Ash made little mewing sounds, interrupting now and then for clarification of some culinary subtlety.

I let her order for us. She knew all the waiters by name and ended up in a long chat with ours about what we should eat. She settled on steamed clams in a broth with Pernod, a salad of field greens lightly dressed, and said we'd think about dessert if we were good girls and cleaned our plates.

While we ate, I told her about my connection to Wood/Warren and the irregularities that had come to light.

"Oh, Kinsey. I feel awful. I hope Lance isn't responsible for the trouble you're in."

"Believe me, I do, too. What's the story on him? Is he the type to burn down the family warehouse?"

Ash didn't leap to his defense as I'd expected her to. "If he did, I don't think he'd snitch on himself," she said.

"Good point. Who'd go after him like that?"

"I don't know. That whole situation got very screwed up once Daddy died. He was crazy about the boys, but Bass was a dilettante and Lance raised hell half the time."

"I seem to remember that. Your father must have had conniption fits."

"Oh, he did. You know how straight he was. Daddy had real strong ideas about parenting, but most of them were wrong. He had no idea how to implement them anyway. He wanted to control and mold and dominate but he couldn't even do that very well. Kids just don't behave like company employees. Daddy thought he'd have more control at home, but the truth was, he had less. Both Lance and Bass were determined to thwart him. Bass never has straightened out."

"He's still in New York?"

"Oh, he comes home now and then—he was here for a week at Thanksgiving—but for the most part, he's gone. New York, Boston, London. He spent a year in Italy and swears he's going back. Much as I love him, he's a waste of time. I don't think he's ever going to get his act together. Of course, Lance was that way for years. They're both smart enough, but they always partied hard and Lance had a few scrapes with the law. It drove Daddy up the wall."

The clams arrived. Each of us was presented with a plate piled high with small, perfect shells, swaddled in cloth to keep the broth piping hot. She speared a tender button of clam flesh and placed it on her tongue, her eyes closing in a near-swoon as she swallowed. I watched her butter a crescent of French bread and dip it in the bowl, sopping up clam liquor. As she bit into it, she made a little sound low in her throat like something out of an X-rated video.

"Your lunch okay?" I asked dryly.

"Fine," she said. "Good." She realized belatedly that I was teasing her and she smiled, her cheeks tinted becomingly with pink. "Someone asked me once which I'd rather have—sex or a warm chocolate-chip cookie. I still can't decide."

"Go for the cookies. You can bake 'em yourself."

She wiped her mouth and took a sip of wine. "Anyway, about the last six or seven years, Lance took hold, more or less, and started showing an interest in the business. Daddy was thrilled. Wood/Warren was Daddy's life. He loved us, but he couldn't manage us the way he did the business. By the time Bass came along, the last in line, Daddy'd pretty much given up any hopes for a successor."

"What about Ebony?"

"Oh, she's been passionate about the company since she was a kid, but she didn't believe Daddy'd ever let her have a hand in it. He was old-fashioned. A man leaves his business to his oldest son. Period. He knew Ebony was smart, but he didn't think she was tough enough, and he didn't think she'd stay with it. Women get married and have babies and spend money. That was his attitude. Women join the country club and play tennis and golf. They don't go head-to-head with chemical engineers and systems analysts. She even went off to Cal Poly and started working on an engineering degree, but Daddy made it clear it wouldn't help her cause, so she went to Europe and got married instead."

"Thus fulfilling his prophecy," I said.

"That's right. Of course, at that point, Daddy did a turnaround and swore he'd have left her the company if she'd stuck it out. She hated him for that, and I didn't blame her a bit. He was a real shit sometimes."

"She's back now, isn't she?"

"Right. She got home in August, minus Julian, which is no big loss. He was a dud if I ever saw one. A real bore. I don't know how she put up with him."

"Lance says she wants to take over."

"I've heard that, too, though it's not anything she talks to me about. I get along with Ebony, but we're not real close."

"What about Olive? Is she interested?"

"Peripherally, I guess. She married one of the chemical engineers who worked for Daddy. He's vice-president now, but they met when she was still in college and he'd just hired on."

"Is that Terry Kohler?"

She nodded. "You met him?"

"When I was out there. What's he like?"

"Oh, I don't know. Smart. Moody. Intense. Pleasant enough, but sort of humorless. Good at what he does. Crazy about her, I must say. He worships the ground she walks on. 'Slavish' is the word."

"Lucky girl. Is he ambitious?"

"He used to be. He wanted to go out on his own at one point and form his own company, but I guess it didn't work out. He kind of lost heart after that, and I don't know . . . being married to the boss's daughter probably takes the heat off."

"How does he get along with Lance?"

"They clash now and then. Terry's easily offended. You know the type. He gets his nose bent out of shape at the least little thing."

"What about John Salkowitz?"

"He's a sweetie. He's what Daddy wanted Lance to be."

"You said Lance had a couple of scrapes with the law. What was that about?"

"He stole some things from the plant."

"Really. When was this?"

"In high school. He came up with a scheme to make some money, but it didn't work out. It was part of an economics class and I guess his grade depended on how well he did. When he realized his little enterprise was failing, he stole some equipment—nothing big—but he tried to sell it to a fence. The guy got uneasy and called the cops."

"Not too smart."

"That's what pissed Daddy off, I suspect."

"Did he press charges?"

"Are you kidding? Of course. He said that was the only way Lance would ever learn."

"And did he?"

"Well, he got in trouble again, if that's what you

mean. Lots of times. Daddy finally threw his hands up and sent him off to boarding school."

The subject veered off. We finished lunch, chatting about other things. At two, Ash glanced at her watch. "Oh Lord. I've got to go. I promised Mother I'd take her shopping this afternoon. Come along if you like. I know she'd love to see you." She signaled for the check.

"I better take care of some other business first, but I do want to talk to her."

"Give us a call and come up to the house."

"Are you living there now?"

"Temporarily. I just bought a place of my own and I'm having some work done. I'll be staying with Mother for another six weeks."

When the check arrived, I reached for my handbag, but she waved me off. "I'll take care of it. I'll claim it as a business lunch and charge it off to the company. It's the least I can do with the bind you're in."

"Thanks," I said. I got Ebony's personal telephone number from her and we walked out together. I was relieved that the valet service brought her car first. I watched her pull away in a little red Alfa-Romeo. My car appeared. I tipped the fellow more than I should have and got in with care, humping myself onto the seat to avoid snagging my panty hose behind the knee. The valet slammed the door and I turned the key. Honest to God, it started right up and I felt a surge of pride. The damn thing is paid for and only costs me ten bucks a week in gas.

I drove home and let myself in the gate, steadfastly disregarding the yawning air of emptiness about the place. The winter grass seemed ragged and the dead heads on the zinnias and marigolds had multiplied. Henry's house stood silent, his back door looking blank. Usually the scent of yeast or cinnamon lies on the air like a heady perfume. Henry's a retired commercial baker who can't quite give up his passion for kneading dough and proofing bread. If he isn't in the kitchen, I can usually find him on the patio, weeding the flower beds or stretched out on a chaise inventing crossword puzzles filled with convoluted puns.

I let myself into my apartment and changed back into jeans, my whole body sighing with relief. I hauled the mower out of the toolshed and had a run at the yard, and then I got down on my hands and knees and clipped all the dead blossoms from the beds. This was very boring. I put the lawn mower away. I went inside and typed up my notes. As long as I was investigating in my own behalf, I decided to do it properly. This was boring, too.

Since Rosie's was closed, I ate dinner at home, preparing a cheese-and-pickle sandwich, which entertained me to no end.

I'd finished the Len Deighton and I didn't have

anything else in the house to read, so I switched on my little portable television set.

Sometimes I wonder if my personal resources aren't wearing a little thin.

6

Tuesday morning, I went into the gym at 6:00 A.M. As I no longer had an office to go to, I could well have waited until later in the morning, but I like the place at that hour. It's quiet and half empty, so there's no competition for equipment. The free weights are neatly reracked. The mirrors are clean and the air doesn't smell like yesterday's sweat socks. Weight-lifting apparatus are a curious phenomenon—machines invented to replicate the backbreaking manual labor the Industrial Revolution relieved us of. Lifting weights is like a meditation: intermittent periods of concentrated activity, with intervals of rest. It's a good time for thinking, as one can do little else. I did ab crunches first; thirty-five, then thirty, then twenty-five. I adjusted the bench on one of the Nautilus machines and started doing seated military presses, three sets, ten reps each, using two plates. The guys lift anywhere from ten to twenty plates, but I work just as hard, and I'm not really preparing for the regional body-building championship.

I was thinking back over the details of the frame-up . . . a clever piece of work, dependent on a number of events coming together just as they had. The phone call to Mac must have come from Ava Daugherty, but who put her up to it? Surely she didn't cook up that trouble by herself. Someone had access to the Wood/Warren file, and while it was possible that the office keys had been lifted from my bag, who at Wood/Warren knew enough to make a mockup of a fire-department report? That must have been done by someone who knew the procedure at CFI. Insurance investigations usually follow a format. An outsider simply couldn't guarantee that all the paper switching could be done in the necessary sequence. Darcy could have managed it. Andy might have, or even Mac. But why?

I worked through biceps and triceps. Since I jog six days a week, my prime interest in the gym is the three A's—arms, abs, and ass—a routine that takes forty-five minutes three times a week. I was finished by 7:15. I went home to shower and then I started out again, dressed in jeans, turtleneck, and boots. Darcy was due at work at 9:00, but I'd spotted her three days out of five having breakfast first, coffee and a Danish in the coffee shop across the street. She used the time to chitchat, read the newspaper, and do her nails.

There was no sign of her when I got there at 8:00. I bought a paper and settled into the back booth where she usually sits. Claudine came by and I ordered breakfast. At 8:12, Darcy came through the door in a lightweight wool coat. She stopped when she saw me, checked her stride, and slid into an empty booth halfway down. I picked up my coffee cup and joined her, loving the sour look that crossed her face when she realized what I was up to.

"Mind if I join you?" I asked.

"Well, actually, I'd prefer to have the time to myself," she said, avoiding my gaze.

Claudine arrived with a steaming plate of bacon and scrambled eggs, which she set down in front of me. Claudine is in her fifties, with a booming voice and calves knotted with varicose veins.

"Morning, Darcy. What'll you have today? We're out of cheese Danish, but I laid back a cherry in case you're interested."

"That's fine. And a small orange juice."

Claudine made a note and tucked her order pad in her apron pocket. "Just a second and I'll bring you a coffee cup." She was gone again before Darcy could protest. I could see her do a quick visual survey, looking for an empty seat. The place was filling up rapidly and it looked like she was trapped.

While I ate, I studied her in a manner that I hoped was disconcerting. She eased out of her coat, making a big deal out of standing up so she could fold it just so. She's one of those women a glamour magazine should "make-over" as a challenge to their in-house experts. She has baby-fine hair that defies styling, a high, bulging forehead, pale-blue eyes. Her skin is milky white and translucent, with a tracery of veins showing through like faded laundry marks. I'd heard Darcy's boyfriend was a mail carrier, dealing drugs on the side, and I wondered if he delivered junk mail and junk on the same run. I could tell I was ruining her day, which improved my appetite.

"I'm assuming you heard about the trouble I'm in."

"It'd be hard not to," she said.

I opened a plastic locket of grape jelly and spread half on a triangle of whole-wheat toast. "Got any ideas about who set me up?"

Claudine returned with a cup and saucer and the coffeepot. Darcy judiciously elected to refrain from comment until her cup was filled and mine had been topped off. When Claudine departed, Darcy's expression turned prim and her coloring altered like a mood ring, shifting down a grade from woeful to glum. Actually, the change was not unappealing. She's big on pastel shades, imagining, I suppose, that washed-out colors are somehow more flattering to her than bold ones. She wore a pale-yellow sweater about the hue of certain urine samples I've seen where the prognosis isn't keen. The pink in her cheeks gave her back an air of health.

She leaned forward. "I didn't do anything to you," she said.

"Great. Then maybe you can help."

"Mac told us specifically not to talk to you."

"How come?"

"Well, obviously, he doesn't want you to get information you're not supposed to have."

"Such as?"

"I'm not going to discuss it with you."

"Why don't I tell you my theory," I said sociably. I half expected her to stick her fingers in her ears and start singing aloud to drown me out, but I noticed that she was not completely uninterested and I took heart from that. "I suspect maybe Andy's at the bottom of this. I don't know what he's getting out of it, but it's probably some form of financial gain. Maybe somebody's throwing business his way, or giving him a kickback. Of course, it crossed my mind that it might be you, but I don't really think so at this point. I think if you'd done it you'd be friendly, to convince me of your goodwill, if nothing else."

Darcy opened a paper sugar packet and measured

out half a teaspoon, which she stirred into her coffee. I went right on, talking aloud as if she were a pal of mine and meant to help.

"CFI hires other outside investigators so I'm imagining that any one of us could have been implicated. It was just my dumb luck that I was up at bat. Not that Andy wouldn't take a certain satisfaction from the fact. He's never been fond of me and he always hated it that Mac let me have office space. Andy wanted to knock the wall out and take that corner for himself. At any rate, I have to assume Lance Wood is the real focus of the frame, though I don't know why yet. What I'll probably do is try working both sides of the street here and just see where all the paths intersect. Should be fun. I've never worked for me before and I'm looking forward to it. Cuts down on the paperwork."

I checked her reaction. Those pale eyes were focused on mine and I could see that her mental gears were engaged.

"Come on, Darcy. Help me out," I coaxed. "What do you have to lose?"

"You don't even like me."

"You don't like me either. What's that got to do with it? We both hate Andy. *That's* the point. The guy's a shit-heel."

"Actually he is," she said.

"You don't think Mac had anything to do with it, do you?"

"Well, no."

"So who else could it be?"

She cleared her throat. "Andy has been hanging around my desk a lot."

Her voice was so low I had to lean forward. "Go on."

"It started the day Jewel left on vacation and Mac told him to farm out her work. Andy was the one who suggested you for the Wood/Warren fire claim."

"He probably thought it'd be easier to pressure me."

Claudine brought Darcy's OJ and the cherry Danish. Darcy broke the Danish into small pieces, buttering each with care before she popped it in her mouth. Jesus, maybe I'd have one.

She was just warming up on the subject of Andy Motycka, who was apparently no fonder of her than he was of me. "What irritates me," she said, "is that I got in trouble with Mac because Andy said the file sat on my desk for three days before it got to you. That's an outright lie. Andy took it home with him. I saw him put it in his briefcase Tuesday when the fire-department report came in."

"Did you tell Mac that?"

"Well, no. Why bother? It sounds like I'm trying to defend myself by pushing all the blame off on him."

"You're right. I found myself in the same position," I said. "Look, if Andy falsified the fire-department report, he probably did the dirty work at home, don't you think?"

"Probably."

"So maybe we can turn up some proof if we look. I'll nose around at his place if you'll try his office."

"He moved, you know. He's not at the house. He and Janice are in the process of splitting up."

"He's getting divorced?"

"Oh, sure. It's been going on for months. She's hosing him, too."

"Really. Well, that's interesting. Where's he living?"

"One of those condos out near Sand Castle."

I'd seen the complex: one hundred and sixty units across from a public golf course called Sand Castle, out beyond Colgate in the little community of Elton. "What about his office? Is there any way you could check that out?"

Darcy smiled for the first time. "Sure. I'll do that. It would serve him right."

I got her home number and said I'd call later. I paid both checks and took off, figuring it wouldn't be a good idea to get caught in Darcy's company. While I was downtown, I hoofed it over to the credit bureau and had a discreet chat with a friend of mine who works as a key-punch operator. I'd done some work for her years before, checking into the background of a certain seedy gent who had hoped to relieve her of a burdensome savings account. She'd had the bucks in hand to pay me, but I sensed that both of us would benefit from a little bartering—"professional courtesies," as they're known. Now I check out any new fellow in her life and, in return, she pirates occasional confirmation copies of computer runs. One drawback is that I have to wait until a periodic updating of the master file is scheduled, which usually happens once a week. I asked her to give me anything she had on Lance Wood and she promised me something in a day. On an impulse, I asked her to check out Andy Motycka while she was at it. Financial information on Wood/Warren I'd have to get from the local equivalent of Dun & Bradstreet. My best source of information was going to be California Fidelity itself, for whom Lance Wood had no doubt filled out countless forms in applying for coverage. I was hoping I could enlist Darcy's aid again on that one. It was amazing to me how much more appealing she seemed now that she was on my team. I trotted back to pick up my car.

As I pulled out of the parking lot behind the building, Andy was just pulling in, pausing while the machine stamped and spat a ticket through the slot. He pretended he didn't see me.

I drove back to my apartment. I'd never paid much attention to the looming importance of the office in my life. I conduct maybe 40 percent of all business in my swivel chair, telephone in the crook of my neck, files close at hand. Sixty percent of the time I'm probably on the road, but I don't like feeling cut off from my reference points. It puts me at a subtle disadvantage.

It was only 10:05 and the day loomed ahead. Out of habit, I hauled out my little portable Smith-Corona and started typing up my notes. That done, I caught up with some filing, prepared some bills for a couple of outstanding accounts, and then tidied up my desk. I hate sitting around. Especially when I could be out getting into trouble. I gave Darcy a call at CFI and got Andy's new address and telephone number. She assured me he was sitting in his office even as we spoke.

I dialed his apartment and was reassured to hear the answering machine pick up. I changed into a pair of blue-gray slacks with a pale stripe along the seam and a matching pale-blue shirt with Southern California Services stitched around a patch on the sleeve. I added hard black shoes left over from my days on traffic detail with the Santa Teresa Police Department, tacked on a self-important key ring with a long chain, and grabbed up a clipboard, my key picks, and a set of master keys. I checked myself out in the mirror. I looked like a uniformed public servant just about to make a routine service check—of what, I wasn't sure. I looked like I could read meters and make important notes. I looked like I could verify downed lines and order up repair crews on the mobile phone in my county-owned maintenance vehicle. I hopped in my car and headed out to Andy's condominium for a little B & E.

7

The Copse at Hurstbourne is one of those fancy-sounding titles for a brand-new tract of condominiums on the outskirts of town. "Copse" as in "a thicket of small trees." "Hurst" as in "hillock, knoll, or mound." And "bourne" as in "brook or stream." All of these geological and botanical wonders did seem to conjoin within the twenty parcels of the development, but it was hard to understand why it couldn't have just been called Shady Acres, which is what it was. Apparently people aren't willing to pay a hundred and fifty thousand dollars for a home that doesn't sound like it's part of an Anglo-Saxon land grant. These often quite utilitarian dwellings are never named after Jews or Mexicans. Try marketing Rancho Feinstein if you want to lose money in a hurry. Or Paco Sanchez Park. Middle-class Americans aspire to tone, which is equated, absurdly, with the British gentry. I had already passed Essex Hill, Stratford Heights, and Hampton Ridge.

The Copse at Hurstbourne was surrounded by a high wall of fieldstone, with an electronic gate meant to keep the riffraff out. The residents were listed on a mounted panel beside a telephone handset with push-buttons, and an intercom. Each occupant was assigned a personal entry code that one had to have in order to gain admittance. I know because I tried several sequences at random and got nowhere. I pulled over and waited until another car approached. The driver punched in his code. When the gate rolled back, I tucked my car in behind his and sailed through. No alarms went off. I wasn't set upon by dogs. Security measures, like the property's pedigree, were largely in the mind of the marketing team.

There were maybe twenty buildings in all, eight units each, gray frame with white trim in a Cape Cod style, all angles, mullioned windows, and wooden balconies. Sycamore and eucalyptus trees still graced the terrain. Winding roads led in two directions, but it was clear that both came together in the same rear parking lot rimmed with carports. I found a visitor's space and pulled in, checking the building directory which sported a plot map of units.

Andy Motycka's was number 144, located, happily, at the far reaches of the property. I took my clipboard and a flashlight and tried to look as officious as I could. I passed the recreational facility, the spa, the laundry rooms, the gym, and the sales office. There were no signs of children. Judging from the number of empty carports, my guess was that many of the residents were off at work somewhere else. Wonderful. A band of thugs could probably sweep through and clean the place out in half a day.

I moved around some Cape Cod-style garbage bins and went up a set of outside stairs to the second floor of building number 18. The landing of the apartment next door to Andy's was attractively furnished with shoulder-high ficus and assorted potted plants. Andy's porchlet was bare. Not even a doormat. The drapes were open, and there were no interior lights on. No sound of a television set, stereo, or toilets flushing. I rang the bell. I waited a decent interval, easing back slightly so I could check for tenants on either side. No signs of activity. It looked like I had the building to myself.

The front-door lock was a Weiss. I sorted through my key picks and tried one or two without luck. Picking a lock is time-consuming shit and I didn't feel I could stand out there indefinitely. Someone might pass and wonder why I was jiggling that length of thin metal in the keyhole and cursing mildly to myself. On an impulse I raised my hand and felt along the top of the doorjamb. Andy'd left me his key. I let myself in.

I dearly love being in places I'm not supposed to be. I can empathize with cat burglars, housebreakers, and second-story men, experiencing, as I've heard some do, adrenaline raised to a nearly sexual pitch. My heart was thudding and I felt extraordinarily alert.

I did a quick walking survey, eyeballing the two bedrooms, walk-in closets, and both bathrooms, just to determine that no one was tossing the apartment but me. In the master bedroom, I opened the sliding glass door and the screen. I went out on the balcony that connected the two bedrooms and devised an escape route in case Andy came home unexpectedly. Against the side wall, around the corner to the right, was an ornamental trellis with a newly planted bougainvillea at its base. In a pinch, I could scamper down like an orangutan and disappear.

I eased back into the apartment and began my search. Andy's bedroom floor was densely matted with dirty clothes, through which a narrow path had been cleared. I picked my way past socks, dress shirts, and boxer shorts in a variety of vulgar prints. In lieu of a chest of drawers, he kept his clean clothes in four dark-blue plastic stacking crates. His newfound bachelorhood must be taking him back to his college days. None of the bins contained anything of interest. I spent fifteen minutes sliding my hand into all the coat pockets on his hanging rod, but all I came up with were some woofies, a handkerchief full of old boogers, and a ticket for a batch of cleaning he hadn't yet retrieved. The second bedroom was smaller. Andy's bicycle was propped against one wall, the back tire flat. He had a rowing machine, eight cardboard moving boxes, unlabeled and still taped shut. I wondered how long he'd been separated.

I'd met Andy's wife, Janice, at a couple of California Fidelity office parties and hadn't thought much of her until I saw what she'd left him with. The lady had really done a thorough shakedown. Andy had always complained about her extravagance, making sure we all knew she shopped at the best stores in town. It was a measure of his success, of course, that she could charge with impunity. What was clear now was that she played for keeps. Andy'd been granted a card table, four aluminum lawn chairs with webbed seats, a mattress, and some flatwear with what must have been his mother's monogram. It looked like Janice had been sticking it in the dishwasher for years because the finish was dull and the silver plate was worn off the handles.

The kitchen cabinets held paper plates and insulated cups, along with a sorry assortment of canned goods. This guy ate worse than I did. Since the condos were brand-new, the appliances were up-to-date and immaculate: self-cleaning oven, big refrigerator (empty except for two six-packs of no-brand beer) with an ice-maker clattering away, dishwasher, microwave, disposal, trash compactor. The freezer was stacked with cartons of Lean Cuisine. He favored Spaghetti and Chicken Cacciatore. A bottle of aquavit lay on its side and he had a bag of frozen rock-hard Milky Way bars that were just an invitation to break off a tooth.

The dining area was actually a simple extension of the small living room, the kitchen separated by a pass-through with bi-fold shutters painted white. There was very little in the way of furnishings. The card table seemed to double as dining-room table and home office. The telephone sat there, plugged into the answering machine, which showed no messages. The surface was littered with typing supplies, but there was no typewriter in sight. His bottle of white-out was getting as sluggish as old nail polish. The wastebasket was empty.

I went back into the kitchen and slid open the compactor, which was loosely packed, but full. Gingerly, I rooted through, spotting crumpled sheets of paper about three layers down. I removed the liner and inserted a fresh one. I doubted Andy would remember whether he'd emptied his trash or not. He'd probably spent most of his married life being waited on hand and foot, and my guess was he took household chores for granted, as if the elves and fairies crept in at night and cleaned pee off the rim of the toilet bowl whenever he missed. I glanced at my watch. I'd been in the place thirty-five minutes and I didn't want to press my luck.

I closed and locked the sliding glass door again, made a final pass to see if I'd overlooked anything, and then let myself out the front, taking his trash bag with me.

By noon, I was home again, sitting on Henry's back patio with Andy's garbage spread around me like a beggar's picnic. Actually, the debris was fairly benign and didn't make me feel I needed a tetanus booster just to sort through. He was heavy into pickles, olives, anchovies, jalapeño peppers, and other foodstuffs in which no germs could live. There were no coffee grounds or orange peels. No evidence whatever that he ate anything fresh. Lots of beer cans. There were six plastic Lean Cuisine pouches, layers of junk mail, six dunning notices rimmed in red or pink, a notice of a Toastmaster's roast of a local businessman, a flyer from a carwash, and a letter from Janice that must have left him incensed, as he had crumpled it into a tiny ball and bitten down on it. I could see the perfect impression of his teeth in the wadded paper. She was bugging him about a temporary support check that was late *again*, said she, underlined twice and bracketed with exclamation points.

At the bottom of the bag was the back end of a pad of checks, deposit slips still attached, with the name of Andy's bank and his checking-account number neatly printed thereon. I saved that for future reference. I had set aside the crumpled papers that were shoved into the bag halfway down. I smoothed them out now—six versions of a letter to someone he referred to variously as "angel," "beloved," "light of my life," "my darling," and "dearest one." He seemed to remember her anatomy in loving detail without much attention to her intellect. Her sexual enthusiasms still had him all aflame and had thus, apparently, impaired his typing skills—lots of strikeovers in the lines where he reviewed their "time together," which I gathered was on or about Christmas Eve. In recalling the experience, he seemed to struggle with a paucity of adjectives, but the verbs were clear enough.

"Well, Andy, you old devil," I murmured to myself.

He said he longed to have her suckle the something-something from his xxxxxxxx . . . all crossed out. My guess was that it was related to flower parts and that his botanical knowledge had failed him. Either that or the very idea had caused emotional dyslexia. Also, he couldn't quite decide what tone to take. He vacillated somewhere between groveling and reverential. He said several things about her breasts that made me wonder if she might benefit from surgical reduction. It was embarrassing reading, but I tried not to shrink from my responsibilities.

Having finished, I made a neat packet of all the papers. I'd make a separate holding file for them until I could decide if any might be of use. I shoved the trash back in the bag and tossed it in Henry's garbage can. I let myself into my apartment and checked my answering machine. There was one message.

"Hi, Kinsey. This is Ash. Listen, I talked to my mother yesterday about this business with Lance and she'd like to meet with you, if that's okay. Give me a call when you get in and we'll set something up. Maybe this afternoon sometime if that works for you. Thanks. Talk to you soon. Bye."

I tried the number at the house, but the line was busy. I changed into my jeans and made myself some lunch.

By the time I got through to Ash, her mother was resting and couldn't be disturbed, but I was invited to tea at 4:00.

I decided to drive up the pass to the gun club and practice target shooting with the little .32 I keep locked in my top desk drawer in an old sock. I shoved the gun, clip, and a box of fifty cartridges into a small canvas duffel and tucked it in the trunk of my car. I stopped for gas and then headed north on 101 to the junction of 154, following the steep road that zigzags up the mountainside. The day was chilly. We'd had several days of unexpected rain and the vegetation was a dark green, blending in the distance to an intense navy blue. The clouds overhead were a cottony white with ragged underpinnings, like the torn lining on the underside of an old box spring. As the road ascended, fog began to mass and dissipate, traffic slowing to accommodate the fluctuating visibility. I downshifted twice and pulled the heater on.

At the summit, I turned left onto a secondary road barely two lanes wide, which angled upward, twisting half a mile into back country. Massive boulders, mantled in dark-green moss, lined the road, where the overhanging trees blocked out the sun. The trunks of the live oaks were frosted with fungus the color of a greened-out copper roof. I could smell heather and bay laurel and the frail scent of woodsmoke drifting from the cabins tucked in along the ridge. Where the roadside dropped away, the canyons were blank with fog. The wide gate to the gun club was open and I drove the last several hundred yards, pulling into the gravel parking lot, deserted except for a lone station wagon. Aside from the man in charge, I was the only person there.

I paid my four bucks and followed him down to the cinder-block shed that housed the restrooms. He opened the padlock to the storage room and extracted an oblong of cardboard mounted on a piece of lathing, with a target stapled to it.

"Visibil'ty might be tough now in this fog," he warned.

"I'll chance it," I said.

He eyed me with misgivings, but finally handed over the target, a staple gun, and two additional targets.

I hadn't been up to the practice range for months, and it was nice to have the whole place to myself. The wind had picked up and mist was being blown across concrete bunkers like something in a horror movie. I set up the target at a range of twenty-five yards. I inserted soft plastic earplugs and then put on hearing protectors over that. All outside noises were damped down to a mild hush, my breathing audible in my own head as though I were swimming. I loaded eight cartridges into the clip of my .32 and began to fire. Each round sounded like a balloon popping somewhere close by, followed by the characteristic whiff of gunpowder I so love.

I moved up to the target and checked to see where I was hitting. High and left. I circled the first eight holes with a Magic Marker, went back to the bench rest and loaded the gun again. A sign just behind me read: "Guns as we use them here are a source of pleasure and entertainment, but one moment of careless-

ness or foolishness can bring it all to an end forever."
Amen, I thought.

The hard-packed dirt just in front of me was as littered with shells as a battlefield. I saved my brass, collecting the casings after each firing, tucking them
neatly back into the Styrofoam brick that cradled the
live rounds.

By 3:15 I was cold, and most of my ammunition
was gone. I can't claim that my little semiautomatic is
wildly accurate at twenty-five yards, but at least I was
feeling connected to the process again.

8

At 3:55, I was turning into the circular drive to the Wood family home, located on seven acres of land that sat on the bluffs overlooking the Pacific. Their fortunes on the rise, they'd moved since I'd last visited. This house was enormous, done in a French Baroque style—a two-story central structure flanked by two prominent tower wings. The stucco exterior was as smooth and white as frosting on a wedding cake, roofline and windows edged with plaster garlands, rosettes, and shell motifs that might have been piped out of a pastry tube. A brick walk led from the driveway around to the seaward-facing front of the house and up two steps to a wide uncovered brick porch. A series of arched French doors spanned the facade, which curved outward around a conservatory on one end and a gazebo on the other. A heavy black woman in a white uniform admitted me. I followed her, like a stray pup, across a foyer tiled in black and white marble squares.

"Mrs. Wood asked if you'd wait in the morning room," the maid said, without pausing for a reply. She departed on thick crepe soles that made no sound on the polished parquet floors.

Oh, sure, I thought, that's where I usually hang out at my place . . . the morning room, where else?

The walls were apricot, the ceiling a high dome of white. Large Boston ferns were arranged on stands between high curving windows through which light streamed. The furniture was French Provincial; round table, six chairs with cane backs. The circle of Persian carpeting was a pale blend of peach and green. I stood at one of the windows, looking out at the rolling sweep of the grounds (which is what rich people call their yards). The C-shape of the room cupped a view of the ocean in its lower curve and a view of the mountains in its hook so that the windows formed a cyclorama. Sky and sea, pines, a pie wedge of city, clouds spilling down the distant mountain-side . . . all of it was perfectly framed, wheeling gulls picked out in white against the dark hills to the north.

What I love about the rich is the silence they live in—the sheer magnitude of space. Money buys light and high ceilings, six windows where one might actu-ally do. There was no dust, no streaks on the glass, no scuff marks on the slender bowed legs of the matching French Provincial chairs. I heard a whisper of sound, and the maid returned with a rolling serving cart, loaded with a silver tea service, a plate of assorted tea sandwiches, and pastries the cook had probably whipped up that day.

"Mrs. Wood will be right with you," she said to me.

"Thanks," I said. "Uh, is there a lavatory close by?"

"Bathroom" seemed like too crude a term.

"Yes, ma'am. Turn left into the foyer. Then it's the first door on the left."

I tiptoed to the loo and locked myself in, staring at my reflection in the mirror with despair. Of course, I was dressed wrong. I never could guess right when it came to clothes. I'd gone to the Edgewater Hotel in my all-purpose dress to eat lunch with Ashley, who'd worn an outfit suitable for bagging game. Now I had down-dressed to the point where I looked like a bum. I didn't know what I'd been thinking of. I knew the Woods had money. I'd just forgotten how much. The trouble with me is I have no class. I was raised in a two-bedroom stucco bungalow, maybe eight hundred and fifty square feet of space, if you counted the little screened-in utility porch. The yard was a tatty fringe of crabgrass surrounded by the kind of white picket fence you bought in sections and stuck in the ground where you would. My aunt's notion of "day-core" was a pink plastic flamingo standing on one foot, which I'd thought was pretty classy shit until I was twelve.

I blocked the bathroom out of my visual field, but not before I got a glimpse of marble, pale-blue porcelain, and gold-plated hardware. A shallow dish held six robin's-egg-sized ovals of soap that had never been touched before by human hands. I peed and then just ran my hands under the water and shook them off, not wanting to soil anything. The terry hand towels looked as though they'd just had the price tags removed from the rims. There were four guest towels laid out beside the basin like big decorative paper napkins, but I was way too smart to fall for that trick. Where would I put a used one afterward— in the trash? These people didn't make trash. I finished drying my hands on the backside of my jeans and returned to the morning room feeling damp around the rear. I didn't dare sit down.

Presently, Ash appeared with Mrs. Wood holding on to her arm. The woman walked slowly, with a halting gait, as if she'd been forced to ambulate with a pair of swim fins for shoes. I was startled to realize she must be in her early seventies, which meant that she'd had her children rather late. Seventy isn't that old out here. People in California seem to age at a different rate than the rest of the country. Maybe it's the passion for diet and exercise, maybe the popularity of cosmetic surgery. Or maybe we're afflicted with such a horror of aging that we've halted the process psychically. Mrs. Wood apparently hadn't developed the knack. The years had knocked her flat, leaving her knees weak and her hands atremble, a phenomenon that seemed to cause her bitter amusement. She appeared to watch her own progress as if she were having an out-of-body experience.

"Hello, Kinsey. It's been a long time," she said. She lifted her face to mine at that point, her gaze dark and snappish. Whatever energy had been drained from her limbs was being concentrated now in her eyes. She had high cheekbones and a strong chin. The skin hung from her face like tissue-thin kid leather, lined and seamed, yellowing with the years like a pair of cotillion gloves. Like Ashley, she was big: wide through the shoulders, thick through the waist. Like Ash, too, she might have been a redhead in her youth. Now her hair was a soft puff of white, gathered on top and secured by a series of tortoiseshell combs. Her clothes were beautifully made—a softly draped kimono of navy silk over a dark red silk wraparound dress. Ashley helped her into a chair, pulling the tea cart within range so her mother could supervise the pouring of tea.

Ash glanced over at me. "Would you prefer sherry? The tea is Earl Grey."

"Tea's fine."

Ash poured three cups of tea while Helen selected a little plate of cookies and finger sandwiches for each of us. White bread spread with butter, sprigs of watercress peeping out. Wheat bread with curried chicken salad. Rye layered with herbed cream cheese and lox. There was something about the ritual attention to detail that made me realize neither of them cared what I was wearing or whether my social status was equivalent to theirs.

Ashley flashed me a smile when she handed me my tea. "Mother and I live for this," she said, dimples appearing.

"Oh, yes," Helen said, with a smile. "Food is my last great vice and I intend to sin incessantly as long as my palate holds out."

We munched and sipped tea and laughed and chatted about old times. Helen told me that both she and Woody had sprung from the commonplace. His father had owned a hardware store in town for years. Her father was a stone-mason. Each had inherited a modest sum which they'd pooled to form Wood/Warren sometime in the forties. The money they'd amassed was all fun and games as far as they were concerned. Woody was dead serious about the running of the company, but the profits had seemed like a happy accident. Helen said he'd carried nearly two million dollars' worth of life insurance on himself, considering it a hot joke as it was the only investment he knew of with a guaranteed payoff.

At 5:00, Ash excused herself, leaving the two of us alone.

Helen's manner became brisk. "Now tell me about this business with Lance."

I brought her up-to-date. Ash had apparently filled her in, but Helen wanted to hear it all again from me.

"I want you to work for me," she said promptly when I finished.

"I can't do that, Helen. For starters, my attorney doesn't want me anywhere near Lance, and I certainly can't accept employment from the Wood family. It already looks like I'm being paid off."

"I want to know who's behind this," she said.

"So do I. But suppose it turns out to be one of you. I don't mean to offend, but we can't rule that out."

"Then we'd have to put a stop to it. I don't like under-handed dealings, especially when people outside the company are affected. Will you keep me informed?"

"If it's practical, of course. I'm willing to share anything I find. For once, I don't have a client to protect."

"Tell me how I can help."

"Fill me in on the details of Woody's will, if that's not too personal. How was his estate divided? Who controls the company?"

A flash of irritation crossed her face. "That was the only thing we argued about. He was determined to leave the business to Lance, which I didn't disagree with in principle. Of all the children, Lance seemed to be the best qualified to carry on once his father was gone. But I felt Woody should have given him the clout to go with it. Woody wouldn't do it. He absolutely refused to give him control."

"Meaning what?"

"Fifty-one percent of the stock, that's what. I said, 'Why give him the position if you won't give him the power to go along with it? Let the boy run it his way, for God's sake, you old goat!' But Woody wouldn't hear of it. Wouldn't even *consider* the possibility. I was livid, but that old fool wouldn't budge. Lord, he could be stubborn when he made his mind up."

"What was he so worried about?"

"He was afraid Lance would run the business into the ground. Lance's judgment *is* sometimes faulty. I'd be the first to admit it. He doesn't seem to have a feel for the market like Woody did. He doesn't have the relationships with suppliers or customers, not to mention employees. Lance is impetuous and he has very grandiose schemes that never quite pan out. He's better now, but those last few years before Woody died, Lance would go off on a tear, all obsessed with some muddleheaded idea he'd got hold of. While Woody was alive, he could rein him in, but he was petrified that Lance would make a disastrous mistake."

"Why leave him the company in the first place? Why not put someone he trusted at the helm?"

"I suggested that myself, but he wouldn't hear of it. It had to be one of the boys, and Lance was the logical choice. Bass was . . . well, you know Bass. He had no desire to follow in Woody's footsteps unless they led straight to the bank."

"What about Ebony? Ash mentioned she was interested."

"I suppose she was, but by the time Woody made out this last will of his, she was off in Europe and showed no signs of coming back."

"How was the stock divided?"

"Lance has forty-eight percent. I have nine, our attorney has three percent, and Ebony, Olive, Ash, and Bass each have ten."

"An odd division, isn't it?"

"It's set up so Lance can't act alone. To make up a majority, he has to persuade at least one of us that what he's proposing makes good business sense. For the most part he's free to do as he sees fit, but we can always rally and outvote him in a pinch."

"That must drive him crazy."

"Oh, he hates it, but I must say I begin to see Woody's point. Lance is young yet and he's not that experienced. Let him get a few years under his belt and then we'll see how things stand."

"Then the situation could change?"

"Well, yes, depending on what happens to my

shares when I die. Woody left that entirely up to me. All I have to do is leave three shares to Lance. That would make him a majority stockholder. No one could touch him."

"Sounds like the stuff of which soap operas are made."

"I can wield power like a man if it comes to that. Next to eating, it's what I enjoy best." She glanced at the watch that was pinned to her dress, then reached over to the wall and pressed a button that apparently signaled the maid somewhere in the house. "Time for my swim. Would you care to join me? We have extra suits and I'd enjoy the company. I can still do a mile, but it bores me to death."

"Maybe another time. I tend to be a land animal, given my choice." I got up and shook her hand. "Tea was lovely. Thanks for the invitation."

"Come again, any time. Meanwhile, I'll see that Ebony and Olive give you any information you need."

"I'd appreciate that. I'll see myself out."

As I moved toward the foyer, the maid was returning with a portable wheelchair.

Behind her the front door opened, and Ebony came in. I hadn't seen her since I was seventeen. She must have been twenty-five then, which seemed very mature and sophisticated to me. She still had the power to intimidate. She was tall, rail-thin, high cheekbones, dark-red lipstick. Her hair was jet-black and pulled back dramatically, worn with a bow at her neck. She'd gone to Europe originally as a fashion model and she still walked like she was whipping down a runway. She'd been at Cal Poly for two years, had quit, had tried photography, dance, design school, and free-lance journalism before she turned to modeling. She'd been married maybe six years to a man whose name had recently been linked with Princess Caroline of Monaco. As far as I knew, Ebony had no children and, at forty, seemed an unlikely prospect for motherhood.

She paused when she caught sight of me, and for a moment I wasn't sure if she remembered who I was. She flicked me a chill smile and continued toward the stairs.

"Hello, Kinsey. Come upstairs. I think we should talk."

I followed her. She was wearing a wide-shouldered black suit, nipped in at the waist, a stark white shirt, knee-high glossy black boots with heels sharp enough to pierce a cheap floor covering. She smelled of a high-powered perfume, dark and intense, faintly unpleasant at close range. A trail of it wafted back at me like diesel fuel. This was going to give me a headache, I could tell. I was already annoyed by her attitude, which was peremptory at best.

The second floor was carpeted in pale beige, a wool pile so dense I felt as if we were slogging through dry sand.

The hallway was wide enough to accommodate a settee and a massive antique armoire. It surprised me somehow that she was living at home. Maybe, like Ash, she was here temporarily until she found a permanent residence somewhere else.

She opened a bedroom door and stepped back, waiting for me to pass in front of her. She should have been a school principal, I thought. With a tiny whip, she could have done a thriving trade in dominance. As soon as I'd entered the room, she closed the door and leaned against it, still holding onto the knob at the small of her back. Her complexion was fine, loose powder lending a matte finish to her face, like the pale cast of hoarfrost.

9

There was an alcove to the left, done up as a little sitting room with a coffee table and two easy chairs. "Sit down," she said.

"Why don't you just tell me what you want and let's get on with it?"

She shrugged and crossed the room. She leaned down and plucked a cigarette from the crystal box on the coffee table. She sat down in one of the upholstered chairs. She lit her cigarette. She blew the smoke out. Every gesture was separate and deliberate, designed to call maximum attention to herself.

I moved to the door and opened it. "Thanks for the trip upstairs. It's been swell," I said, as I started out the door.

"Kinsey, wait. Please."

I paused, looking back at her.

"I'm sorry. I apologize. I know I'm rude."

"I don't care if you're rude, Ebony. Just pick up the pace a bit."

Her smile was wintry. "Please sit, if you would."

I sat down.

"Would you like a martini?" She set her burning cigarette in the ashtray and opened a small refrigerator unit built into the coffee table. She extracted chilled glasses, a jar of pitted green olives, and a bottle of gin. There was no vermouth in sight. Her nails were so long they had to be fake, but they allowed her to extract the olives without getting her fingers wet. She inserted an acrylic tip and pierced the olives one by one, lifting them out. I watched her pour gin with a glint in her eye that suggested a thirst springing straight from her core.

She handed me a drink. "What happened with you and Lance?"

"Why do you ask?"

"Because I'm curious. The company's affected by whatever affects him. I want to know what's going on." She picked up her cigarette again and took a deep drag. I could tell the nicotine and alcohol were soothing some inner anxiety.

"He knows as much as I do. Why don't you ask him?"

"I thought you might tell me, as long as you're here."

"I'm not sure that's such a good idea. He seems to think you're part of it."

Her smile returned, but it held no mirth. "In this family, I'm not part of anything. I wish I were."

I felt another surge of impatience. I said, "Jesus, let's quit fencing. I hate conversations like this. Here's the deal. Someone set me up and I don't like it. I have no idea why and I don't much give a shit, but I'm going to find out who it was. At the moment I'm self-employed, so the only client I have to answer to is me. If you want information, hire a private detective. My services are spoken for."

Her expression hardened like plaster of Paris, dead white. I suspected if I reached out to touch her, her skin would have had the same catalytic heat. "I hoped you'd be reasonable."

"What for? I don't know what's going on, and what I've seen so far, I don't like. For all I know, you're at the bottom of this or you know who is."

"You don't mince words, do you?"

"Why should I mince words? I don't work for you."

"I made a simple inquiry. I can see you've decided to take offense." She stubbed out her cigarette at the halfway mark.

She was right. I was hot and I wasn't sure why. I took a deep breath and calmed myself. Not for her sake, but for mine. I tried again. "You're right. I'm out of line. I didn't think I was pissed off, but clearly I am. Somehow I've gotten caught up in family politics and that doesn't sit well with me."

"What makes you so sure it's family politics? Suppose it's someone outside the company?"

"Like who?"

"We have competitors like anybody else." She took a sip of her martini and I could see her savor the icy liquid as it flooded through her mouth. Her face was narrow, her features fine. Her skin was flawless and unlined, giving her the bland expression of a Madame Alexander doll. Either she'd already had plastic surgery or she'd somehow learned not to have the kinds of feelings that leave telltale marks. It was hard to imagine that she and Ash were sisters. Ash was earthy and open with a sunny disposition, generous, good-natured, easygoing, relaxed. Ebony was as lean as a whip, all edged—brittle, aloof, controlled, arrogant. It was possible, I thought, that the differences between them were related, in part, to their relative positions in the family constellation. Ebony was the oldest daughter, Ash the youngest. Woody and Helen had probably expected perfection of their first child. By the time they got down to Ash, and beyond her to Bass, they must have given up expecting anything.

Ebony touched the olive in her drink, turning it. She eased the fingernail into the hole and plucked it out, laying the green globe on her tongue. Her lips closed around her finger and she made a faint sucking noise. The gesture had obscene overtones and I wondered suddenly if she was coming on to me.

She said, "I don't suppose you'll tell me what Mother wanted."

I could feel my temper climb again. "Don't you people talk to each other? She invited me for tea. We had a few laughs about old times. I'm not going to run straight up here and spill it all to you. If you want to know what we talked about, ask her. When I find out what's going on, I'll be delighted to dump the whole thing in your lap. In the meantime, I don't think it's smart to run around telling everything I know."

Ebony was amused. I could see the corners of her mouth turning up.

I stopped what I was saying. "Have you got some kind of problem with that?"

She laughed. "I'm sorry. I don't mean to condescend, but you were always like this. All that energy. So fiery and defensive."

I stared at her, stumped for a response.

"You're a professional," she went on pleasantly. "I understand that. I'm not asking you to divulge any confidences. This is my family and I'm concerned about what goes on. That's my only point. If I can be of any help, just tell me how. If something you discover has a bearing on me, I'd like to hear about it. Is that so unreasonable?"

"Of course not. Sorry," I said. I circled back through our conversation, returning to something she'd said earlier. "You mentioned that the trouble might originate from someone outside the company. Were you talking in general or specific terms?"

She shrugged languidly. "General, really, though I do know of someone who hates us bitterly." She paused, as though trying to decide how to frame her explanation. "There was an engineer who worked for us for many years. A fellow named Hugh Case. Two years ago, a couple of months before my father died, as a matter of fact, he—um, killed himself."

"Was there a connection?"

She seemed faintly startled. "With Daddy's death? Oh, no, I'm sure not, but from what I'm told, Hugh's wife was convinced Lance was responsible."

"How so?"

"You'd have to ask someone else for the details. I was in Europe at the time, so I don't know much except that Hugh shut himself up in his garage and ran his car until he died of carbon monoxide poisoning." She paused to light another cigarette and then sat for a moment, using the spent match to rake the ash into a neat pile in the ashtray.

"His wife felt Lance drove him to it?"

"Not quite. She thought Lance murdered him."

"Oh, come on!"

"Well, he was the one who stood to benefit. There was a rumor floating around at the time that Hugh Case intended to leave Wood/Warren and start a company of his own in competition with us. He was in charge of research and development, and apparently he was on the track of a revolutionary new process. The desertion could have caused us serious harm. There are only fifteen or so companies nationwide in our line of work so the defection would have set us back."

"But that's ridiculous. A man doesn't get murdered because he wants to change jobs!"

Ebony arched an eyebrow delicately. "Unless it represents a crippling financial loss to the company he leaves."

"Ebony, I don't believe this. You'd sit there and say such a thing about your own brother?"

"Kinsey, I'm reporting what I heard. I never said *I* believed it, just that she did."

"The police must have investigated. What did they find?"

"I have no idea. You'd have to ask them."

"Believe me, I will. It may not connect, but it's worth checking out. What about Mrs. Case? Where is she at this point?"

"I heard she left town, but that might not be true. She was a bartender, of all things, in that cocktail lounge at the airport. Maybe they know where she went. Her name is Lyda Case. If she's remarried or gone back to her maiden name, I don't know how you'd track her down."

"Anybody else you can think of who might want to get to Lance?"

"Not really."

"What about you? I heard you were interested in the company. Isn't that why you came back?"

"In part. Lance has done some very foolish things since he took over. I decided it was time to come home and do what I could to protect my interests."

"Meaning what?"

"Meaning just what it sounds like. He's a menace. I'd like to get him out of there."

"So if he's charged with fraud, it won't break your heart."

"Not if he's guilty. It would serve him right. I'm after his job. I make no bones about it, but I certainly wouldn't need to go about it in an underhanded way, if that's what you're getting at," she said, almost playfully.

"I appreciate your candor," I said, though her attitude irritated me. I'd expected her to be defensive. Instead, she was amused. Part of what offended me in Ebony was the hint of superiority that underscored everything she did. Ash had told me Ebony was always considered "fast." In high school, she'd been daring, a dazzler and wild, one of those girls who'd try anything once. At an age when everyone else was busy trying to conform, Ebony had done whatever suited her. "Smoked, sassed adults, and screwed around," was the way Ash put it. At seventeen she'd learned not to give a shit, and now she seemed indelibly imprinted with an air of disdain. Her power lay in the fact that she had no desire to please and she didn't care what your opinion of her was. Being with her was exhausting and I was suddenly too tired to press her about the little smile that played across her mouth.

It was 6:15. High tea wasn't doing much for someone with my low appetites. I was suddenly famished. Martinis give me a headache anyway and I knew I smelled of secondhand cigarette smoke.

I excused myself and headed home, stopping by McDonald's to chow down a quarter-pounder with cheese, large fries, and a Coke. This was no time to torment my cells with good nutrition, I thought. I finished up with one of those fried pies full of hot glue that burns the fuck out of your mouth. Pure heaven.

When I got back to my place, I experienced the same disconcerting melancholy I'd felt off and on since Henry got on the plane for Michigan. It's not my style to be lonely or to lament, even for a moment, my independent state. I like being single. I like being by myself. I find solitude healing and I have a dozen ways to feel amused. The problem was I couldn't think of one. I won't admit to depression, but I was in bed by 8:00 P.M. . . . not cool for a hard-assed private eye waging a one-woman war against the bad guys everywhere.

10

By 1:00 the next afternoon, I had tracked Lyda Case by telephone to a cocktail lounge at the Dallas/Fort Worth airport, where she was simultaneously tending bar and hanging up in my ear with a force that made me think I'd have to have my hearing rechecked. Last May I'd been compelled to shoot someone from the depths of a garbage bin and my ears have been hissing ever since. Lyda didn't help this . . . especially as she said a quite rude word to me before she smacked the phone down. I was deeply annoyed. It had taken me a bit of doing to locate her and she'd already hung up on me once that day.

I'd started at 10:00 A.M. with a call to the Culinary Alliance and Bartenders Local 498, which refused to tell me anything. I've noticed lately that organizations are getting surly about this sort of thing. It used to be you could ring them right up, tell a plausible tale, and get the information you wanted within a minute or two. Now you can't get names, addresses, or telephone numbers. You can't get service records, bank balances, or verification of employment. Half the time, you can't even get confirmation of the facts you already have. Don't even bother with the public schools, the Welfare Department, or the local jail. They won't tell you nothin'.

"That's privileged," they say. "Sorry, but that's an invasion of our client's privacy."

I hate that officious tone they take, all those clerks and receptionists. They *love* not telling you what you want to know. And they're smart. They don't fall for the same old song and dance that worked a couple of years ago. It's too aggravating for words.

I reverted to routine. When all else fails, try the county clerk's office, the public library, or the DMV. They'll help. Sometimes there's a small fee involved, but who cares?

I whipped over to the library and checked back through old telephone directories year by year until I found Hugh and Lyda Case listed. I made a note of the address and then switched to the crisscross and found out who their neighbors had been two years back. I called one after another, generally bullshitting my way down the block. Finally, someone allowed as how Hugh had died and they thought his widow moved to Dallas.

It worried me briefly that Lyda Case might be un-listed, but I dialed Information in Dallas and picked up a home phone number right away. Hot damn, this was fun. I tried the number and someone answered on the third ring.

"Hello."

"May I speak to Lyda Case?"

"This is she."

"Really?" I asked, amazed at my own cleverness.

"Who is this?" Her voice was flat.

I hadn't expected to get through to her and I hadn't yet made up a suitable fib, so I was forced to tell the truth. Big mistake. "My name is Kinsey Mill-hone. I'm a private detective in Santa Teresa, Califor-nia. . . ."

Bang. I lost some hearing in the mid-range. I called back, but she refused to answer the phone.

At this point, I needed to know where she was em-ployed and I couldn't afford to call every bar in the Dallas/Forth Worth area, if indeed that's the sort of work she still did. I tried Information again and picked up the telephone number of the Hotel and Restaurant Employees Union Local 353 in Dallas. I had my index finger poised to dial when I realized I would need a ruse.

I sat and thought for a moment. It would help to have Lyda Case's Social Security number, which might lend a little air of credibility to my bogus pur-

suit. Never try to get one of these from the Social Security Office. They're right up there with banks in
their devotion to thwarting you at every turn. I was
going to have to get the information through access
to public records of some sort.

I grabbed my handbag, a jacket, and my car keys
and headed over to the courthouse. The Registrar of
Voters is located in the basement, down a flight of
wide red-tile steps with a handrail made out of antique rope as big around as a boa constrictor.

I followed the signs down a short corridor to the
right, pushing into the office through a glass door.
Two clerks were working behind the counter, but no
one paid any attention to me. There was a computer
terminal on the counter and I typed in Lyda Case's
name. I closed my eyes briefly, offering up a small
prayer to whichever of the gods is in charge of bu-
reaucracies. If Lyda had registered to vote any time in
the last six years, the revised form wouldn't show her
Social Security number. That question had been
deleted in 1976.

The name flashed up, line after line of green print
streaking out. Lyda Case had first registered to vote
October 14, 1974. The number of the original affidavit was listed on the bottom line. I made a note of
the number and gave it to the clerk who had approached when she saw I needed help.

She disappeared into a back corridor where the old

files are kept. She returned a few minutes later with the affidavit in hand. Lyda Case's Social Security number was neatly filled in. As a bonus, I also picked up her date of birth. I started laughing at the sight of it. The clerk smiled and I knew from the look we exchanged that she felt as I did about some things. I love information. Sometimes I feel like an archaeologist, digging for facts, uncovering data with my wits and a pen. I made notes, humming to myself.

Now I could go to work.

I went home again and picked up the phone, redialing the Bartenders Local in Santa Teresa.

"Local Four-Ninety-eight," the woman said.

"Oh, hi," said I. "Who am I speaking to, please?"

"I'm the administrative assistant," she said primly. "Perhaps you'll identify yourself."

"Oh, sorry. Of course. This is Vicky with the Chamber of Commerce. I'm addressing invitations for the annual Board of Supervisors dinner and I need your name, if you'd be so kind."

There was a dainty silence. "Rowena Feldstaff," she said, spelling it out for me carefully.

"Thank you."

I dialed Texas again. The phone on the other end rang four times while two women in teeny, tiny voices laughed about conditions in the Inky Void. Someone picked up.

"Hotel and Restaurant Employees Local Three-

Five-Three. This is Mary Jane. Can I he'p you?" She had a soft voice and a mild Texas accent. She sounded like she was about twenty.

"You sure can, Mary Jane," I said. "This is Rowena Feldstaff in Santa Teresa, California. I'm the administrative assistant for Bartenders Local Four-Ninety-eight and I'm trying to do a status check on Lyda Case. That's C-A-S-E . . ." Then I rattled out her date of birth and her Social Security number, as though from records of my own.

"Can I have a number so I can call you back?" said the ever-cautious Mary Jane.

"Sure," I said and gave her my home phone.

Within minutes, my phone rang again. I answered as Bartenders Local 498, and Mary Jane very kindly gave me Lyda Case's current place of employment, along with the address and phone number. She was working at one of the cocktail lounges at the Dallas/Fort Worth airport.

I called the bar and one of the waitresses told me Lyda would be there at 3:00 Dallas time, which was 1:00 where I was.

At 1:00, I called back and lost another couple of decibels' worth of hearing. Whoo, that lady was quick. I'd have to walk around with a horn sticking out of my ear at this rate.

If I'd been working off an expense account, I'd have hied myself out to the Santa Teresa airport and jumped on a plane for Dallas. I can be pretty cavalier with someone else's money. My own, I think about first, as I'm very cheap.

I hopped in my car and drove over to the police station. Jonah Robb, my usual source of illicit information, was out of town. Sergeant Schiffman, sitting in for him, was not all that swift and didn't really like to bend the rules, so I bypassed him and went straight to Emerald, the black clerk in Records and Identification. Technically she's not supposed to give out the kind of information I needed, but she's usually willing to help if no one's around to catch her.

I leaned on the counter in the reception area, waiting while she finished typing a department memo. She took her time getting to me, probably sensing that I was up to no good. She's in her forties, with a medium complexion about the color of a cigar. Her hair is cut very short and it curls tensely around her head, a glistening, wet-looking black with gray frizz at the tips. She's probably fifty pounds overweight and it's all solidly packed into her waist, her belly, and her rump.

"Uh-uhn," she said to me as she approached. Her voice is higher than one would imagine for a woman her size, and it has a nasal cast to it, with just the faintest suggestion of a lisp. "What do you want? I'm almost afraid to ask."

She was wearing a regulation uniform, a navy-blue skirt and a white short-sleeved blouse that looked very stark and clean against the tobacco brown of her arms. The patch on her sleeve said Santa Teresa Police Department, but she's actually a civilian clerk.

"Hello, Emerald. How are you?"

"Busy. You better cut right down to what you want," she said.

"I need you to look something up for me."

"Again? I'm gonna get myself fired one of these days because of you. What is it?" Her tone was offset by a sly smile that touched off dimples in her cheeks.

"A suicide, two years back," I said. "The guy's name was Hugh Case."

She stared at me.

Uh-oh, I thought. "You know who I'm talking about?"

"Sure, I know. I'm surprised you don't."

"What's the deal? I assume it wasn't routine."

She laughed at that. "Oh, honey, no way. No way. Uh-un. Lieutenant Dolan still gets mad when he hears the name."

"How come?"

"How come? Because the evidence disappeared, that's how come. I know two people at St. Terry's got fired over that."

Santa Teresa Hospital, St. Terry's, is where the hospital morgue is located.

"What evidence came up missing?" I asked.

"Blood, urine, tissue samples, the works. His

weren't the only specimens disappeared. The courier picked 'em up that day and took 'em out to County and that's the last anybody ever saw of the whole business."

"Jesus. What about the body? Why couldn't they just redo the work?"

Emerald shook her head. "Mr. Case'd been cremated by the time they found out the specimens were missing. Mrs. Case had the ashes what-do-you-call-'em . . . scattered at sea."

"Oh, shit, you're kidding."

"No ma'am. Autopsy'd been done and Dr. Yee already released the body to the mortuary. Mrs. Case didn't want any kind of funeral, so she gave the order to have him cremated. He was gone. People had a fit. Dr. Yee turned St. Terry's upside down. Nothing ever did show. Lieutenant Dolan was beside himself. Now I hear they got this whole new policy. Security's real tight."

"But what was the assumption? Was it an actual theft?"

"Don't ask me. Like I said, lot of other stuff disappeared at the same time so the hospital couldn't say what went on. It could have been a mistake. Somebody might have thrown all that stuff out by accident and then didn't want to admit it."

"Why was Dolan involved? I thought it was a suicide."

"You know nobody will make a determination on the manner and cause of death until the reports come back."

"Well, yeah," I said. "I just wondered if the lieutenant had any initial doubts."

"Lieutenant always has doubts. He'll have some more he catches you sniffin' around. Now I got work to do. And don't you tell nobody I told you this stuff."

I drove over to the Pathology Department at St. Terry's, where I had a quick chat with one of the lab techs I'd dealt with before. She confirmed what Emerald had told me, adding a few details about the mechanics of the episode. From what she said, a courier from the coroner's office did a daily run in a blood-transport vehicle, making a sweep of labs and law-enforcement agencies. Specimens to be picked up were sealed, labeled, and placed in insulated cold packs, like picnic supplies. The "hamper" itself was stored in the lab refrigerator until the driver showed up. The lab tech would fetch the hamper. The courier would sign for the evidence and away he'd go. The Hugh Case "material," as she so fastidiously referred to it, was never seen again once it left the hospital lab. Whether it disappeared en route or after it was delivered to the coroner's lab, no one ever knew. The clerk at St. Terry's swore she gave it to the driver and she had a signed receipt to show for it. She assumed the hamper reached its destination as it had every day for years. The courier remembered putting it in the vehicle and assumed it was among the items delivered at the end of his run. It was only after some days had passed and Dr. Yee began to press for lab results on the toxicological tests that the disappearance came to light. By then, of course, as Emerald had indicated, Hugh Case's remains had been reduced to ashes and flung to the far winds.

I used one of the pay phones in the hospital lobby to call my travel agent and inquire about the next flight to Dallas. There was one seat left on the 3:00 shuttle from Santa Teresa to Los Angeles, arriving at LAX at 3:35. With a two-hour layover, I could pick up a United flight that would get me into Dallas that night at 10:35, CST. If Lyda clocked into the bar at 3:00 and worked an eight-hour shift, she should be getting off at 11:00. A delay at any point in the journey would get me there too late to connect with her. I couldn't get a flight back to Santa Teresa until morning anyway, because the airport here shuts down at 11 P.M. I was going to end up spending a night in Dallas in any event. The air fare itself was nearly two hundred bucks, and the notion of paying for a hotel room on top of that made me nearly giddy with anxiety. Of course, I could always sleep listing sideways in one of those molded-plastic airport chairs, but I didn't relish the idea. Also, I wasn't quite sure how I could contrive to eat on the ten bucks in cash I had on me. I probably couldn't even afford to retrieve my VW from the long-term parking lot when I got home again.

My travel agent, Lupe, was breathing patiently into my ear while I did these lightning-quick calculations.

"I don't want to bug you, Millhone, but you got about six minutes to make up your mind about this."

I glanced at my watch. It was 2:17. I said, "Oh hell, let's go for it."

"Done," she said.

She booked the seats. I charged the tickets to my United credit card which I had just gotten paid off. Curses, I thought, but it had to be done. Lupe said the tickets would be waiting for me at the ticket counter. I hung up, left the hospital, and headed out to the airport.

My handsome travel wardrobe that day consisted of my boots, my ratty jeans, and a cotton turtleneck, navy blue with the sleeves only slightly stretched out of shape. I had an old windbreaker in the back seat of my car. Happily, I hadn't used it recently to clean off my windshield. I also keep a small overnight case in the back seat, with a toothbrush and clean underwear.

I boarded the plane with twelve minutes to spare and tucked my overnight case under the seat in front of me. The aircraft was small and all fifteen seats were occupied. A hanging curtain separated the passengers from the cockpit. Since I was only two seats back, I could see the whole instrument panel, which didn't look any more complicated than the dashboard of a new Peugeot. When the flight attendant saw me rubbernecking, she pulled the curtain across the opening, as if the pilot and copilot were doing something up there we were better off not knowing about.

The engines sounded like lawn mowers and reminded me vaguely of the Saturday mornings of my youth when I would wake late to hear my aunt out cutting the grass. Over the din, the intercom system was worthless. I couldn't hear a word the pilot said, but I suspected he was reciting that alarming explanation of what to do in the "unlikely" event of a water landing. Most planes crash and burn on land. This was just something new to worry about. I didn't think my seat cushion was going to double as a flotation device of any kind. It was barely adequate to keep my rear end protected from the steel-reinforced framework of the seat itself. While the pilot droned on, I looked at the plastic card with its colorful cartoon depicting the aircraft. Someone had placed two X's on the diagram. One said, "You are here." A second X out on the wing tip said, "Toilet is here."

The flight only took thirty-five minutes so the flight attendant, who wore what looked like a Girl Scout uniform, didn't have time to serve us complimentary drinks. Instead, she whipped down the aisle, passing a little basket of Chiclets chewing gum in tiny boxes. I spent the flight time trying to get my ears to unpop, looking, I'm sure, like I was suffering from some kind of mechanical jaw disease.

My United flight left right on time. I sat in the no-smoking section being serenaded by a duet of crying babies. Lunch consisted of a fist of chicken breast on a pile of rice, covered with what looked like rubber cement. Dessert was a square of cake with a frosting that smelled like Coppertone. I ate every bite and tucked the cellophane-wrapped crackers in my purse. Who knew when I'd get to eat again.

Once we landed in Dallas, I grabbed up my belongings and eased my way toward the front of the plane as we waited for the jetway to thump against the door. The stewardess released us like a pack of noisy school kids and I dogtrotted toward the gate. By the time I actually hit the terminal, it was 10:55. The cocktail lounge I was looking for was in another satellite, typically about as far away as you could get. I started running, grateful, as usual, that I keep myself fit. I reached the bar at 11:02. Lyda Case had left. I'd missed her by five minutes and she wasn't scheduled to work again until the weekend. I won't repeat what I said.

11

I had Lyda paged. I had passed a Traveler's Aid station, an L-shaped desk, where the airline-terminal equivalent of a candy-striper was posted. This woman was in her fifties, with an amazingly homely face: gaunt and chinless, with one eye askew. She was wearing a Salvation Army uniform, complete with brass buttons and epaulets. I wasn't sure what the deal was. Maybe distraught mothers of lost toddlers and foreign-speaking persons in need of Kaopectate were meant to garner spiritual comfort along with the practical kind. She was just shutting down her station for the night, and at first she didn't seem to appreciate my request for help.

"Look," I said, "I just flew in from California to speak with a woman who's on her way out of the terminal. I've got to catch her before she hits the parking lot, and I have no idea which exit she's using. Is there any way to have her paged?"

The woman fixed me with the one eye while the other moved to the one-page directory she kept taped to her desk top. Without a word, she picked up the phone and dialed. "What's the name?" she asked.

"Lyda Case."

She repeated the name and within moments, I heard Lyda Case being paged to the Traveler's Aid station, terminal 2. I was profuse in my thanks, though she didn't seem to require much in the way of appreciation. She finished packing up and, with a brief word, departed.

I had no idea if Lyda Case would show. She might have been out of the building by the time her name was called. Or she might have been too tired and cranky to come back for any reason. On an impulse, I rounded the desk and sat down in the chair. A man passed with a rolling suitcase that trailed after him reluctantly, like a dog on its way to the vet. I glanced at my watch. Twelve minutes had passed. I checked the top desk drawer, which was unlocked. Pencils, pads of paper, tins of aspirin, cellophane-wrapped tissue, a Spanish-language dictionary. I read the list of useful phrases inside the back cover. "*Buenas tardes*," I murmured to myself. "*Buenas noches*." Good nachos. I was starving to death.

"Somebody paging me? I heard my name on the

public-address system and it said to come here." The accent was Texan. Lyda Case was standing with her weight on one hip. Petite. No makeup. All freckles and frizzy hair. She was dressed in dark slacks and a matching vest—one of those all-purpose bartender uniforms that you can probably order wholesale from the factory. Her name was machine-embroidered on her left breast. She had on a diamond-crusted watch, and in her right hand she held a lighted cigarette, which she dropped and crushed underfoot.

"What's the matter, baby? Did I come to the wrong place?" Mid-thirties. Lively face. Straight little nose and a sharp, defiant chin. Her smile revealed crooked eyeteeth and gaps where her first molars should have been. Her parents had never gone into debt for *her* orthodontia work.

I got up and held my hand out. "Hello, Mrs. Case. How are you?"

She allowed her hand to rest in mine briefly. Her eyes were the haunting, surreal blue of contact lenses. Distrust flickered across the surface. "I don't believe I know you."

"I called from California. You hung up on me twice."

The smile drained away. "I thought I made it clear I wasn't interested. I hope you didn't fly all this way on my account."

"Actually, I did. You'd just gone off duty when I

got to the lounge. I'm hoping you'll spare me a few minutes. Is there some place we can go to talk?"

"This is called talkin' where I come from," she snapped.

"I meant, privately."

"What about?"

"I'm curious about your husband's death."

She stared at me. "You some kind of reporter?"

"Private detective."

"Oh, that's right. You mentioned that on the phone. Who all are you working for?"

"Myself at the moment. An insurance company before that. I was investigating a warehouse fire at Wood/Warren when Hugh's name came up. I thought you might fill me in on the circumstances of his death."

I could see her wrestling with herself, tempted by the subject. It was probably one of those repetitious nighttime tales we tell ourselves when sleep eludes us. Somehow I imagined there were grievances she recited endlessly as the hours dragged by from 2:00 to 3:00. Something in the brain comes alive at that hour and it's usually in a chatty mood.

"What's Hugh got to do with it?"

"Maybe nothing. I don't know. I thought it was odd his lab work disappeared."

"Why worry about it? No one else did."

"It's about time then, don't you think?"

She gave me a long look, sizing me up. Her expression changed from sullenness to simple impatience. "There's a bar down here. I got somebody waiting so I'll have to call home first. Thirty minutes. That's all you get. I worked my butt off today and I want to rest my dogs." She moved off and I followed, trotting to keep up.

We sat in captain's chairs at a table near the window. The night sky was thick with low clouds. I was startled to realize it was raining outside. The plate glass was streaked with drops blown sideways by a buffeting wind. The tarmac was as glossy as black oilcloth, with runway lights reflected in the mirrored surface of the apron, pebbled with raindrops. Three DC-10s were lined up at consecutive gates. The area swarmed with tow tractors, catering vehicles, boom trucks, and men in yellow slickers. A baggage trailer sped by, pulling a string of carts piled high with suitcases. As I watched, a canvas duffel tumbled onto the wet pavement, but no one seemed to notice. Somebody was going to spend an irritating hour filling out "Missing Baggage" claim forms tonight.

While Lyda went off to make her phone call, I ordered a spritzer for me and a Bloody Mary for her, at her request. She was gone a long time. The waitress brought the drinks, along with some Eagle Snack pretzels in a can. "Lyda wanted somethin' to snack on, so I brought you these," she said.

"Can we run a tab?"

"Sure thing. I'm Elsie. Give a holler if you need anything else."

Ground traffic was clearing and I saw the jetway retract from the side of the plane nearest us. On the runway beyond, an L-1011 lumbered by with a stripe of lighted windows along its length. The bar was beginning to empty, but the smoke still sat on the air like a visible smudge on a photograph. I heard high heels clopping toward the table, and Lyda was back. She'd peeled off her vest, and her white blouse was now unbuttoned to a point just between her breasts. Her chest was as freckled as a bird's egg and it made her look almost tanned.

"Sorry it took me so long," she said. "I got this roommate in the middle of a nervous breakdown, or so she thinks." She used her celery stalk to stir the pale cloud of vodka into the peppered tomato juice down below. Then she popped the top off the can of pretzels.

"Here, turn your hand up and lemme give you some," she said. I held my hand out and she filled my palm with tiny pretzels. They were shaped like Chinese pagodas encrusted with rock salt. Her hostility had vanished. I'd seen that before—people whose mistrust takes the form of aggressiveness at first, their resistance like a wall in which a sudden gate appears.

She'd decided to talk to me and I suppose she saw no point in being rude. Besides, I was buying. With ten bucks in my pocket, I couldn't afford more than thirty minutes' worth of drinks anyway.

She had taken out a compact and she checked her makeup, frowning at herself. "God. I am such a mess." She plunked her bag up on the table and rooted through until she found a cosmetics pouch. She unzipped it and took out various items, and then proceeded to transform herself before my very eyes. She dotted her face with liquid foundation and smoothed it on, erasing freckles, lines, discolorations. She took out an eyeliner and inked in her upper and lower lids, then brushed her lashes with mascara. Her eyes seemed to leap into prominence. She dusted blusher high on each cheek, lined the contour of her mouth with dark red and then filled her lips in with a lighter shade. Less than two minutes passed, but by the time she glanced at me again, the rough edges were gone and she had all the glamour of a magazine ad. "What do you think?"

"I'm impressed."

"Oh, honey, I could make you over in a minute. You ought to do a little more with yourself. That hair of yours looks like a dog's back end."

I laughed. "We better get down to business if thirty minutes is all I get."

She waved dismissively. "Don't worry about that. I changed my mind. Betsy's workin' on an overdose and I don't feel like going home yet."

"Your roommate took an overdose?"

"She does that all the time, but she never can get it right. I think she got a little booklet from the Hemlock Society and takes half what she needs to do the job. Then I get home and have to deal with it. I truly hate paramedics trooping through my place after midnight. They're all twenty-six years old and so clean-cut it makes you sick. Lot of times she'll date one afterward. She swears it's the only way to meet nurturing men."

I watched while she drained half her Bloody Mary. "Tell me about Hugh," I said.

She took out a pack of chewing gum and offered me a piece. When I shook my head, she unwrapped a stick and doubled it into her mouth, biting down. Then she lit a cigarette. I tried to imagine the combination . . . mint and smoke. It was an unpleasant notion even vicariously. She wadded up the gum wrapper and dropped it in the ashtray.

"I was just a kid when we met. Nineteen. Tending bar. I went out to California on the Greyhound bus the day I turned eighteen, and went to bartending school in Los Angeles. Cost me six hundred bucks. Might have been a rip-off. I did learn to mix drinks but I probably could have done that out of one of them little books. Anyway, I got this job at LAX and I've been working airport bars ever since. Don't ask me why. I just got stuck somehow. Hugh came in one night and we got talkin' and next thing I knew, we fell in love and got married. He was thirty-nine years old to my nineteen, and I was with him sixteen years. I knew that man. He didn't kill himself. He wouldn't do that to me."

"What makes you so sure?"

"What makes you sure the sun's coming up in the east ever' day? It just does, that's all, and you learn to count on that the way I learned to count on him."

"You think somebody killed him?"

" 'Course I do. Lance Wood did it, as sure as I'm sittin' here, but he's not going to admit it in a million years and neither will his family. Have you talked to them?"

"Some," I said. "I heard about Hugh's death for the first time yesterday."

"I always figured they paid off the cops to keep it hush. They got tons of money and they know ever'one in town. It was a cover-up."

"Lyda, these are honorable people you're talking about. They'd never tolerate murder and they wouldn't protect Lance if they thought he had anything to do with it."

"Boy, you're dumber than I am, if you believe that. I'm tellin' you it was murder. Why'd you fly all this way if you didn't think so yourself?"

"I don't know what to think. That's why I'm asking you."

"Well, it wasn't suicide. He wasn't depressed. He wasn't the suicidal type. Why would he do such a thing? That's just dumb. They knew him. They knew what kind of man he was."

I watched her carefully. "I heard he was planning to leave the company and start a business of his own."

"He talked about that. He talked about a lot of things. He worked for Woody fifteen years. Hugh was loyal as they come, but everybody knew the old man meant to leave the company to Lance. Hugh couldn't stand the idea. He said Lance was a boob and he didn't want to be around to watch him mess up."

"Did the two of them have words?"

"I don't know for sure. I know he gave notice and Woody talked him out of it. He'd just bid on a big government contract and he needed Hugh. I guess Hugh said he'd stay until word came through whether Woody got the bid or not. Two days later, I got home from work, opened the garage door, and there he was. It looked like he fell asleep in the car, but his skin was cherry red. I never will forget that."

"There's no way it could have been an accident?"

She leaned forward earnestly. "I said it once and I'll

say it again. Hugh wouldn't kill himself. He didn't have a reason and he wasn't depressed."

"How do you know he wasn't holding something back?"

"I guess I don't, if you put it like that."

"The notion of murder doesn't make any sense. Lance wasn't even in charge at that point, and he wouldn't kill an employee just because the guy wants to move on. That's ludicrous."

Lyda shrugged, undismayed by my skepticism. "Maybe Lance worried Hugh would take the business with him when he went."

"Well, aside from the fact he wasn't gone yet, it still seems extreme."

She bristled slightly. "You asked for my opinion. I'm tellin' you what I think."

"I can see you believe it, but it's going to take more than that to talk me into it. If Hugh was murdered, it could have been someone else, couldn't it?"

"Of course it could. I believe it was Lance, but I can't *swear* to it. I don't have any proof, anyhow. Sometimes I think it's not worth foolin' with. It's over and done, so what difference does it make?"

I shifted the subject. "Why'd you have him cremated so fast?"

She stared at me. "Are you thinking *I* had a hand in it?"

"I'm just asking the questions. What do I know?"

"He *asked* to be cremated. It wasn't even my idea. He'd been dead for two days. The coroner released the body and the funeral director suggested we go ahead with it, so I took his advice. You can talk to him yourself if you don't believe me," she said. "Hugh was drugged. I'd bet money that's how they pulled it off. His lab work was stolen so nobody'd see the test results."

"Maybe he was drunk," I suggested. "He might have pulled into the garage and fallen asleep."

She shook her head. "He didn't drink. He'd given that up."

"Did he have a problem with alcohol?"

"Once upon a time, he did," she said. "We *met* in a bar. Two in the afternoon, in the middle of the week. He wasn't even travelin'. He just liked to come watch the planes, he said. I should have suspected right then, but you know what it's like when you fall in love. You see what you want to see. It took me years to figure out how far gone he was. Finally I said I'd leave him if he didn't straighten up. He went into this program . . . not AA, but something similar. He got sobered up and that's how he stayed."

"Is there a chance he'd gone back to drinking? It wouldn't be unheard of."

"Not with him on Antabuse. He'da been sick as a pup."

"You're sure he took the stuff?"

"I gave it to him myself. It was like a little game we played. Every morning with his orange juice. He held his hand out and I gave him his pill and watched him swallow it right down. He wanted me to see he didn't cheat. He swore, the day he quit drinking, he'd never go back to it."

"How many people knew about the Antabuse?"

"I don't know. He never made a big deal of it. If people around him were drinking, he just said 'No thanks.'"

"Tell me what was happening the week he died."

"Nothing. It seemed like an ordinary week to me. He talked to Woody. Two days later, he was dead. After the funeral, I packed up, put everything in a U-Haul, and hit the road for home. This is where I've been ever since."

"And there was nothing among his things to suggest what was going on? No letter? A note?"

She shook her head. "I went through his desk the day he died, and I didn't see a thing."

12

The flight home was uneventful. I'd spent an hour and a half with Lyda, and the rest of the night in the airport terminal with its red carpeting, high glass ceiling, real trees, and an actual bird that flew back and forth, chirping incessantly. It was sort of like camping out, only I was sitting upright and I didn't have any wienies to roast. I made notes of my conversation with Lyda, which I'd transcribe for the files when I got home. I was inclined to believe Hugh Case had been murdered, though I had no idea how, why, or by whom. I also tended to think his death was related to current events at Wood/Warren, though I couldn't imagine what the connection might be. Lyda had promised to get in touch if she remembered anything of note. All in all, it was not an unproductive trip. It had generated more questions than it answered, but that was fine with me. As long as there are threads to unravel, I'm in business. The frustration starts when all the leads dry up and the roads turn out to be dead ends. With Hugh Case, I felt like I'd just found one of the corner pieces of a jigsaw puzzle. I had no idea what the final picture would look like, but at least I had a place to start.

I boarded the plane at 4:30 A.M. and arrived at LAX at 5:45. I had to wait for a 7:00 A.M. shuttle to Santa Teresa, and by the time I dragged my sorry ass home, I was dead on my feet. I let myself into the apartment an hour later, checked for messages (none), pulled my boots off, and curled up in the folds of my quilt, fully dressed.

At approximately 9:02, there was a knock at my door. I staggered up out of sleep and shuffled to the door, dragging my quilt behind me like a bridal train. My mouth tasted foul and my hair was standing straight up, as spiky as a punker's, only not as clean. I peered through the fish-eye, too clever to be caught unawares by an early-morning thug. Standing on my doorstep was my second ex-husband, Daniel Wade.

"Shit," I murmured. Briefly, I leaned my head against the door and then peeked again. All I could see in truncated form was his face in profile, blond hair curling around his head like an aura. Daniel Wade is quite possibly the most beautiful man I've ever seen—a bad sign. Beautiful men are usually either gay or impossibly narcissistic. (Sorry for the generalization, folks, but it's the truth.) I like a good face or an interesting face or a face with character, but not this sculpted perfection of his . . . the straight, well-proportioned nose, high cheekbones, strong jawline, sturdy chin. His hair was sun-bleached, his eyes a remarkable shade of blue, offset by dark lashes. His teeth were straight and very white, his smile slightly crooked. Get the picture, troops?

I opened the door. "Yes?"

"Hi."

"Hello." I gave him a rude stare, hoping he'd disappear. He's tall and slim and he can eat anything without gaining weight. He stood there in faded jeans and a dark-red sweatshirt with the sleeves pushed up. His skin had a golden sheen, tanned and windburned, so his cheeks glowed darkly. Just another boring California golden boy. The hair on his arms was bleached nearly white. His hands were tucked in his pockets, which was just as well. He's a jazz pianist with long, bony fingers. I fell in love with his hands first and then worked my way up.

"I've been in Florida." Good voice, too . . . just in case his other virtues fail to excite. Reedy and low. He sings like an angel, plays six instruments.

"What brought you back?"

"I don't know. Homesick, I guess. A friend of mine

was heading this way so I tagged a ride. Did I wake you up?"

"No, I often walk around looking like this."

A slight smile here, perfectly timed. His manner seemed hesitant, which was unusual for him. He was searching the sight of me, looking (perhaps) for some evidence of the girl I used to be.

"I like the haircut," he said.

"Gee, this is fun. I like yours, too."

"I guess I caught you at a bad time. I'm sorry about that."

"Uh, Daniel, could we skip to the punch line here? I'm operating on an hour's sleep and I feel like shit."

It was clear he'd rehearsed this whole conversation, but in his mind my response was tender instead of down-right rude. "I wanted you to know I'm clean," he said. "I have been for a year. No drugs. No drinking. It hasn't been easy, but I really have straightened up."

"Super. I'm thrilled. It's about bloody time."

"Could you knock off the sarcasm?"

"That's my natural way of speaking ever since you left. It's real popular with men."

He rocked slightly on his heels, looking off across the yard. "I guess people don't get a second chance with you."

I didn't bother to respond to that.

He tried a new tack. "Look. I have a therapist

named Elise. She was the one who suggested I clean up the unfinished business in my life. She thought maybe you might benefit, too."

"Oh, hey. That's swell. Give me her address and I'll write her a bread-and-butter note."

"Can I come in?"

"Jesus Christ, Daniel, of course not! Don't you get it yet? I haven't seen you for eight years and it turns out that's not long enough."

"How can you be so hostile after all this time? I don't feel bad about you."

"Why would you feel bad? I didn't do anything to you!"

A look of injury crossed his face and his bewilderment seemed genuine. There's a certain class of people who will do you in and then remain completely mystified by the depth of your pain. He shifted his weight. This apparently wasn't going as he thought it would. He reached up to pick at a wood splinter in the door frame above my head. "I didn't think you'd be bitter. That's not like you, Kinsey. We had some good years."

"Year. Singular. Eleven months and six days, to be exact. You might move your hand before I slam the door on it."

He moved his hand.

I slammed the door and went back to bed.

After a few minutes, I heard the gate squeak.

I thrashed about for a while, but it was clear I wouldn't get back to sleep. I got up and brushed my teeth, showered, shampooed my hair, shaved my legs. I used to have fantasies about his showing up. I used to invent long monologues in which I poured out my sorrow and my rage. Now I was wishing he'd come back again so I could do a better job of it. Being rejected is burdensome that way. You're left with emotional baggage you unload on everyone else. It's not just the fact of betrayal, but the person you become . . . usually not very nice. Jonah had survived my tartness. He seemed to understand it had nothing to do with him. He was so blunt himself that a little rudeness didn't bother him. For my part, I really thought I'd made my peace with the past until I came face to face with it.

I called Olive Kohler and made an appointment to see her later in the day. Then I sat down at my desk and typed up my notes. At noon, I decided to get some errands done. Daniel was sitting in a car parked just behind mine. He was slouched down in the passenger seat, his booted feet propped up on the dashboard, a cowboy hat tilted over his face. The car was a ten-year-old Pinto, dark blue, dented, rusted, and stripped of its hubcaps. The sheepskin car-seat covers looked like badly matted dog. A decal on the bumper indicated that the car was from Rent-A-Ruin.

Daniel must have heard the gate squeak as I came

out. He turned his head, pushing his hat back lazily. He sometimes affects that aw-shucks attitude. "Feeling better (Miss Kitty)?"

I unlocked my car and got in, started the engine and pulled away. I avoided the apartment for the rest of the day. I can't remember now half of what I did. Mostly I wasted time and resented the fact that I was not only out an office but banned from my own residence.

At 5:00, with the aid of a street map, I found the Kohlers' house on an obscure leafy lane in Montebello. The property was hidden by a ten-foot hedge, the driveway barred by an electronically controlled wrought-iron gate. I parked out on the street and let myself in through a wooden gate embedded in the shrubbery. The house was a two-story, English Tudor style, with a steeply pitched shingled roof, half-timbered gables, and a handsome pattern of vertical beams across the front. The lot was large, shaded with sycamores and eucalyptus trees as smooth and gray as bare concrete. Dark-green ivy seemed to grow everywhere. A gardener, a graduate of the Walt Disney school of landscape maintenance, was visible, trimming the shrubs into animal shapes.

The newspaper was resting on the doormat. I picked it up and then I rang the bell. I expected a maid, but Olive opened the door herself in a gray satin robe and low-heeled satin mules. I'd mostly seen those in Joan Crawford movies, and they looked like they'd be a trick to wear. I had brief visions of plopping around my apartment in backless bedroom slippers. Cigarette holder. Marcelled hair. I could have my eyebrows plucked back to ogee arches.

"Hello, Kinsey. Come in. Terry's on his way. I forgot we were due at a cocktail party at six." She stepped away from the door and I followed her in.

"We can do this another time if you like," I said. I handed her the paper.

"Thanks. No, no. This is fine. It's not for an hour anyway and the people don't live far. I've got to finish dressing, but we can talk in here." She glanced at the paper briefly and then tossed it on the hall table next to a pile of mail.

She clattered her way along the dark stone-tile hallway toward the master suite at the rear of the house. Olive was slim and blond, her shoulder-length hair blunt-cut and thick. I wondered sometimes if Ash was the only sister whose hair remained its natural shade. Olive's eyes were bright blue, her lashes black, her skin tone gold. She was thirty-three or so, not as brittle as Ebony, but with none of Ash's warmth. She was talking back over her shoulder to me.

"I haven't seen you for ten years. What have you been up to?"

"Setting up my own agency," I said.

"Married? Kids?"

"No, on both counts. You have kids?"

She laughed. "God forbid."

The bedroom we entered was spacious. Beamed ceiling, big stone fireplace, French doors opening onto a walled-in patio where a small deck had been added on. I could see a round two-person hot tub, surrounded by ferns. A white Persian cat was curled up on a chaise, its face tucked into the circling plume of its tail.

The bedroom floor was polished teak with area rugs of a long white wool that probably came from yaks. The entire wall behind the bed was mirrored and I flashed on an image of Terry Kohler's sexual performances. What did Olive stare at, I wondered, while he watched himself? I glanced at the ceiling, checking to see if there was a cartoon tacked up there, like the one in my gynecologist's examining room: "Smile. It gives your face something to do!" This does not amuse.

I eased into an easy chair and watched while Olive moved into a walk-in closet the size of a two-car garage. Quickly she began to sort through a rack of evening clothes, rejecting sequined outfits, floor-length organza gowns, beaded jackets with long, matching skirts. I could see an assortment of shoes stacked in clear plastic boxes on the shelf overhead, and at one end of the rack, several fur coats of various lengths and types. She selected a knee-length cocktail dress with spaghetti straps and returned to the bedroom where she scrutinized her reflection. The dress was avocado green, infusing her skin with sallow undertones.

"What do you think?" she said, eyes still pinned to her own image in the glass.

"Makes you look green."

She stared at herself, squinting critically. "You're right. Here. You take this. I never liked it anyway." She tossed the dress on the bed.

"I don't wear clothes like that," I said uncomfortably.

"Take it. We'll have a New Year's Eve party and you can wear it then." She pulled out a black taffeta dress cut straight across the front. She stepped into it, then zipped it up the back in a motion that snapped everything into place. She was so slender I didn't see how the globelike breasts could possibly be hers. She looked like she'd had softballs surgically implanted on her chest. Hug a woman like that and she was bound to leave dents.

She sat down on the dressing-table bench and pulled on black panty hose, then slipped her feet into four-inch black spike heels. She looked gorgeous, all curves and flawless skin, the pale-blond hair brushing against her bare shoulders. She sorted through her jewelry box and selected clip-on diamond earrings shaped like delicate silver branches hung with sparkling fruit.

She returned to the closet and emerged in a soft, white fur coat the same length as the dress. When she pulled the coat around her, she looked like a flasher decked out in white fox.

She half-smiled when she caught my look. "I know what you're thinking, sweetie, but they were already dead when I got to the furrier's. Whether or not I bought the coat had no effect on their fates."

"If women didn't wear them, they wouldn't be killed in the first place," I said.

"Oh, bullshit. Don't kid yourself. In the wild, these animals get torn to shreds every day. Why not preserve the beauty, like a piece of art? The world's a vicious place. I don't pretend otherwise. And don't argue with me," she said, firmly. She pointed a finger. "You came to talk, so talk." She slipped the coat off and tossed it on the bed, then sat down on the bench and crossed her legs. She eased off one high heel and let her shoe flap against the bottom of her foot.

I said, "How much do you know about the situation at Wood/Warren?"

She gestured impatiently. "Business is a bore. I use that section of the paper to line the cat box."

"You have no interest in the family split?"

"What split? You mean with Lance? I have nothing

invested one way or the other. He and Ebony disagree. She wants me to vote with her. The way she explains it, it's to my advantage. Lance will have a fit, of course, but who gives a shit? He's had his chance."

"You're siding with her?"

"Who knows? Probably. She's smarter than he is and it's time for new blood. He's got his head in the toilet half the time."

"Meaning what?"

"Let me give you the lowdown on my brother, honey-bun. He's a salesman at heart. He can charm your socks off when it suits him. He's enthusiastic about anything that interests him, which isn't much. He has no head for figures. Absolutely none. He hates sitting in an office and he can't stand routine. He's good at generating business and lousy at follow-through. End transmission."

"You've seen this firsthand or is this Ebony's claim?"

"I hear about what happens at the plant every day. Terry's a workaholic and most of what he talks about is business."

"How do he and Lance get along?"

"They knock heads all the time. Terry's obsessive. It drives him crazy when people fuck up. Excuse the scientific term. Lance has poor judgment. Everyone knows that. Meet the woman he married if you have any doubts."

"What about the rest of the family? Can't they vote him out?"

"Nope. The rest of us combined only own forty-nine percent of the stock. Ebony wants to put the squeeze on him, but she can't actually force him out. She can bring him to heel, which I suspect is what she wants."

"I take it Bass isn't involved since he lives in New York."

"He shows up for board meetings occasionally. He enjoys playing mogul, but he's harmless enough. He and Lance are usually thick."

"Who will Ashley side with?"

"She could go either way. Obviously, Ebony's hoping she can persuade us all to mutiny."

"How does your mother feel? This couldn't sit well with her."

"She hates it. She wants Lance in charge. Not because he's good, but because it's less hassle."

"Do you think he's honest?"

"Lance? Are you kidding? No way."

"How do you and he get along?"

"I can't stand him. He's a very tense person and he's soooo paranoid. I hate to be around him. He gets on my nerves. He's my brother and I love him, don't get me wrong. I just don't like him much." She wrinkled her nose. "He always smells like garlic and sweat and that nasty Brut cologne. I don't know why men wear it. Such a turnoff."

"Have you heard any gossip about the warehouse blaze?"

"Just what Terry's told me. You know Lance borrowed money against the company two years ago and now he's losing his shirt. He'd love half a million bucks."

"Oh really. That's the first I heard of it."

She shrugged carelessly. "He went into the printing business, which is foolish in itself. I've heard printing and restaurants are the quickest way to go broke. He's lucky the warehouse burned down. Or is that the point?"

"Why don't you tell me?"

She rested her elbow on her knee and propped her chin up on her fist. "If you're looking for answers, I've just run out. I don't care about Lance. I don't care about Wood/Warren, to tell you the truth. Sometimes the politics amuse me in a soap-opera kind of way, like *Dynasty*, but it's still boring stuff."

"What *do* you care about?"

"Tennis. Travel. Clothes. Golf. What else is there?"

"Sounds like a fun life."

"Actually, it is. I entertain. I do charity work when I have the time. There are people who think I'm a spoiled, lazy bitch, but I have what I want. That's more than most can say. It's the have-nots who wreak havoc. I'm a real pussycat."

"You're fortunate."

"Like they say, there's no such thing as a free ride. I pay a price, believe me."

I could see what an exhausting proposition that must be.

We heard someone at the entrance, then footsteps along the hall. By the time Terry Kohler reached the bedroom door, he was already in the process of removing his coat and tie.

"Hello, Kinsey. Olive mentioned you'd be stopping by. Let me grab a quick shower and then we can talk." He looked at Olive. "Could you fetch us a drink?" he said, his tone peremptory.

She didn't exactly perk up and pant, but that's the impression she gave. Maybe her job was harder than I thought. I wouldn't do that for anyone.

13

I waited in the living room while Olive stepped into the kitchen. The place was handsome; beveled windowpanes, pecan paneling, a fieldstone fireplace, traditional furniture in damask and mahogany. Everything was rose and dusty pink. The room smelled faintly spicy, like carnations. I couldn't imagine the two of them sitting here doing anything. Aside from the conventional good taste, there was no indication that they listened to music or read books. No evidence of shared interests. There was a current copy of *Architectural Digest* on the coffee table, but it looked like a prop. I've never known rich people to read *Popular Mechanics*, *Family Circle*, or *Road & Track*. Come to think of it, I have no idea what they do at night.

Olive returned in ten minutes with a tray of hors d'oeuvres and a silver cooler with a wine bottle nestled in ice. Her entire manner had changed since Terry walked in the door. She still had an air of elegance, but her manner was tinged now with servitude. She fussed with small linen cocktail napkins, arranging them in a pattern near the serving plate she'd placed at one end of the coffee table. She'd prepared ripe figs stuffed with mascarpone cheese, triangles of phyllo, and chilled new potato halves topped with sour cream and caviar. If I called this my dinner, would all of my nutritional needs be met?

Olive crossed briskly to a sideboard and set out liquor bottles so we'd have a choice of drinks. The room was beginning to darken and she turned on two table lamps. The panels of her taffeta skirt made a silky scritching sound every time she moved. Her legs were well muscled and the spike heels threw her calves into high relief.

I glanced over to see Terry standing in the doorway, freshly showered and dressed, his gaze lingering on the picture she presented. He caught my eye, smiling with the barest suggestion of proprietorship. He didn't look like an easy man to please.

"Gorgeous house," I said.

Olive looked over with a rare smile. "Thanks," she said.

"Have a seat," he said.

"I don't want to hold you up."

Terry waved dismissively, as if the pending conversation took precedence. The gesture had the same in-gratiating effect as someone who tells his secretary to hold all the calls. It's probably bullshit . . . maybe no one ever calls anyway . . . but it gives the visitor a feeling of importance.

"He'd never pass up a chance to talk business," Olive said. She handed him a martini and then glanced at me. "What would you like?"

"The white wine, if I may."

While I looked on, she opened the bottle, pouring a glass for me and then one for herself. She handed me mine and then eased out of her shoes and took a seat on the couch, tucking her feet up under her. She seemed softer, less egotistical. The role of helpmeet suited her, which surprised me, somehow. She was a woman who had no apparent purpose beyond in-dulging herself and pampering "her man." The no-tion seemed outdated in a world of career women and supermoms.

Terry perched on the arm of the couch, staring at me with guarded interest. He took charge of the con-versation, a move he must have been accustomed to. His dark eyes gave his narrow face a brooding look, but his manner was pleasant. He made only an occa-sional digital reference to the fact of his moustache. I've seen men who stroke their facial hair incessantly, as if it were the last remnant of a baby bunting, com-forting and soft. "Lance says someone tried to frame you," he said. He ate a new-potato half and passed the plate to me.

"Looks that way," I said. I helped myself to a fig. Heaven on the tongue.

"What do you need from us?"

"For starters, I'm hoping you can fill me in on Ava Daugherty."

"Ava? Sure. What's she got to do with it?"

"She was there the day I did the fire-scene inspection. She also saw Heather give me the envelope full of inventory sheets, which have since disappeared."

His gaze shifted and I watched him compose his reply before he spoke. "As far as I know, Ava's straight as an arrow. Hardworking, honest, devoted to the company."

"What about Lance? How does she get along with him?"

"I've never heard them exchange a cross word. He's the one who hired her, as a matter of fact, when it was clear we needed an office manager."

"How long ago was that?"

"God, it must be two, three years now," he said. He looked down at Olive, sitting close by. "What's your impression? Am I reporting accurately?"

Olive shrugged. "Well, I wouldn't say she's crazy about him. She thinks he plays too much when he ought to be getting work done, but I don't think she'd devise any scheme to do him in." Olive passed the hors d'oeuvre tray to me. I thought it only gracious to sample something else so I selected a potato half and popped it in my mouth.

"Who might?" I asked, licking sour cream from my thumb. This shit was great. If they'd just leave the room for a minute, I'd have a go at the rest.

Both seemed to come up blank.

"Come on. He must have enemies. Somebody's gone to a lot of trouble over this," I said.

Terry said, "At the moment, I couldn't name one, but we can give it some thought. Maybe something will occur to us."

"What can you tell me about the Wood/Warren engineer who killed himself?"

"Hugh Case," Olive said.

Terry seemed surprised. "What brought that up? I just got a call from Lyda Case this afternoon."

"Really?" I said. "What did she have to say?"

"It wasn't what she said so much as her attitude. She was completely freaked out, screaming at the top of her lungs. Said his death was my fault."

Olive looked at him in disbelief. "Yours? What bullshit! Why would she say that?"

"I have no idea. She sounded drunk. Ranting and raving. Foulmouthed, shrill."

"That's curious," I said. "Is she here in town?"

Terry shook his head. "She didn't say. The call was long distance from the sound of it. Where's she live?"

"Dallas, I believe."

"I got the impression she intended to fly out. Do you want to talk to her if she shows up?"

"Yes, I'd like that," I said, careful to omit any reference to the fact that I'd met with her the night before. She hadn't seemed paranoid to me at all and she'd never mentioned Terry's name.

Olive stirred on the couch, shifting positions. "Just in time for New Year's. Everyone'll be here." She glanced at Terry. "Did I tell you Bass gets in tonight?"

A look of annoyance flashed across his face. "I thought he was broke. I hope you didn't pay his way."

"Me! Absolutely not. Ebony sends him money, but you wouldn't catch me doing it," she remarked. And then to me, "Bass and I had a falling-out at Thanksgiving and we haven't spoken since. He's got a big mouth in matters that are none of his business. I think he's loathsome, and he's just about that fond of me."

Terry glanced at his watch and I took that as my cue. "I should let you go if you've got a party," I said.

"I don't feel we've been any help," Olive said.

"Don't worry about it. I've got other sources. Just let me know if you come up with anything you think might pertain."

I left my card on the coffee table. Terry walked me to the door while Olive excused herself to fetch her coat. He watched her disappear into the bedroom. "I didn't want to mention this in front of her,"

he said, "but Lyda Case scared the shit out of me this
afternoon."

"How so?"

"I don't want to make Olive nervous, but the
woman threatened me. I don't think it has anything
to do with Lance or I'd have said so up front. This is
different. I don't know what it's about, but she really
sounded cracked."

"What kind of threat?" I asked.

"Out of nowhere, she asked me how old I'd be on
my next birthday. I didn't know what she was getting
at, but when I told her I'd be forty-six, she said, 'Don't
count on it.' And then she laughed like a fiend. Jesus,
the sound made my blood run cold. I can't believe she
was serious, but my God! What a thing to say."

"And you have no idea why she suddenly got in
touch?"

"I haven't talked to her for years. Since Hugh died,
I guess."

"I understand there's some question about the
manner of his death."

"I've heard that too and I don't know what to
think."

"How well did you know him?"

"I wouldn't say we were close, but I worked with
him, oh, probably five years or so. He never struck
me as the sort who'd commit suicide. Of course, you
never know what someone under pressure will do."

"Pressure?"

"Lyda'd threatened to leave him. Hugh was a sweet guy, but he was terribly dependent on her and I think it just knocked the props out from under him."

"Why was she leaving? What was that about?"

"I wasn't privy to the details. Lance might know."

Olive reappeared, white fur coat across her shoulders, the green dress over her arm. Terry and I abandoned the topic of Lyda Case. He made no comment when she gave me the dress. Maybe Olive always gave away her clothes. The three of us left the house together, confining ourselves to small talk.

It was fully dark by then and the night was chilly. I turned on the heater in my car and drove to a pay phone in Montebello Village, putting a call in to Darcy at home. I wanted to stop off and see her before I went back to my place. But she told me Andy'd worked late, so she hadn't had a chance to search his office. She was going in early the next morning, and said she'd call if she came up with anything.

I hung up, realizing then how exhausted I felt. In addition to the jet lag, I was operating on a bad night's sleep, and the fragmentary nap I'd picked up this morning wasn't helping anything. I headed home. As I turned the corner onto my street, I spotted Daniel's rental car, still sitting at the curb in front of my apartment. I parked and got out. Even in the dark, I could see him slouched in the front seat, feet on the dash as they had been before. I was just opening the gate when he rolled down his window. "Can I talk to you?"

I felt something snappish rise up in me, but I forced it back down again. I don't like being bitchy, and I hated admitting to myself that he still had the power to distress. "All right," I said. I approached the car and halted about six feet away. "What is it?"

He unfolded himself and emerged from the car, leaning his elbows on the open car door. The pale glow from the street light gilded his cheekbones, touching off strands of silver in the cloud of blond hair.

"I'm in a bit of a bind," he said. His face was dappled with shadows that masked the remembered clear blue of his eyes. After eight years, it was amazingly painful just to be in his company.

I thought the safest course was to repeat information back to him without comment. "You're in a bind," I said. There was a brief silence wherein I assumed I was meant to quiz him on the nature of his problem. I clamped my teeth together, waiting patiently.

He smiled ruefully. "Don't worry. I'm not going to ask you for money and I'm not trying to get in your pants."

"This comes as a big relief, Daniel. What *do* you

want?" The bitchy tone was already back, but I swear I couldn't help myself. There's nothing more infuriating than a man who's manipulated your emotions once and now thinks he can do it again. I could still remember the charge that ran between us early in our relationship, sexual electricity infusing the very air we breathed. It had taken years for me to realize that I had generated most of it myself out of my own neediness. Maybe that's what was making me so churlish in retrospect. I was still chafing at myself for what a fool I'd been.

"I need a place to stash my gear," he said.

"What gear?"

He shrugged. "I got a two-thousand-dollar acoustic guitar I can't leave because the trunk lock is busted on the rental car I picked up. It'll get ripped off if it's in the back seat."

"You brought a guitar like that all the way from Florida?"

"I thought maybe I'd pick up a gig out here. I could use the bucks."

"What happened to your friend? I thought you got a ride with someone. Why not take it to his place? Or is it a woman? I guess I never asked you that."

"Well, no, it's a guy," he said. "The problem is, he doesn't actually live here in town. He was just passing through on his way to San Francisco and he won't be back till late on Sunday. That's why I had to rent a car of my own."

"Where are you staying? Don't you have a place?"

"I'm working on that. The town's booked solid because of the holidays. Meantime, I can't even pull into a gas station to take a leak without hauling everything in with me. It's just for a couple of days."

I stared at him. "You always do things like this, you know that? You're always in a bind, shifting your weight from foot to foot, hoping someone'll bail you out of the hole you're in. Try the Rescue Mission. Pick up a woman. That shouldn't be so tough. Or sell the damn thing. Why is it up to me?"

"It's not up to you," he said mildly. "It's a simple favor. What's the big deal?"

I ran out of steam. We'd had this same exchange a hundred times and he'd never heard me before. I might as well save my breath. I might as well give him what he wanted and get it over with. It was probably just an elaborate excuse to prolong our contact. "Never mind," I said. "No big deal. You can park the damn thing in a corner until Sunday and then I want it out of here."

"Sure. No problem. Thanks."

"I'm warning you, Daniel. If you've got a stash anywhere within six blocks of here, I'll call the cops."

"I'm clean. I told you that. You can look for your-self."

"Skip it," I said. I knew him well enough to know he wouldn't bluff on that, because he knew *me* well enough to know I'd have him thrown in the slammer if I caught him.

14

I took a couple of Tylenols and slept like a stone—deep, dreamless sleep that soothed my frazzled nerves and restored my good spirits. I was up at 6:00, ready to jog as usual. There was no sign of Daniel parked at my curb. I did a perfunctory stretch against the fence post and headed toward Cabana Boulevard.

The run felt great. The sky was a pearl gray streaked with pink. To my right, a dark-gray surf boomed against the hard-packed sand, leaving snowy froth in its wake. The wharf was mirrored in the glistening pools that remained when the waves receded. The sea seemed to shush the birds that shrieked overhead. This was the last day of the year and I ran with a sense of optimism the new year always brings. I'd find a way to sort it all out: Lance, Mac's suspicions about me, even Daniel's sudden appearance on my doorstep. I was alive and healthy, physically fit.

Rosie's would open again on Monday. Henry would be home in another six days. I had the sassy green dress Olive had given me, and maybe a New Year's invitation if she came through as hoped. I did my three miles and slowed to a walk, cooling off as I headed home.

I showered and dressed in jeans as usual, savoring the morning at home. By then it was 7:00—too early for phone calls. I ate my cereal and read the *L.A. Times* over two cups of coffee. Daniel's guitar sat in the corner in mute testimony to his renewed presence in my life, but I ignored it for the most part.

Darcy called at 7:35 from California Fidelity. She'd done a thorough search. Andy's office was clean.

"Shit," I said. "What about a typewriter? I was hoping we could get a match on the phony fire department report, but I didn't find one at his apartment."

"Maybe he keeps it in the trunk of his car."

"Oh, I like that. I'll see if I can find a way to check that out. In the meantime, keep an eye peeled. Maybe something will surface. Andy's gotta be tied into this business somehow. It would help a lot to know who he knows at Wood/Warren. Did you go through his Rolodex?"

"That won't help. He knows all those guys because that was his account. He's bound to have the number handy. I'll check it out, though. Maybe something else will come to light." She clicked off.

At 8:00, I put a call through to Lyda Case in Texas. Her roommate said she was out of town, maybe in California, but she wasn't sure. I left my number and asked her to have Lyda get in touch with me if she called home.

I called my pal at the credit bureau, but she was out until Monday. I had the feeling the rest of the day was going to come down about the same way. It was New Year's Eve day. As with Christmas Eve, businesses were closing early, people taking off at noon. Olive called me at 10:00 to say that she was indeed putting together an impromptu cocktail party. "It's mostly family and a few close friends. Half the people I called already had plans. Are you free? We'd love to have you, if you're not already tied up."

"Of course I'm not," I said. "I'd love to come." I hated to sound so eager, but in truth I was. I didn't want to spend this New Year's Eve alone. I was worried Daniel might start looking too good. "Can I bring anything?"

"Actually I could use some help," she said. "I gave the housekeeper the weekend off, so I'm throwing the whole thing together by myself. I can always use an extra set of hands."

"Well, I'm not a cook, but I can sure chop and stir. What time?"

"Four-thirty? I'll be back from the supermarket by then. Ash said she'd come about five to help, too.

Everybody else will be coming about seven. We'll keep going till the food and alcohol give out."

"Great," I said. "And the green dress will be okay?"

"It better be. I'm giving this party so you can wear the damn thing."

I put a call through to Lance. I didn't like initiating the contact with him, but I had to hear his version of the situation with Hugh Case. As soon as he was on the line, I told him what I'd heard. The silence was weighty. "Lance?"

"I'm here," he said. He sighed heavily. "Jesus, I don't know how to deal with this. What the hell is going on? I heard rumors back then she thought I had something to do with his death. It's not true. It's completely untrue, but I don't have a way of proving it. Why would I do that? What could I possibly gain by killing him?"

"Wasn't he leaving the company?"

"Absolutely not. He talked about quitting. He said he wanted to start a company of his own. He even gave notice, but hell, Dad called him in and they had a long talk. Dad offered to make him a vice-president. Gave him a big raise and he was happy as a clam."

"When was this?"

"I don't know. A couple of days before he died."

"Didn't that strike you as peculiar?"

"Sure it did. She swore he didn't kill himself and I agreed. He wasn't the depressive type and he'd just made a hell of a deal for himself. Somehow she got it in her head that I killed the man. I wouldn't harm a soul. You gotta believe me. Somebody's working very hard to get me put away."

"Speaking of which, have you heard anything from California Fidelity?"

His tone changed. "Yeah, yesterday. They're turning everything over to the cops."

I could feel my stomach clench. "Really? Do they have enough to make a case?"

"I don't know. I hope not. Look, I need to talk to you privately and I can't do it here. It's important. Is there any way we can meet?"

I told him I'd be at Olive's later and we agreed to talk then. I wasn't anxious to be seen in his company, but he seemed insistent, and at that point, I didn't see how things could get worse. I wasn't guilty of conspiracy and I was tired of acting like I was. Worry was sitting on my chest like a weight, leaden and oppressive. I had to do something to get my mind off things.

I went out and bought a pair of high heels, anxiety translating into excitement as the day progressed. Being isolated that week had made me aware that I do have a few social impulses—buried deep, perhaps, under layers of caution, but part of me nevertheless.

This was like dress-up time with the big kids, and I was looking forward to it. I'd begun to feel very charitable about Olive, whose life-style only yesterday had seemed superficial and self-indulgent. Who was I to judge? It was none of my business how she made her peace with the world. She'd fashioned a life out of tennis and shopping, but she managed to do occasional charity work, which was more than I could claim. She was right about one thing: the harm in the world is done by those who feel disenfranchised and abused. Contented people (as a rule) don't kite checks, rob banks, or kill their fellow citizens.

I thought about going to the gym, but decided to bag that idea. I hadn't done a workout since Tuesday, but I just didn't give a damn. I puttered and napped through the middle of the day.

At 3:00 I took a long bubble bath . . . well, I used dishwashing liquid, but it did foam right up. I washed my hair and combed it for a change. I did some stuff to my face that passed for makeup in my book, and then wiggled into underwear and panty hose. The dress was grand, and it fit like a charm, rustling the same way Olive's had the night before. I'd never had a role model for this female stuff. After my parents' death when I was five, I'd been raised by a maiden aunt, no expert herself at things feminine. I'd spent the days of my childhood with cap guns and books, learning self-sufficiency, which loomed large with her. By the time I reached junior high I was a complete misfit, and by high school I'd thrown in my lot with some bad-ass boys who cussed and smoked dope, two things I mastered at an early age. In spite of the fact that I'm a social oaf, my aunt instilled a solid set of values, which prevailed in the end. By the time I graduated, I'd straightened up my act and now I'm a model citizen, give or take a civil code or two. At heart, I've always been a prissy little moralist. Private investigation is just my way of acting out.

By 4:30, I was standing on the Kohlers' doorstep, listening to the door chime echo through the house. It didn't look as if anyone was there. There was mail jammed in the box, the newspaper and a brown paper-wrapped parcel on the mat. I peered into one of the long glass panels on either side of the front door. The foyer was dark and no lights were showing at the rear of the house. Olive probably wasn't home from the supermarket yet. The cat appeared from around the side of the house with her long white coat and flat face. Somehow she seemed like a girl to me, but what do I know? I said some cat-type things. She appeared unimpressed.

I heard a car horn toot. The electronic gate was rolled back from the driveway and a white Mercedes 380 SL pulled in. Olive waved and I moved toward the parking pad. She got out of the car and moved around to the rear, looking very classy in her white fur coat.

"Sorry I'm late. Have you been here long?"

"Five minutes."

She opened the trunk and picked up one grocery bag, then struggled to lift a second.

"Here, let me help with that."

"Oh, thanks. Terry should be right behind me with the liquor."

I took the bag, snagging up another one while I was at it. There were two more in the trunk and another two bags visible in the front seat. "God, how many people did you invite?"

"Just forty or so. It should be fun. Let's get these in and we'll have Terry bring the rest. We've got a ton of work to do."

She moved toward the front door while I brought up the rear. There was a crunch of tires on gravel and Terry pulled into the drive in a silver-gray Mercedes sedan. Must be nice, I thought. The gate rolled shut. I waited while Olive emptied the mailbox and shoved the stack of envelopes in the top of her grocery bag. She picked up the newspaper and tucked that in, too, then grabbed the parcel.

"You need help? I can take something else."

"I got it." She laid the parcel across the bag, securing it with her chin while she fumbled for her house key.

The cat was sauntering toward the driveway, plumed tail aloft. I heard the clink of liquor bottles as Terry set his bags down on the concrete. He began to coil up a garden hose the yardman had left on the walk.

"Break your neck on this thing," he said. Olive got the door open and gave it a push. The telephone started to ring. I glanced back as she tossed the parcel toward the hall table.

What happened next was too swift to absorb. There was a flash of light, a great burst that filled my visual field like a sun, followed by a huge cloud of white smoke. Shrapnel shot from a central point, spraying outward with a deadly velocity. A fireball seemed to curl across the threshold like a wall of water with a barrier removed, washing flames into the grass. Every blade of green in its path turned black. At the same time, I was lifted by a shattering low-frequency boom that hurtled me capriciously across the yard. I found myself sitting upright against a tree trunk like a rag doll, shoes gone, toes pointing straight up. I saw Olive fly past me as if she'd been yanked, tumbling in a high comic arc that carried her to the hedge and dropped her in a heap. My vision shimmered and cleared, a light show of the retina, accompanied by the breathless thumping of my heart. My brain, mute with wonder, failed to compute anything but the smell of black powder, pungent and harsh.

The explosion had deafened me, but I felt neither fear nor surprise. Emotions are dependent on comprehension, and while I registered the event, nothing made any sense. Had I died in that moment, I would not have felt the slightest shred of regret, and I understood how liberating sudden death must be. This was pure sensation with no judgment attached.

The front wall of the house was gone and a crater appeared where the hall table had been. The foyer was open to the air, surrounded by coronas of charred wood and plaster, burning merrily. Large flakes of pale blue and pale brown floated down like snow. Grocery items littered the entire yard, smelling of pickles, cocktail onions, and Scotch. I had taken in both sight and sound, but the apparatus of evaluation hadn't caught up with me yet. I had no idea what had happened. I couldn't remember what had transpired only moments before, or how this might relate to past events. Here we were in this new configuration, but how had it come to pass?

From the change in light, I guessed that my eyebrows and lashes must be gone and I was conscious of singed hair and flash burns. I put a hand up, amazed to find my limbs still functioning. I was bleeding from the nose, bleeding from both ears, where the pain was now excruciating. To my left, I could see Terry's mouth working, but no words were coming out. Something had struck him a glancing blow and blood poured down his face. He appeared to be in pain, but the movie was silent, sound reel flapping in-effectually. I turned to see where Olive was.

For one confused moment, I thought I saw a pile of torn foxes, their bloodied pelts confirming what she'd said the day before. It *is* true, I thought, these animals in the wild get ripped to shreds every day. The harsh splattering of red against the soft white fur seemed obscene and out of place. And then, of course, I understood what I was looking at. The blast had opened her body, exposing tangles of bloody flesh, yellow fat, and jagged bone along her backside. I closed my eyes. By then, the smell of black powder was overlaid with the scent of woodsmoke and cooked flesh. Carefully I pondered the current state of affairs.

Olive had to be dead, but Terry seemed okay, and I thought perhaps at some point he would come and help me up. No hurry, I thought. I'm comfy for now. The tree trunk provided back support, which helped, as I was tired. Idly, I wondered where my shoes had gone. I sensed movement, and when I opened my eyes again, confused faces were peering into mine. I couldn't think what to say. I'd already forgotten what was going on, except that I was cold.

Time must have passed. Men in yellow slickers pointed hoses at the house, swords of water cutting through the flames. Worried people crouched in front of me and worked their mouths some more. It was funny. They didn't seem to realize they weren't saying anything. So solemn, so animated, and so intent. Lips and teeth moving to such purpose with no visible effect. And then I was on my back, looking up into tree branches that wobbled through my visual field as I was borne away. I closed my eyes again, wishing that the reeling of the world would stop before I got sick. In spite of the fire, I was shivering.

15

Gradually my hearing returned, pale voices in the distance coming nearer until I understood that it was someone bending over me. Daniel, as radiant as an archangel, appeared above me. The sight of him was baffling, and I felt an incredible urge to put a hand to my forehead, like a movie heroine recovering from a swoon, murmuring, Where am I? I was probably dead. Surely, hell is having your former spouse that close again . . . flirting with a nurse. Ah, I thought, a clue. I was in a hospital bed. She was standing to his right, in polyester white, a vestal virgin with a bedpan, her gaze fixed on his perfect features in profile. I'd forgotten how cunning he was at that sort of thing. While he feigned grave concern for me, he was actually casting backward with his little sexual net, enveloping her in a fine web of pheromones. I moved my lips and he leaned closer. He said, "I think she's conscious."

"I'll get the doctor," the nurse said. She disappeared.

Daniel stroked my hair. "What is it, babe? Are you in pain?"

I licked my lips. "Asshole," I said, but it came out all garbled and I wasn't sure he got the drift. I vowed, in that moment, to get well enough to throw him out. I closed my eyes.

I remembered the flash, the deafening bang, Olive flying past me like a mannequin. She had looked unreal, arms crooked, legs askew, as lumpen as a sandbag flung through the air, landing with a sodden thump.

Olive must be dead. There wasn't any way to mend the parts of her turned inside out by the blast.

I remembered Terry with the blood gushing down his face. Was he dead, too? I looked at Daniel, wondering how bad it was.

Daniel sensed my question. "You're fine, Kin. Everything's okay. You're in the hospital and Terry's here, too," he said. And after a hesitation, "Olive didn't make it."

I closed my eyes again, hoping he'd go away.

I concentrated on my various body parts, hoping that all of them could be accounted for. Many treasured portions of my anatomy hurt. I thought at first I was in some sort of bed restraint, but it turned out to be an immobilizing combination of bruises, whiplash, IV fluids, painkillers, and pressure dressings on the areas where I had suffered burns. Given the fact that I'd been standing ten feet away from Olive, my injuries turned out to be miraculously insignificant—contusions and abrasions, mild concussion, superficial burns on my extremities. I'd been hospitalized primarily for shock.

I was still confused about what had happened, but it didn't take a 160 IQ to figure out that something had gone boom in a big way. A gas explosion. More likely a bomb. The sound and the impact were both characteristic of low explosives. I know now, because I looked it up, that low explosives have velocities of 3,300 feet per second, which is much faster than the average person tends to move. That short trip from Olive's front porch to the tree base was as close to free flight as I was ever going to get.

The doctor came in. She was a plain woman with a good face and sense enough to ask Daniel to leave the room while she examined me. I liked her because she didn't lapse into a slack-jawed stupor at the sight of him. I watched her, as trusting as a child while she checked my vital signs. She must have been in her late thirties, with haphazard hair, no makeup, gray eyes that poured out compassion and intelligence. She held my hand, lacing her cool fingers through mine. "How are you feeling?"

Tears welled up. I saw my mother's face superimposed on hers, and I was four again, throat raw from a tonsillectomy. I'd forgotten what it was like to experience the warmth radiated by those who tend the sick. I was saturated by a tenderness I hadn't felt since my mother died. I don't take well to helplessness. I've worked hard in my life to deny neediness, and there I was, unable to sustain any pretense of toughness or competence. In some ways it came as a great relief to lie there in a puddle and give myself up to her nurturing.

By the time she'd finished checking me, I was somewhat more alert, anxious to get my bearings. I quizzed her in a foggy way, trying to get a fix on my current state.

She told me I was in a private room at St. Terry's, having been admitted, through Emergency, the night before. I remembered, in fragments, some of it: the high keening of sirens as the ambulance swayed around corners, the harsh white light above me in the Emergency Room, the murmurs of the medical personnel assigned to evaluate my injuries. I remembered how soothing it was when I was finally tucked into bed: clean, patched up, pumped full of medications, and feeling no pain. It was now mid-morning of New Year's Day. I was still groggy, and I discovered belatedly that I was dropping off to sleep without even being aware of it.

The next time I woke, the IV had been removed and the doctor had been replaced by a nurse's aide who helped me onto the bedpan, cleaned me up again, changed my gown, and put fresh sheets on the bed, cranking me into a sitting position so I could see the world. It was nearly noon. I was famished by then and wolfed down a dish of cherry Jell-O the aide rustled up from somewhere. That held me until the meal carts arrived on the floor. Daniel had gone down to the hospital cafeteria for lunch, and by the time he got back, I'd requested a "No Visitors" sign hung on the door.

The restrictions must not have applied to Lieutenant Dolan, however, because the next thing I knew, he was sitting in the chair, leafing through a magazine. He's in his fifties, a big, shambling man, with scuffed shoes and a light-weight beige suit. He looked exhausted from the horizontal lines across his forehead to his sagging jawline, which was ill-shaved. His thinning hair was rumpled. He had bags under his eyes and his color was bad. I had to guess that he'd been out late the night before, maybe looking forward to a day of football games on TV instead of interviewing me.

He looked up from his magazine and saw that I was

awake. I've known Dolan for maybe five years, and while we respect each other, we're never at ease. He's in charge of the homicide detail of the Santa Teresa Police Department, and we sometimes cross swords. He's not fond of private investigators and I'm not fond of having to defend my occupational status. If I could find a way to avoid homicide cases, believe me, I would.

"You awake?" he said.

"More or less."

He set the magazine aside and got up, shoving his hands in his coat pockets while he stood by my bed. All my usual sassiness had been, quite literally, blown away. Lieutenant Dolan didn't seem to know how to handle me in my subdued state. "You feel well enough to talk about last night?"

"I think so."

"You remember what happened?"

"Some. There was an explosion and Olive was killed."

Dolan's mouth pulled down. "Died instantly. Her husband survived, but he's blanking on things. Doctor says it'll come back to him in a day or two. You got off light for someone standing right in the path."

"Bomb?"

"Package bomb. Black powder, we think. I have the bomb techs on it now, cataloguing evidence. What about the parcel? You see anything?"

"There was a package on the doorstep when I got there."

"What time was that?"

"Four-thirty. Little bit before. The Kohlers were having a New Year's Eve party and she asked me to help." I filled him in briefly on the circumstances of the party. I could feel myself reviving, my thoughts gradually becoming more coherent.

"Tell me what you remember about the parcel."

"There isn't much. I only glanced at it once. Brown paper. No string. Block lettering, done with a Magic Marker from the look of it. I saw it upside down."

"The address facing the door," he said. He took out a little spiral-bound notebook and a pen.

"Right."

"Who's it sent to?"

"Terry, I think. Not 'Mr. and Mrs.' because the line of print wasn't that long. Even upside down, I'd have noticed the 'O' in Olive's name."

He was jotting notes. "Return address?"

"Uhn-un. I don't remember any postmark either. There might have been a UPS number, but I didn't see one."

"You're doing pretty good," he said. "The regular mailman says he only delivered hand mail yesterday, no packages at all. UPS had no record of a delivery to that address. They didn't even have a truck in the area. You didn't see anyone leave the premises?"

I tried to think back, but I was drawing a blank. "Can't help you there. I don't remember anyone on foot. A car might have passed, but I can't picture it."

I closed my eyes, visualizing the porch. There were salmon begonias in big tubs along the front. "Oh, yeah. The newspaper was on the doormat. I don't know how far up the walk the paperboy comes, but he might have seen the parcel when he was doing his route."

He made another note. "We'll try that. What about dimensions?"

I could feel myself shrug. "Size of a shirt box. Bigger than a book. Nine by twelve inches by three. Was there anything left of it?"

"More than you'd think. We believe there was gift wrap under the brown mailing paper. Blue."

"Oh sure," I said, startled. "I remember seeing flakes of brown and blue. I thought it was snow, but it must have been paper particles." I remembered what Terry had said to me. "Something else," I said. "Terry was threatened. He talked about it when I was there the night before. He had a phone call at the plant from a woman named Lyda Case. She asked him when his birthday was and when he told her, she said he shouldn't count on it."

I filled him in on the rest, unburdening the sequence of events from the first. For once, I loved offloading the information on him. This was big time . . . the heavy hitters . . . more than I could deal with by myself. When it came down to bombs, I was out of my league. Lieutenant Dolan was scratching notes at a quick clip, his expression that mask of studied neutrality all cops tend to wear—taking in everything, giving nothing back. He talked as if he was already on the witness stand. "So there's a chance she's in Santa Teresa. Is that what you're saying?"

"I don't know. He seemed to think she was coming out, but he was pretty vague on that point. He's here, too?" I asked.

"This floor. Other end of the hall."

"You care if I talk to him?"

"No, not a bit. Might help jog his memory."

After Lieutenant Dolan left, I eased into a sitting position on the edge of the bed, feet dangling over the side. My head was pounding at the sudden exertion. I sat and waited for the light show inside my head to fade. I studied as much of my body as I could see.

My legs looked frail under the lightweight cotton of the hospital gown, which tied at the back and let in lots of air. The pattern of bruises across my front looked like someone had taken a powder puff and dusted me with purple talc. My hands were bandaged and I could see an aura of angry red flesh along my inner arms where the burns tapered off. I held onto the handrail and slid off the bed, supporting myself on the bed table. My legs were trembling. I could almost bet they didn't want me getting up this way. I didn't think it was such a hot idea myself, the more I thought of it. Nausea and clamminess were chiming in with the pounding in my head and a fuzzy darkness was gathering along the periphery of my vision. I wasn't going to win an award for this so I sat back down.

There was a tap at the door and the nurse came in. "Your husband's out here. He says he has to leave and he'd like to see you before he goes."

"He's not my husband," I said automatically.

She put her hands in the pockets of her uniform— a tunic over white pants, no cap. I only knew she was a nurse because her plastic name tag had an R.N. after her name, which was Sharie Wright. I studied her covertly, knowing how much Daniel liked women with names like that. Debbie and Tammie and Cindie. Candie loomed large in there, too. I guess Kinsey qualified, now that I thought of it. Kinsie. Infidelity reduces and diminishes, leaving nothing where you once had a sense of self-worth.

"He's been worried sick," she said. "I know it's none of my business, but he was here all night. I thought you should be aware." She saw that I was struggling to get settled in the bed and she gave me a hand. I guessed that she was twenty-six. I was twenty-three when I married him, twenty-four when he left.

No explanation, no discussion. The divorce was no-fault, served up in record time.

"Is there a way I can get a wheelchair? There's someone down the hall I'd like to see. The man who was admitted at the same time I was."

"Mr. Kohler. He's in three-oh-six at the end of the hall."

"How's he doing?"

"Fine. He's going home this afternoon."

"The policeman who was here a little while ago wants me to talk to him."

"What about your husband? He said it would only take two minutes."

"He's not my husband," I said, parrotlike, "but sure. Send him in. After he goes, could you find me a wheelchair? If I try to walk, I'll fall on my puss and have to sue this outfit."

She didn't think I was amusing and she didn't like the reference to lawsuits. She went out without a word. My husband, I thought. I should live so long.

16

He looked tired—an improvement, I thought. Daniel stood by my hospital bed, showing every minute of his forty-two years. "I know this won't sit well with you," he said, "but the doctor says she won't let you go home unless you have someone to look after you."

A feeling very like panic crept up in my chest. "I'll be fine in a day. I don't need anyone looking after me. I hate that idea."

"Well, I knew you would. I'm telling you what she said."

"She didn't mention it to me."

"She never had a chance. You were half zonked. She said she'd talk to you about it next time she made her rounds."

"They can't keep me here. That's disgusting. I'll go nuts."

"I already told her that. I just wanted you to know I'd be willing to help. I could get you signed out of here and settled at home. I wouldn't actually have to stay on the premises. That place of yours looks too small for more than one person anyway. But I could at least check on you twice a day, make sure you have everything you need."

"Let me think about it," I said grudgingly. But I could already see the bind I was in. With Henry gone, Rosie on vacation, and Jonah out of town, I'd be on my own. Truly, I wasn't feeling that good. I just couldn't make my body do what I wanted it to. The elderly, the feeble, and the infirm must experience the same exasperation and bewilderment. For once, my determination had nothing whatever to do with my proficiency. It was exhausting to sit up, and I knew perfectly well I couldn't manage much at home. Staying here was out of the question. Hospitals are dangerous. People make mistakes. Wrong blood, wrong medication, wrong surgeries, wrong tests. I was checking out of this place "toot sweet."

Daniel ran his hand across the top of my head. "Do what you want. I'll be back later."

He was gone again before I could protest.

I buzzed the nurses' station on the intercom.

A hollow voice came on. "Yes?"

"Can Mr. Kohler in three-oh-six have visitors?"

"As far as I know he can." The nurse sounded like she was talking into an old tin can, coughs and rustling in the background.

"Can I get a wheelchair? I'd like to go down and see him."

It was twenty minutes before anybody managed to find me one. In the meantime, I became aware that I was struggling with a depression generated by Olive's death. It wasn't as if we had had a relationship, but she'd been around on the borders of my life for years. I'd first seen her in high school when I met Ashley, but she'd left just before our junior year began. After that she was more rumor than fact . . . the sister who was always off somewhere else: boarding school, Switzerland, skiing in Utah with friends. I don't think we'd exchanged more than superficial chat until two days before, and then I'd found my opinion of her undergoing a shift. Now, death had smashed her like a bug, the blow as abrupt as a fly being swatted on a windowsill. The effect was jarring and the emotional impact hadn't worn off. I found myself turning images in my mind, trying to absorb the finality. I hadn't been consulted in the matter and I hadn't agreed. Death is insulting, and I resented its sudden appearance, like an unannounced visit from a boorish relative. I suspected the knot in my chest would be there for a long time; not grief per se, but a hard fist of regret.

I wheeled myself down the corridor to room 306. The door was closed and Bass was standing in the hall. He turned his head idly as I approached. Bass had the smooth good looks of someone in an eighteenth-century oil painting. His face was oval, boyish, his brow unlined, his eyes a barren brown. His mouth was sensual, his manner superior. Put him in a satin vest, a waistcoat, breeches, and leggings, and he might have been Blue Boy, grown slightly decadent. His hair was fine and dark, receding at the temples, worn slightly long and rather wispy where it gathered in a point on his forehead. He should have had an Afghan at his side, some creature with silky ears and a long, aristocratic snout.

"Hello, Bass. I'm Kinsey Millhone. Do you remember me?"

"Of course," he said. He bent down then and gave my cheek a social buss, more noise than contact. His expression was bleak. There was a dead time in the air, one of those uncomfortable stretched moments when you struggle to find something to say. His sister was dead. This was hardly the time for effusiveness, but I was puzzled by the awkwardness of our encounter.

"Where's Terry?"

He glanced at the door. "He's having his dressing changed. They should be done shortly. He's going home as soon as the doctor signs the release. How are you? We heard you were down the hall."

"I'm all right. I'm sorry about Olive," I said, and I truly was.

"God, this is all so screwed up. I don't know what's going on."

"How's your mother doing? Is she holding up all right?"

"She'll be okay. She's a tough old bird. She's taking it pretty hard, but she's got a spine of steel. Ash is destroyed. She's been leveled. She and Olive were always just like this," he said, holding up crossed fingers. "What about you? You look like you took a beating."

"I'm all right. This is the first time I've been out of bed and I feel like shit."

"You're lucky to be alive from what I hear."

"Lucky is right. I thought about picking the package up myself, but Olive's car pulled in and I went to help her with the groceries instead. Are you staying at your mother's?"

He nodded. "I got in Thursday night and then Olive called yesterday and said she was putting the party together. Seems like years ago. I was having a swim before I got dressed when Ebony showed up at the side of the pool. I couldn't figure out what was wrong with her. You know Eb. Always in control, never a hair out of place. Well, she looked like a wild woman. I pulled myself up on the side of the pool and she said a bomb had gone off at Olive's house and she was dead. I thought she was making the whole thing up. I laughed. It was so far-fetched, I couldn't help myself. She slapped the shit out of me and that's when I realized she was serious. What happened? Terry can't remember and the police won't tell us much."

I told him what I could, omitting the gruesome details of Olive's injuries. Even talking about it made me shake. I clamped my teeth shut, trying to relax. "Sorry," I said.

"It's my fault. I shouldn't have brought it up," he said. "I didn't mean to put you through it all again."

I shook my head. "That's fine. I'm okay. Nobody's told me much either. Honestly, I think it helps. The blanks are frustrating." I was looking for a narrative thread to hang fragments on. I'd lost the night. Everything from 4:30 on had been deleted from my memory bank.

He hesitated for a moment and then filled me in on events from his end. Ash had left. She was on her way to Olive's to help set up for the party. As soon as he heard about the explosion, he pulled some clothes on and he and Ebony jumped in the car. They arrived to find Terry being loaded into the ambulance. I was being bundled onto a stretcher, semiconscious. Olive was still lying near the shrubs, covered by a blanket.

Bass's recital of events was flat, like a news report. He was calm, his tone impersonal. He made no eye contact. I stared down the hall where a doctor with a somber expression was talking to an older couple sitting on a bench. The news must have been bad because the woman clutched and unclutched the purse in her lap.

I remembered then that I had seen Bass . . . one of the faces scrutinizing mine, bobbing above me like a balloon on a string. By then, shock had set in and I was shivering uncontrollably, in spite of the blankets they'd wrapped me in. I didn't remember Ebony. Maybe they had kept her out by the road, refusing to let her any closer to the carnage. The bomb had made tatters of Olive's flesh. Hunks of her body had been blown against the hedges, like clots of snow.

I put a hand against my face, feeling flushed with tears. Bass patted me awkwardly, murmuring nonsense, upset that he'd upset me, probably wondering how to get out of it. The emotion passed and I collected myself, taking a deep breath. "What about Terry's injuries?"

"Not bad. A cut on his forehead. Couple of cracked ribs where the blast knocked him into the garage. They wanted him in for observation, but he seems okay."

There was activity behind us and the door to Terry's room opened. A nurse came out bearing a stainless steel bowl full of soiled bandages. She seemed enveloped in aromas of denatured alcohol, tincture of iodine, and the distinctive smell of adhesive tape.

"You can go in now. Doctor said he can leave any time. We'll get a wheelchair for him when he's ready to go down."

Bass went in first. I wheeled myself in behind. A nurse's aide was straightening the bed table where the nurse had been working. Terry was sitting on the edge of the bed, buttoning up his shirt. I caught sight of his taped ribs through the loose flaps of his shirt and I looked away. His torso was stark white and hairless, his chest narrow and without musculature. Illness and injury seem so personal. I didn't want to know the details of his frailty.

He looked battered, with a dark track sketched along his forehead where the stitches had been put in. One wrist was bandaged, from cuts perhaps, or burns. His face was pale, his moustache stark, his dark hair disheveled. He seemed shrunken, as if Olive's death had diminished him.

Ebony appeared in the doorway, taking in the scene with a cursory glance. She hesitated, waiting for the aide to finish. The room seemed unbearably crowded. I needed fresh air.

"I'll come back in a minute," I murmured. I wheeled myself out. Ebony followed me as far as the visitors' lounge, a small alcove with a green tweed couch, two matching chairs, an artificial palm, and an ashtray. She took a seat, searching through her handbag for her cigarettes. She lit one, sucking in smoke as if it were oxygen. She looked totally composed, but it was clear that the hospital atmosphere unsettled her. She picked a piece of lint from the lap of her skirt.

"I don't understand any of this," she said harshly. "Who'd want to kill Olive? She never did anything."

"Olive wasn't the target. It was Terry. The package with the bomb in it was addressed to him."

Ebony's gaze shot up to mine and hung there. A pale wash of pink appeared in the dead white of her face. The hand with the cigarette gave a lurch, almost of its own accord, and cigarette ash tumbled into her lap. She rose abruptly, brushing at it.

"That's ridiculous," she snapped. "The police said there was nothing left of the package once the bomb went off." She stubbed the cigarette out.

"Well, there was," I said. "Besides which, I saw it. Terry's name was printed on the front, not hers."

"I don't believe it." A wisp of smoke drifted up from the crushed cigarette stub. She snatched it up again, working the live ember out with her fingertips. She was shredding the remains of the cigarette. The strands of raw tobacco seemed obscene.

"I'm just telling you what I saw. Olive could have

been the target, but the package was addressed to him."

"Bullshit! That *bastard*! Don't tell me Olive died because she picked it up instead of him!" Her eyes suffused with tears and she struggled for control. She got up, pacing with agitation.

I turned the wheelchair slightly, tracking her course. "What bastard, Ebony? Who are you referring to?"

She sat down abruptly, pressing the butts of both palms against her eyes. "No one. I'm sorry. I had no idea. I thought someone meant to kill her, which was horrible enough. But to die by mistake. My God! At least she didn't suffer. They swear she died instantly." She sobbed once.

She formed a tent of her hands, breathing hard into her palms.

"Do you know who killed her?"

"Of course not! Absolutely not! What kind of monster do you think I am? My own sister . . ." Her tone of outrage fell away and she wept earnestly. I wanted to believe her, but I couldn't be sure. I was tired, too close to events to sort out the false from the true. She lifted her face, which was washed with tears.

"Olive said she wasn't going to vote with you," I said, trying the possibility on her for size.

"You're such a bitch!" she shrieked at me. "How dare you! Get away from me!"

Bass appeared in the archway, his gaze turning to mine quizzically. I jammed backward on the push rim, pivoting in the wheelchair. I pushed myself down the corridor, passing a room where someone was calling for help in a low, hopeless tone. A clear plastic tube trailed from under the sheet to a gallon jug of urine under the bed. It looked like lemonade.

Olive usually brought the mail in. I'd seen her toss it on the hall table carelessly the day before. She might have been the intended victim even if the package *was* addressed to him. I really couldn't remember what she'd told me about who she was siding with in the power play between Ebony and Lance. Maybe he did it as a means of persuading the others to fall in line.

Darcy was waiting in my room when I got back. "Andy's gone," she said.

17

I eased myself back into bed while Darcy filled me in on the details. Andy had come whipping into the office at about 10:00 the day before. Mac had insisted on keeping office hours until 5:00, despite the fact that it was New Year's Eve day. Andy had a lunch meeting scheduled as well as a 2:00 appointment with one of the company vice-presidents. Darcy said Andy was in panic mode. She tried to give him his phone messages, but he cut her dead, hurried into his office, and began to load his personal items into his briefcase, along with his Rolodex. Next thing she knew, he was gone.

"It was too weird for words," she said. "He's never done anything like that before. And why the Rolodex? I'd already been through it and I didn't find a thing, but what made him think of that?"

"Maybe he's psychic."

"He'd have to be. Anyway, we didn't see him again for the rest of the day, so after work I hopped in my car and drove out to his place."

"You went all the way out to Elton?"

"Well, yeah. I just didn't like his attitude. He really had his undies in a bundle and I wanted to know what it was about. I didn't see his car parked anywhere near his apartment, so I went up and peeked in his front window. The place was a pigsty and all the furniture was gone. Maybe a card table in the living room, but that was it."

"That's all he's got," I said. "It looks like Janice took him for a bundle and she's clamoring for more."

"She can clamor all she wants, Kinsey, the man is gone. His next-door neighbor saw me peering in the window and he came out and asked me what I was up to. I told him the truth. I said I worked with Andy and we were worried because he left the office in a snit without telling us what to do about his appointments. This guy claims he saw Andy going down the steps yesterday morning with two big suitcases banging against his legs. This was maybe nine-thirty, something like that. He must have come straight to the office, packed up his stuff, and taken off. I called his place every couple of hours last night and again this morning. All I get is his machine."

I thought about it briefly. "Did the newspapers carry an account of Olive's death?"

"Not till this morning and he was gone by then."

I could feel a surge of energy, part restlessness, part dread. I pushed the covers back and swung my legs over the side of the bed. "I've gotta get out of here."

"Are you supposed to be up?"

"Sure. No problem. Check the closet and see if Daniel brought me any clothes." The green cocktail dress was gone, probably dissected by a pair of surgical scissors in the emergency room the night before, along with my tatty underwear.

"It's empty, except for this," she said. She held up my handbag.

"Great. We're in business. As long as I've got my keys, I can get some clothes when I get home. I assume you've got a car here."

"Can you leave without a doctor's permission?"

"I got it. She told Daniel I could go as long as he looked in on me, which he said he would."

Darcy studied me uncertainly, probably guessing what I said was part fib.

"God, don't worry about it, Darcy. It's not against the law to check out of a hospital. It's not a prison sentence. I'm a volunteer," I said.

"What about your bill?"

"Would you quit being such a stickler? My insurance pays for this so I don't owe them anything. They've got my address. They'll find me if they need to."

Darcy was clearly unconvinced, but she shrugged and helped me into the wheelchair, pushing me down the corridor toward the elevators. One of the nurse's aides stared at us as we went by, but I gave her a little wave and she apparently decided she didn't need to concern herself.

When we got downstairs, Darcy lent me her coat and left me in the glass foyer while she went to fetch the car. There I sat in my borrowed coat and little paper slippers, handbag in my lap. If my doctor walked by, I wasn't sure what I'd do. People passing through the foyer gave me cursory glances, but nobody said a word. Being sick is bullshit. I had work to do.

By 3:15 I was letting myself into my apartment, which already seemed to have the musty smell of neglect. I'd been gone one day, but it felt like weeks. Darcy came in behind me, her expression tinged with guilt when she saw that I was still shaky on my feet. I perched on the couch, momentarily clammy, and then set about getting dressed.

"What next?" she asked.

I was easing into my blue jeans. "Let's go into the office and see if Andy left anything behind," I said. I pulled on a sweatshirt and went into the bathroom, where I brushed my teeth. My reflection in the bathroom mirror showed a face marked by astonishment where my eyebrows used to be. My cheeks looked sunburned. I could see a few scrapes and bruises, but it was no big deal. I kind of liked having frizz across the front where my hair once was. I opened the medicine cabinet and took out my trusty nail scissors. I clipped the tape off my right arm and unwound the gauze, inspecting what was underneath. Looked okay to me. Burns do better in the open air, anyway. I took a painkiller just in case, and then waved dismissively at the sight of myself. I was fine.

I snagged the file folder I'd made after raiding Andy's trash. I put on some sweatsocks and tennis shoes, grabbing a jacket just before I locked up again. Santa Teresa usually gets chilly once the sun goes down and I wasn't sure how long I'd be gone.

Outside, it felt more like August than January. The sky was clear, the sun high overhead. There was no breeze at all, and the sidewalks were functioning like solar panels, absorbing the sunlight, throwing off heat. There was no sign of Daniel, for which I was grateful. He would no doubt have disapproved of my hospital defection. I spotted my little VW parked two doors down and I was glad somebody'd had the foresight to drive it back to my place. I wasn't up to driving yet, but it was nice to know the car was there.

Darcy drove us over to the office. There was

scarcely any traffic. The whole downtown area seemed deserted, as if in the wake of nuclear attack. The parking lot was empty, except for a series of beer bottles clustered near the kiosk, the dregs of a New Year's Eve revelry.

We went up the back stairs. "You know what bothers me?" I asked Darcy as we climbed.

She unlocked the door to the building, glancing back at me. "What's that?"

"Well, suppose we assume Andy's guilty of conspiracy in this. It does look that way even though we don't have proof at this point, right?"

"I'd say so."

"I can't figure out why he agreed to it. We're talking major insurance fraud. He gets caught, it's his livelihood. So what's in it for him?"

"It has to be a payoff," Darcy said. "If Janice hosed him, he's probably desperate for cash."

"Maybe," I said. "It means somebody knew him well enough to think he'd tumble to a bribe. Andy's always been a jerk, but I never really thought of him as dishonest."

We'd reached the glass doors of California Fidelity. "What are you saying?" she asked as she unlocked the door and let us in. She flipped the overhead lights on and tossed her handbag on a chair.

"I don't really know. I'm wondering if something

else was going on, I guess. He's in a perfect position to fiddle with the claim forms, but it's still a big risk. And why the panic? What went wrong?"

"He probably didn't count on Olive getting killed. That's gotta fit in somewhere," she said.

We went into Andy's office. Darcy watched with interest as I went through a systematic search. It looked like his business files were still intact, but all of his personal effects had been removed: the photograph of his kids that had sat on his desk, his leather-bound appointment calendar, address book, Rolodex, even the framed APSCRAP and MDRT awards he'd gotten some years before. He'd left a studio portrait of Janice, a five-by-seven color head shot, showing bouffant blond hair, a heart-shaped face, and a pointed chin. She did have a spiteful look about her, even grinning at the camera. Andy had blackened one front tooth and penned in some handsome hairs growing out of her nose. By widening her nostrils slightly, he'd created a piggy effect. The ever-mature Andy Motycka expressing his opinion of his ex-wife.

I sat in his swivel chair and surveyed the place, wondering how I was going to get a line on him. Where would he go and why take off like that? Had he made the bomb? Darcy was quiet, not wanting to interrupt my thought processes, such as they were.

"You have a number for Janice?" I asked.

"Yeah, at my desk. You want me to call and see if she knows where he is?"

"Let's do that. Make up an excuse if you can, and don't give anything away. If she doesn't know he's skipped out, let's don't tip it at this point."

"Right," Darcy said. She moved out to the reception area. I picked up the file I'd brought and pulled out all the papers. It was clear that Andy was in serious financial straits. Between Janice's harangue over the late support check, and the pink- and red-rimmed dunning notices, it was safe to assume that the pressure was on. I reread the various versions of his love letter to his inamorata. That must have been quite a Christmas eve they'd had. Maybe he'd run away with her.

Andy's calendar pad still sat at the uppermost edge of his blotter, two date sheets side by side, connected by arched clips that allowed the pages to lie flat. He'd taken his leather month-by-month appointment book, but he'd left this behind. Apparently he made a habit of noting appointments on both places so his secretary could keep track of his whereabouts. I leafed back through the week, day by day. On Friday, December 24, he'd circled 9:00 P.M. and penciled in the initial L. Was this his beloved? I worked my way back through the last six months. The initial cropped up at irregular intervals, with no pattern that I could discern.

I went out to the reception area, taking the calendar pad and the file folder with me.

Darcy was on the phone, in the midst of a chat with Janice, from what I gathered.

"Uh-hun. Well, I wouldn't know anything about that. I don't know him all that well. Uh-hun. What's your attorney telling you? I guess that's true, but I don't know what good it would do you. Look, I'm going to have to run, Janice. I've got somebody standing here waiting to use the phone. Uh-hun, I'd appreciate that and I'll let you know what we hear on this end. I'm sure he just went off for the weekend and forgot to mention it. Thanks much. You, too. Bye-bye. Right."

Darcy replaced the receiver and let out a deep breath. "Good God, that woman can talk! It's lucky I called when I did because I got an earful. She's p.o.'d. He was supposed to come by last night and pick the kids up and he never showed. She was all set to go out and had to cancel her plans. No call, no apologies, nothing. She's convinced he's skipped town and she's all set to call the cops."

"Wouldn't do any good unless he's been missing seventy-two hours," I said. "He's probably shacked up somewhere with this bimbo he's so crazy about." I showed Darcy the letters I'd picked out of his trash.

It was wonderful watching her expression shift from amusement to distaste. "Oh God, would you let him suckle your hmphm-hmph?"

"Only if I doused it with arsenic first."

Darcy's brow wrinkled. "Her bazookas must be huge. He couldn't think what to compare 'em to."

I looked over her shoulder. "Well, 'footballs,' but he crossed that out. Probably didn't seem romantic."

Darcy shoved the papers back in the file. "That was titillating stuff. Oh, bad joke. Now what?"

"I don't know. He took his address book with him, but I do have this." I flipped through the calendar pad and showed her the penciled initials scattered through the months. I could see Darcy's mental wheels start to turn.

"Wonder if she ever called him here," she said. "She must have, don't you think?"

She opened her top right-hand desk drawer and took out the log for incoming telephone calls. It was a carbonless system with a permanent record in yellow overlaid by white perforated originals. If a call came in for someone out of the office, she made a note of the date and time, the caller, and the return number, checking off one of the responses to the right, "Please call," "Will call back," or "Message." The top slip was then torn out and given to the relevant recipient. Darcy turned back to December 1.

It didn't take us long to find her. By comparing the

log of Andy's calls with the calendar pad, we came up with one repeat caller who left a number, but no name, always a day or two prior to Andy's assignations . . . if indeed that's what they were.

"Do you keep crisscross around here?" I asked.

"I don't think so. We used to have one, but I haven't seen it for months."

"I've got last year's in my office. Let's see who's listed at this number. We better hope it's not a business."

I pulled my keys out of my handbag as Darcy followed me.

"You were supposed to turn those keys in," she said in mild reproof.

"Oh really? I didn't know that."

I unlocked my office door and moved to the file cabinet, pulling the crisscross from the bottom drawer. The number, at least the year before, belonged to last name, Wilding, first name Lorraine.

"You think it's her?" Darcy asked.

"I know a good way to find out," I said. The address listed was only two blocks from my apartment, down near the beach.

"Are you sure you're okay? I don't think you should be running around like this."

"Don't sweat it. I'm fine," I said. The truth was, I wasn't feeling all that terrific, but I didn't want to lay my little head down until a few questions had been answered first. I was running on adrenaline—not a bad source of energy. When it ran out, of course, you were up shit creek, but for the time being it seemed better to be on the move.

18

I had Darcy drop me off. In an interview situation I prefer to work alone, especially when I'm not quite sure who I'm dealing with. People are easier to manage one on one; there's more room to ad-lib and more room to negotiate.

The apartment building was Spanish style, probably dating from the thirties. The red-tile roof had aged to the color of rust and the stucco had mellowed from stark white to cream. There were clumps of beaky-looking bird of paradise plants in front. A towering, sixty-foot pine tree enveloped the yard in shade. Bougainvillea was massed at the roofline, a tumble of magenta blossoms that spread out along the gutters and trailed like Spanish moss. Wood shutters, painted dark brown, flanked the windows. The loggia was chilly and smelled of damp earth.

I knocked at apartment D. There was no sign of

Andy's car on the street, but there was still a possibility that he was here. I had no idea what I'd say if he appeared at the door. It was nearly six and I could smell someone's supper in the making, something with onions and celery and butter. The door opened and I felt a little lurch of surprise. Andy's ex-wife was staring out at me.

"Janice?" I said, with disbelief.

"I'm Lorraine," she said. "You must be looking for my sister."

Once she spoke, the resemblance began to fade. She had to be in her mid-forties, her good looks just beginning to dehydrate. She had Janice's blond hair and the same pointed chin, but her eyes were bigger and her mouth was more generous. So was her body. She was my height, probably ten pounds heavier, and I could see where she carried the excess. Her eyes were brown and she'd lined them with black, adding false lashes as dense as paintbrushes. She wore snug white twill shorts and a halter top. Her legs had been shapely once, but the muscles had taken on that stringy look that connotes no exercise. Her tan looked like the comprehensive sort you acquire at a tanning salon—the electric beach.

Andy must have been in heaven. I've known men who fall in love with the same type of woman over and over again, but the similarities are usually not so obvious. She looked hauntingly like Janice. The difference was that Lorraine was voluptuous where the former Mrs. Motycka tended toward the small, the dry, and the mean. Judging from Andy's letter, Lorraine was freer with her affections than Janice ever was. She did things to him that made his syntax turn to hiccups. I wondered if his affair with Lorraine came before or after his divorce. Either way, the liaison was dangerous. If Janice found out about it, she would extract a pretty price. It crossed my mind briefly that someone might have used this as leverage to secure his cooperation.

"I'm looking for Andy," I said.

"Who?"

"Andy Motycka, your brother-in-law. I'm from the insurance company where he works."

"Why look at me? He and Janice are divorced."

"He gave me this address in case I ever needed to get in touch."

"He did?"

"Why else would I be here?"

She looked at me with suspicion. "How well do you know Janice?"

I shrugged. "I don't really. I used to see her at company parties before they split. When you first opened the door, I thought it was her, you look so much alike."

She took that in and digested it. "What do you want Andy for?"

"He disappeared yesterday and no one seems to know where he went. Did he say anything to you?"

"Not really."

"Mind if I come in? Maybe we can figure what's happening."

"All right," she said reluctantly. "I suppose that's okay. He never told me he gave anyone this address."

She stepped back and I followed her into the apartment. A small tiled entry dropped down two steps into a large living room. The apartment looked as if it had been furnished from a rental company. Everything was new, handsome, and impersonal. A foot-high live spruce decked with candy canes sat on the glass-and-brass coffee table, but that was the only indication that Christmas had come and gone.

Lorraine flicked the television off and motioned me to a chair. The upholstery had the tough, rubbery feel of Scotchgarding. Neither tears, blood, or spilled booze could penetrate such a finish. She sat down, giving the crotch of her shorts a pull so the inseam wouldn't bury itself in her private parts. "How'd you say you know Andy? Do you work for him?"

"Not really for him, but the same company. When did you see him last?"

"Three days ago. I talked to him on the phone Thursday night. He was taking his kids on New Year's Eve so I wasn't going to see him till late tomorrow anyway, but he always calls, regardless of what's going on. When I didn't hear by this morning, I drove out to his place, but there's no sign of him. Why would you need him New Year's Day?"

I stuck as close to the truth as I could, filling her in on the fact that he'd departed Friday morning without giving any indication where he meant to go. "We need one of the files. Do you know anything about the claim he was working on? There was a fire out at Wood/Warren about a week ago and I think he was doing some of the paperwork."

There was a startled silence and the barriers shot up again. "Excuse me?"

"Did he mention that to you?"

"What'd you say your name was?"

"Darcy. I'm the receptionist. I think I've talked to you a couple of times on the phone."

Her manner became formal, circumspect. "I see. Well, Darcy, he doesn't talk to me about his work. I know he loves the company and he's fine at what he does."

"Oh, absolutely," said I. "And he's very well liked, which is why we were concerned when he went off without a word. We thought maybe some kind of family matter came up. He didn't say anything about going out of town for a few days?"

She shook her head.

Judging from her attitude, I was almost certain she knew about the scam. I was equally certain she'd never give a hint of confirmation.

She said, "I wish I could help you, but he never said a word to me. In fact, I'd appreciate a call myself when the man turns up. I don't like to have to sit here and fret."

"I don't blame you," I said. "You can reach me at this number if you need to, and I'll check back with you if I hear anything." I jotted down Darcy's name and my telephone number.

"I hope nothing's wrong." This seemed like the first sincere comment she'd made.

"I'm sure not," I said. Personally, I was betting something had scared the hell out of him and he'd taken off.

She'd had a few minutes now to focus on my brow-less, burned face. "Uh, I hope this doesn't seem rude, but were you in some kind of accident?"

"A gas heater blew up in my face," I said. She made some sympathetic noises and I hoped the lie wouldn't come back to haunt me. "Well, I'm sorry I had to bother you on a holiday. I'll let you know if we hear from him." I got up and she rose as well, crossing with me to the front door.

I walked home through streets beginning to darken, though it was not quite 5:00. The winter sun had sunk and the air temperature was dropping with it. I was exhausted, secretly wishing I could check back into the hospital for the night. Something about the clean white sheets seemed inviting. I was hungry, too, and for once would have welcomed something more nutritious than peanut butter and crackers, which was what I was looking forward to.

Daniel's car was parked at the curb out in front of my apartment. I peered in, half expecting to find him asleep on the back seat. I went in through the gate and around the side of the building to Henry's back-yard. Daniel was sitting on the cinder-block wall that separated Henry's lot from our neighbor to the right. Daniel, his elbows on his knees, was blowing a low, mournful tune on an alto harmonica. With the cowboy boots, the jeans, and a blue-denim jacket, he might have been out on the range.

" 'Bout time you got home," he remarked. He tucked the harmonica in his pocket and got up.

"I had work to do."

"You're always working. You should take better care of yourself."

I unlocked my front door and went in, flipping on the light. I slung my handbag on a chair and sank down on the couch. Daniel moved into my kitchenette and opened the refrigerator.

"Don't you ever grocery-shop?"

"What for? I'm never home."

"Lord." He took out a stub of butter, some eggs,

and a packet of cheese so old it looked like dark plastic around the edge. While I watched, he searched my kitchen cabinets, assembling miscellaneous foodstuffs. I slouched down on my spine, leaning my head against the back of the couch with my feet propped up on the ottoman. I was fresh out of snappy talk and I couldn't conjure up a shred of anger. This was a man I'd loved once, and though the feelings were gone, a certain familiarity remained.

"How come this place smells like feet?" he said idly. He was already chopping onions, his fingers nimble. He played piano the same way, with a careless expertise.

"It's my air fern. Somebody gave it to me as a pet."

He picked up the tag end of a pound of bacon, sniffing suspiciously at the contents. "Stiff as beef jerky."

"Lasts longer that way," I said.

He shrugged and extracted the three remaining pieces of bacon, which he dropped into the skillet with a clinking sound. "God, one thing about giving up dope, food never has tasted right," he said. "Smoke dope, you're always eating the best meal you ever had. Helps when you're broke or on the road."

"You really gave up the hard stuff?"

"'Fraid so," he said. "Gave up cigarettes, gave up coffee. I do drink a beer now and then, though I notice you don't have any. I used to go to AA meetings five times a week, but that talk of a higher power got to me in the end. There isn't any power higher than heroin, you can take my word for it."

I could feel myself drifting off. He was humming to himself, a melody dimly remembered, that blended with the scent of bacon and eggs. What could smell better than supper being cooked by someone else?

He shook me gently and I woke to find an omelet on a warmed plate being placed in my lap. I roused myself, suddenly famished again.

Daniel sat cross-legged on the floor, forking up eggs while he talked. "Who lives in the house?"

"My landlord, Henry Pitts. He's off in Michigan."

"You got something goin' with him?"

I paused between bites. "The man is eighty-one."

"He have a piano?"

"Actually, I think he does. An upright, probably out of tune. His wife used to play."

"I'd like to try it, if there's a way to get in. You think he'd care?"

"Not at all. I've got a key. You mean tonight?"

"Tomorrow. I gotta be somewhere in a bit."

The way the light fell on his face, I could see the lines near his eyes. Daniel had lived hard and he wasn't aging well. He looked haggard, a gauntness beginning to emerge. "I can't believe you're a private detective," he said. "Seems weird to me."

"It's not that different from being a cop," I said. "I'm not part of the bureaucracy, that's all. Don't wear a uniform or punch a time clock. I get paid more, but not as regularly."

"A bit more dangerous, isn't it? I don't remember anyone ever tried to blow you up back then."

"Well, they sure tried everything else. Traffic detail, every time you pull someone over, you wonder if the car's stolen, if the driver's got a gun. Domestic violence is worse. People drinking, doing drugs. Half the time they'd just as soon waste you as one another. Knock on the door, you never know what you're dealing with."

"How'd you get involved in a homicide?"

"It didn't start out like that. You know the family, by the way," I said.

"I do?"

"The Woods. Remember Bass Wood?"

He hesitated. "Vaguely."

"His sister Olive is the one who died."

Daniel set his plate down. "The Kohler woman is *his* sister? I had no idea. What the hell is going on?"

I sketched it out for him, telling him what I knew. If I have a client, I won't talk about a case, but I couldn't see the harm here. Just me. It felt good, giving me a chance to theorize to some extent. Daniel was a good audience, asking just the right questions.

It felt like old times, the good times, when we talked on for hours about whatever suited us.

Finally a silence fell. I was cold and feeling tense. I reached for the quilt and covered my feet. "Why'd you leave me, Daniel? I never have understood."

He kept his tone light. "It wasn't you, babe. It wasn't anything personal."

"Was there someone else?"

He shifted uneasily, tapping with the fork on the edge of his dinner plate. He set the utensil aside. He stretched his legs out in front of him and leaned back on his elbows. "I wish I knew what to tell you, Kinsey. It wasn't that I didn't want you. I wanted something else more, that's all."

"What?"

He scanned my face. "Anything. Everything. What-ever came down the pike."

"You don't have a conscience, do you?"

He broke off eye contact. "No. That's why we were such a mismatch. I don't have any conscience and you have too much."

"No, not so. If I had a conscience, I wouldn't tell so many lies."

"Ah, right. The lies. I remember. That was the one thing we had in common," he said. His gaze came up to mine. I was chilled by the look in his eyes, clear and empty. I could remember wanting him. I could remember looking at his face, wondering if there could ever be a man more beautiful. For some reason I never expect the people I know to have any talent or ability. I'd been introduced to Daniel and dismissed him until the moment I heard him play. Then I did a long double-take, astonished, and I was hooked. There just wasn't any place to go from there. Daniel was married to his music, to freedom, to drugs, and briefly, to me. I was about that far down on the list.

I stirred restlessly. A palpable sexual vapor seemed to rise from his skin, drifting across to me like the scent of woodsmoke half a mile away. It's a strange phenomenon, but true, that in sleeping with men, none of the old rules apply to a man you've slept with before. Operant conditioning. The man had trained me well. Even after eight years, he could still do what he did best . . . seduce. I cleared my throat, struggling to break the spell. "What's the story on your therapist?"

"No story. She's a shrink. She thinks she can fix me."

"And this is part of it? Making peace with me?"

"We all have delusions. That's one of hers."

"Is she in love with you?"

"I doubt it."

"Must be early in the game," I said.

The dimple appeared and a smile flashed across his face, but it was mirthless, evasive, and I wondered if I hadn't touched on some pain of his. Now, he was the restless one, glancing at his watch.

"I got to get," he said abruptly. He gathered both plates and the silverware, toting dishes to the kitchen. He'd cleaned up while he cooked, an old habit of his, so he didn't have much to do. By 7:00, he was gone. I heard the thunder and rattle of his car as he started it and pulled away.

The apartment seemed dark. Extraordinarily quiet.

I locked up. I took a bath, keeping the water away from my burns. I closed myself into the folds of my quilt and turned out the light. Being with him had brought back the pain in fossil form, evidence of ancient emotional life, embedded now in rock. I studied the sensations as I would some extinct subspecies, for the curiosity, if nothing more.

Being married to a doper is as close to loneliness as you can get. Add to that his chronic infidelity and you've got a lot of sleepless nights on your hands. There are certain men who rove, men who prowl the night, who simply don't show up for hours on end. Lying in bed, you tell yourself you're worried that he's wrecked the car again, that he's drunk or in jail. You tell yourself you're worried he's been rolled, mugged, or maimed, that he's overdosed. What really worries you is he might be with someone else. The hours creep by. From time to time, you hear a car approaching, but it's never his. By 4:00 A.M., it's a toss-up which is uppermost in your mind—wishing he would come home or wishing he were dead.

Daniel Wade was the one who taught me how to value solitude. What I endure now doesn't hold a candle to what I endured with him.

19

The memorial service for Olive was held at 2:00 P.M. on Sunday at the Unitarian Church, a spartan ceremony in a setting stripped of excess. Attendance was limited to family and a few close friends. There were lots of flowers, but no casket in evidence. The floors were red tile, glossy and cold. The pews were carved and polished wood, without cushions. The lofty ceiling of the church lent a sense of airiness, but the space was curiously devoid of ornamentation and there were no religious icons at all. Even the stained-glass windows were a plain cream with the barest suggestion of green vines curling around the edges. The Unitarians apparently don't hold with zealousness, piety, confession, penance, or atonement. Jesus and God were never mentioned, nor did the word "amen" cross anybody's lips. Instead of scriptures, there were readings from Bertrand Russell and Kahlil Gibran. A man with a flute played several mournful classical tunes and ended with a number that sounded suspiciously like "Send In the Clowns." There was no eulogy, but the minister chatted about Olive in the most conversational of tones, inviting those congregated to stand up and share recollections of her. No one had the nerve. I sat near the back in my all-purpose dress, not wanting to intrude. I noticed that several people nudged one another and turned to look at me, as if I'd achieved celebrity status by being blown up with her. Ebony, Lance, and Bass remained perfectly composed. Ash wept, as did her mother. Terry sat alone in the front row, leaning forward, head in his hands. The whole group didn't occupy more than about the first five rows.

Afterward we assembled in the small garden courtyard outside, where we were served champagne and finger sandwiches. The occasion was polite and circumspect. The afternoon was hot. The sun was bright. The garden itself was gaudy with annuals, gold, orange, purple, and red marching along the white stucco wall that enclosed the churchyard. The stone-and-tile fountain plashed softly, a breeze occasionally blowing spray out onto the surrounding paving stones.

I moved among the mourners, saying little, picking up fragments of conversation. Some were discussing the stock market, some their recent travels, one the divorce of a mutual acquaintance who'd been married twenty-six years. Of those who thought to talk about Olive Wood Kohler, the themes seemed to be equally divided between conventional sentiment and cattiness.

". . . he'll never recover from the loss, you know. She was everything to him . . ."

". . . paid seven thousand dollars for that coat . . ."

". . . shocked . . . couldn't believe it when Ruth called me . . ."

". . . poor thing. He worshiped the ground she walked on, though I never could quite see it myself . . ."

". . . tragedy . . . so young . . ."

". . . well, I always wondered about that, as narrow as she was through the chest. Who did the work?"

I found Ash sitting on a poured-concrete bench near the chapel door. She looked drawn and pale, her pale-red hair glinting with strands of premature gray. The dress she wore was a dark wool, loosely cut, the short sleeves making her upper arms seem as shapeless as bread dough. In another few years she'd have that matronly look that women sometimes get, rushing into middle age just to get it over with. I sat down beside her. She held out her hand and we sat there together like grade-school kids on a field trip. "Line up in twos and no talking." Life itself is a peculiar out-ing. Sometimes I still feel like I need a note from my mother.

I scanned the crowd. "What happened to Ebony? I don't see her."

"She left just after the service. God, she's so cold. She sat there like a stone, never cried a tear."

"Bass says she was a mess when she first heard the news. Now she's got herself under control, which is probably much closer to the way she lives. Were she and Olive close?"

"I always thought so. Now I'm not so sure."

"Come on, Ashley. People deal with grief differently. You never really know what goes on," I said. "I went to a funeral once where a woman laughed so hard she wet her pants. Her only son had died in a car accident. Later, she was hospitalized for depression, but if you'd seen her then, you never would have guessed."

"I suppose." She let her gaze drift across the courtyard. "Terry got another phone call from that woman."

"Lyda Case?"

"I guess that's the one. Whoever threatened him."

"Did he call the police?"

"I doubt it. It came up a little while ago, before we left the house to come here. He probably hasn't had a chance."

I spotted Terry talking to the minister. As if on cue, he turned and looked at me. I touched Ash's arm. "I'll be right back," I said.

Terry murmured something and broke away, moving toward me. Looking at him was like looking in my mirror . . . the same bruises, same haunted look about the eyes. We were as bonded as lovers after the trauma we'd been through. No one could know what it was like in that moment when the bomb went off. "How are you?" he said, his voice low.

"Ash says Lyda Case called."

Terry took my arm and steered me toward the entrance to the social hall. "She's here in town. She wants to meet with me."

"Bullshit. No way," I whispered hoarsely.

Terry looked at me uneasily. "I know it sounds crazy, but she says she has some information that could be of help."

"I'm sure she does. It's probably in a box and goes boom when you pick it up."

"I asked her about that. She swears she didn't have anything to do with Olive's death."

"And you believed her?"

"I guess I did in a way."

"Hey, you were the one who told me about the threat. She scared the life out of you and here she is again. If you won't call Lieutenant Dolan, I will."

I thought he would argue, but he sighed once. "All right. I know it's the only thing that makes any sense. I've just been in such a fog."

"Where's she staying?"

"She didn't say. She wants to meet at the bird refuge at six. Would you be willing to come? She asked for you by name."

"Why me?"

"I don't know. She said you flew to Texas to talk to her. I can't believe you didn't mention that when the subject came up."

"Sorry. I guess I should have. That was early in the week. I was trying to get a line on Hugh Case, to see how his death fits in."

"And?"

"I'm not sure yet. I'd be very surprised if it didn't connect. I just can't figure out how."

Terry gave me a skeptical look. "It's never been proven he was murdered, has it?"

"Well, that's true," I said. "It just seems highly unlikely that the lab work would disappear unless somebody meant to conceal the evidence. Maybe it's the same person with a different motive this time."

"What makes you say that? Carbon-monoxide poisoning is about as far away from bombs as you can get. Wouldn't the guy use the same method if it worked so well the first time?"

I shrugged. "I don't know. If it were me, I'd do whatever was expedient. The point is, this is not something we should fool around with on our own."

I saw Terry's gaze focus on something behind me. I turned to see Bass. He looked old. Everybody had aged in the wake of Olive's death, but on Bass the lines of weariness were the least flattering— something puffy about the eyes, something pouty about the mouth. He had one of those boyish faces that didn't lend itself to deep emotion. On him, sorrow looked like a form of petulance. "I'm taking Mother home," he said.

"I'll be right there," Terry said. Bass moved away and Terry turned back to me. "Do you want to call Lieutenant Dolan or should I?"

"I'll do it," I said. "If there's any problem, I'll let you know. Otherwise, I'll meet you down at the bird refuge at six."

I was home by 3:35, but it took me almost an hour to track down the lieutenant, who was certainly interested in having a chat with Lyda Case. He said he'd be there at 5:00 in an unmarked car, on the off-chance that she was feeling truly skittish about contact with the police. I changed into jeans and a sweatshirt and pulled on my tennis shoes. I was tired, and the residual pain from my injuries was like a slow leak from a tire, depleting. Over the course of the day, I could feel myself go flat. In some ways I shared Terry's sentiments. It was hard to believe Lyda was responsible for the package bomb, let alone her husband's death two years before. In spite of her accusations and the veiled threat to Terry, she didn't seem like the homicidal type, for whatever that's worth. I've been surprised by killers again and again, and I try not to generalize, but there it was. Maybe she was just what she claimed to be . . . someone with information that might be of help.

By the time I reached the meeting place, the sun was almost down. The bird refuge is a landscaped preserve near the beach, established to protect geese, swans, and other fowl. The forty-three-acre property abuts the zoo and consists of an irregular-shaped freshwater lagoon, surrounded by a wide lane of clipped grass through which a bike trail runs. There's a small parking lot at one end where parents bring little children with their plastic bags of old popcorn and stale bread. Male pigeons puff and posture in jerky pursuit of their inattentive female counterparts who manage to strut along just one step away from conception.

I pulled into the lot and parked. I got out of my car. Sea gulls swirled and settled in an oddly choreographed dance of their own. Geese honked along the shore in search of crumbs while the ducks paddled through the still waters, sending out ripples around them. The sky was a deepening gray, the ruffled silver surface of the lagoon reflecting the rising wind.

I was glad when Lieutenant Dolan's car pulled in beside mine. We chatted idly until Terry appeared, and then the three of us waited. Lyda Case never showed. At 8:15, we finally gave it up. Terry took Dolan's number and said he'd be in touch if he heard from her. It was a bit of a letdown, as all three of us had hoped for a break in the case. Terry seemed grateful for the activity and I had to guess that it was going to be hard for him to spend his first night alone. He'd been in the hospital Friday night and with his mother-in-law on Saturday while the bomb squad finished their crime-scene investigation and a work crew came in to board up the front wall of the house.

My own sense of melancholy had returned in full force. Funerals and the new year are a bad mix. The painkillers I'd been taking dulled my mental processes and left me feeling somewhat disconnected from reality. I needed companionship. I wanted lights and noise and a good dinner somewhere with a decent glass of wine and talk of anything except death. I fancied myself an independent soul, but I could see how easily my attachments could form.

I drove home hoping Daniel would appear again. With him, you never knew. The day he walked out of the marriage eight years before, he hadn't even left a note. He didn't like to deal with anger or recrimination. He said it bummed him out to be around people who were sad, depressed, or upset. His strategy was to let other people cope with unpleasantness. I'd seen him do it with his family, with old friends, with gigs that no longer interested him. One day he wasn't there, and you might not see him for two years. By then, you couldn't even remember why you'd been so pissed off.

Sometimes, as in my case, there'd be some residual rage, which Daniel usually found puzzling. Strong emotion is hard to sustain in the face of bafflement. You run out of things to say. Most of the time, in the old days, he was stoned anyway, so confronting him was about as productive as trying to discipline a cat for spraying on the drapes. He didn't "get it." Fury didn't make any sense to him. He couldn't see the connection between his behavior and the wrath that was generated as a consequence. What the man did really well was play. He was a free spirit, whimsical, inventive, tireless, sweet. Jazz piano, sex, travel, parties, he was wonderful at those . . . until he got bored, of course, or until reality surfaced, and then he was gone. I had never been taught how to play, so I learned a lot from him. I'm just not sure it was anything I really needed to know.

I found a parking spot six doors away. Daniel's car was parked in front of my place. He was leaning against the fender. There was a paper bag with twine handles near his feet, a baguette of French bread sticking out of it like a baseball bat.

"I thought you might be gone by today," I said.

"I talked to my friend. It looks like I'll be here a couple days more."

"You find a place to stay?"

"I hope so. There's a little motel here in the neighborhood that will have a room free later. Some folks are checking out."

"That's nice. You can reclaim your stuff."

"I'll do that as soon as I know for sure."

"What's that?" I said, pointing at the baguette.

He looked down at the sack, his gaze following mine. "Picnic," he said. "I thought I'd play the piano some, too."

"How long have you been here?"

"Since six," he said. "You feel all right? You look beat."

"I am. Come on in. I hope you have wine. I could use some."

He pushed away from the car, toting the bag as he followed me through the gate. We ended up at Henry's, sitting on the floor in his living room. Daniel had bought twenty-five votive candles and he arranged those around the room until I felt like I was sitting in the middle of a birthday cake. We had wine, pâté, cheeses, French bread, cold salads, fresh raspberries, and sugar cookies the size of Frisbees. I stretched out afterward in a food-induced reverie while Daniel played the piano. Daniel didn't play music so much as he discovered it, calling up melodies, pursuing them across the keys, embroidering, embellishing. His background was in classical piano, so he warmed up with Chopin, Liszt, the intricacies of Bach, drifting over into improvisation without effort.

Daniel stopped abruptly.

I opened my eyes and looked at him.

His expression was pained. He touched at the keyboard carelessly, a sour chord. "It's gone. I don't have it anymore. I gave up drugs and the music went with 'em."

I sat up. "What are you talking about?"

"Just what I said. It was the choice I had to make, but it's all bullshit. I can live without drugs, babe, but not without music. I'm not made that way."

"It sounded fine. It was beautiful."

"What do you know, Kinsey? You don't know anything. That was all technique. Mechanics. I got no soul. The only time music works is when I'm burning with smack, flying. This is nothing. Half-life. The other is better . . . when I'm on fire like that and give it all away. You can't hold back. It's all or nothin'."

I could feel my body grow still. "What are you saying?" Dumb question. I knew.

His eyes glowed and he pinched his thumb and index finger together near his lips, sucking in air. It was the gesture he always used when he was about to roll a joint. He looked down at the crook of his elbow and made a fist lovingly.

"Don't do that," I said.

"Why not?"

"It'll kill you."

He shrugged. "Why can't I live the way I want? I'm the devil. I'm bad. You should know that by now. There isn't anything I wouldn't do just for the hell of it . . . just to stay *awake*. Fuck. I'd like to fly again, you know? I'd like to feel good. I'll tell you something about being straight . . . it's a goddamn drag. I don't know how you put up with it. I don't know how you keep from hangin' yourself."

I crumpled up paper napkins and stuffed them in the sack, gathered paper plates, plastic ware, the empty wine bottle, cardboard containers. He sat on the piano bench, his hands held loosely in his lap. I doubted he'd live to see forty-three.

"Is that why you came back?" I asked. "To lay this on me. What do you want, permission? Approval?"

"Yeah, I'd like that."

I started blowing out candles, darkness gathering like smoke around the edges of the room. You can't argue with people who fall in love with death. "Get out of my life, Daniel. Would you just do that?"

20

I got up Monday morning at 6:00 and did a slow, agonizing five-mile jog. I was in bad shape and I had no business being out there at all, but I couldn't help myself. This had to be the worst Christmas I'd ever spent and the new year wasn't shaping up all that great as far as I could see. It was now January 3, and I wanted my life back the way it was. With luck, Rosie would reopen later in the day, and maybe Jonah would return from Idaho. Henry was flying home on Friday. I recited my blessings to myself as I ran, ignoring the fact that my body hurt, that I had no office at the moment, and a cloud of suspicion was still hanging over my head.

The sky was clear, a torpid breeze picking up. The day seemed unseasonably warm even at that hour, and I wondered if we were experiencing Santa Ana conditions, winds gusting in from the desert, hot

drafts like the blast from an oven. It was the wrong
time of year for it, but the air had that dry, dusty feel
to it. The sweat on my face evaporated almost at once
and my T-shirt was clinging to my back like a hot,
soggy rag. By the time I got back to my neighborhood, I felt I'd blown some of the tension away. Kinsey Millhone, perpetual optimist. I jogged all the way
to Henry's gate and took a few minutes walking back
and forth, catching my breath, cooling down. Daniel's
car was gone. In its place was a vehicle I hadn't seen
before—a compact, judging from the shape, anonymous under a pale-blue cotton car cover. Off-street
parking in the area is restricted and garages are rare.
If I ever got a new car, I'd have to invest in a cover
myself. I leaned against the fence, stretching my
hamstrings dutifully before I went in to shower.

Lance Wood called me at 8:00. The background
noise was that hollow combination of traffic and en-
closure that suggests a phone booth.

"Where are you?" I asked, as soon as he'd identified himself.

"On a street corner in Colgate. I think my phone at
work is tapped," he said.

"Have you had it checked?"

"Well, I'm not really sure how to go about it and I
feel like a fool asking the phone company to come
out."

"I'll bet," I said. "That's like asking the fox to secure the henhouse. What makes you think you've got a tap?"

"Odd stuff. I'll have a conversation and the next thing I know, something I've said is all over the place. I'm not talking about office gossip. It's something more insidious than that, like comments I've made to out-of-state customers that people here would have no way of knowing."

"Could it be a simple case of someone listening in? A lot of employees have access to the phones out there."

"Not my private line. It isn't like anything we do is top secret, but we all say things we'd rather not have spread around. Someone's making me look very bad. Is there some way you can check it out?"

"I can try," I said. "What about the phone itself? Have you tried unscrewing the mouthpiece?"

"Sure, but I don't know what the inside of a receiver's supposed to look like. I'm not picking up any odd noises or clicks, I will say that."

"You wouldn't if the tap is set up properly. It'd be virtually undetectable. Of course, it might not be that at all," I said. "Maybe the office itself is bugged."

"In which case, what? Is that something you can spot?"

"Sometimes, with luck. It's also possible to buy an electronic device that will scan for bugs. I'll see if I can locate one before I come out. Give me a couple of hours and I'll meet you at the plant. I've got some other things I probably ought to take care of first."

"Right. Thanks."

I took the next hour to type up my notes, clipping the newspaper article about the explosion to include with my files. I tried Lyda Case's telephone number in Texas on the off chance that her roommate had heard from her. It would help if I knew how to find her here in Santa Teresa.

At 9:10, my phone rang. It was Darcy calling from California Fidelity and talking as if she had a hand cupped over the mouthpiece. "Big trouble," she said.

I could feel my heart sink. "Now what?"

"If I change the subject abruptly, you'll know Mac walked in," she murmured. "I overheard a conversation between him and Jewel. He says someone tipped the cops about the warehouse inventory. It looks like Lance Wood moved all the merchandise to another location before his warehouse burned down. The inventory he claimed reimbursement for was all worthless junk."

"That's bullshit," I said. "I saw some of it myself. I must have gone through five or six boxes when I inspected the place."

"Well, I guess he had a few real boxes seeded in among the fake. He's going to be charged, Kinsey. Arson and fraud, and you're being named as co-conspirator. Mac turned everything over to the D.A.

this morning. I thought you'd like to know in case you need to talk to an attorney."

"What's the timetable? Do you know?"

"Mr. Motycka isn't in today, but I can leave a message on his desk," she said.

"Is that Mac?"

"He didn't say exactly, but we're expecting him some time today. Uh-hun. Yes, I'll do that. All right, thanks," she said and hung up.

I put a call through to Lonnie Kingman and alerted him. He said he'd check with the D.A.'s office and find out if a warrant was being issued. His advice was to surrender voluntarily, thus avoiding the ignominy and uncertainty of a public arrest.

"Jesus, I can't believe this is happening," I said.

"Well, it hasn't yet. Don't worry about it until I tell you to," he said.

I grabbed my handbag and car keys and headed out the door. I had disconnected my emotions again. There was no point in letting anxiety get in my way. I hopped in my car and drove over to an electrical-supply place on Granita. My knowledge of electronic surveillance was bound to be out-of-date, limited to information picked up in a crash course at the Police Academy nearly ten years before. The advances in miniaturization since then had probably revolutionized the field, but I suspected the basics were always going to be the same. Microphone, transmitter, recorder of some type, probably voice-activated these days. The planting can be done by a technician disguised as any commonly seen service person: telephone lineman, meter reader, cable-television installer. Electronic surveillance is expensive, illegal unless authorized by the court, and looks a lot easier on television than it is in real life. Bug detection is another matter altogether. It was always possible, of course, that Lance Wood was imagining the whole thing, but I doubted it.

The small all-band receiver I bought was about the size of a portable radio. While not truly all-band, it was sufficient to cover most bugging frequencies—30–50 MHz and 88–108 MHz. If the bug in his office was wired, I was going to have to find the wire myself, but if the bug was wireless, the receiver would start emitting a high-pitched squeal when it was within range.

I drove out to Colgate with my windows rolled down, parched air whipping through the interior of the VW like a convection oven. The weather forecaster on the car radio seemed as baffled as I was. It felt like August, asphalt shimmering in the heat. January in Santa Teresa is usually our best month. Everything is green, flowers in full bloom, the temperatures in the low seventies, mild and pleasant. The time-and-temp sign on the bank building was showing 89 degrees and it wasn't yet noon.

I parked in front of Wood/Warren and went in. Lance came out of his office in a wilted shirt with the sleeves rolled up.

"Do we need to watch what we say once we go in there?" he asked, indicating the office door.

"I don't think so. Let's let 'em know we're hot on the trail. Maybe it'll shake 'em up."

Before we started work, I did a quick check of both interior and exterior office walls on the off-chance that someone had installed a spike mike, a small probe that can be inserted between the studs, or hidden in a hollow door, the door panel itself serving as a diaphragm to transmit sound. Lance's office was located in the right-front corner of the building. The construction on those two sides was block and fieldstone, which didn't lend itself to easy installation. Somebody would have had to drill through solid rock. Inside, one office wall was contiguous with the reception area, where the pickup unit would have been difficult to conceal. The fourth wall was clean.

Company employees watched the two of us incuriously as we moved through the preliminary phases of the search. If anyone was worried about surveillance equipment coming to light, there was no indication of it.

We went into the office. I examined the telephone first, taking the plate off the bottom, unscrewing the mouth and ear pieces. As far as I could tell, the instrument was clean.

"I take it it's not the phone," Lance said, watching me.

"Who knows? The bug might be downstream," I said. "I don't have any way to find out if somebody's tapped into the line at the pole. We'll have to operate on the premise that the bug's somewhere in the room. It's just a matter of coming up with it."

"What exactly are we looking for?" Lance asked.

I shrugged. "Microphone, transmitter. If you're being spied on by the FBI or the CIA, we probably won't find anything. I'm assuming those guys are good. On the other hand, if your eavesdropper's an amateur, the device might be fairly crude."

"What's that thing?"

"My handy little all-band receiver," I said. "This should pick up any sound being transmitted by the bug in a feedback loop that'll result in a high-pitched squeal. We'll try this first, and if nothing comes to light, we'll take the office apart item by item."

I flipped the receiver on and began to work my way through the popular bugging frequencies, moving around the office like someone dowsing for water. Nothing.

I tucked the debugger in the outside pocket of my handbag and started searching in earnest, working my way around the periphery of the room, then toward the center in an imaginary grid pattern that covered every square foot.

Nothing.

I stood for a moment, perplexed, my eye traveling along the ceiling, down the walls, along the base-board. Where was the sucker? I felt my attention tugged by the phone jack just to the right of the door. There was no telephone cord coming from it.

"What's that?"

"What? Oh. I had the jack moved when I changed the office around. The telephone used to be over there."

I got down on my hands and knees and inspected the jack. It looked okay. I took out my screwdriver and popped off the cover. A small section of the base-board had been cut away. Tucked into the space was a microcassette recorder about the size of a deck of playing cards.

"Hello," I said. The tape gave a half-turn and stopped. I moved the microsensor button away from the voice-activated setting and placed the recorder on his desk. Lance sank heavily into his swivel chair. He and I exchanged a long look.

"Why?" he said, baffled.

"I don't know. You tell me."

He shook his head. "I can't even think where to start. I don't have enemies as far as I know."

"Apparently you do. And it isn't just you. Hugh

Case is dead and Terry *would* have been if he'd picked up that package instead of Olive. What do the three of you have in common?"

"Nothing, I swear. We're all connected to Wood/Warren, but none of us even do the same kind of work. We make hydrogen furnaces. That's all we do. And Hugh died two years ago. Why then? If somebody wants control of the company, why kill off the key personnel?"

"Maybe that's not the motive. It could be something wholly unrelated to the work. Give it some thought. I'll talk to Terry and have him do the same. Maybe there's something you've overlooked."

"There must be," he said, his face florid with heat and tension. He pushed at the tape recorder with one finger. "Thanks for this."

"Be careful. There could be another one. Maybe this one was planted someplace obvious to distract us from the other." I picked up my handbag and started toward the door, pausing at the threshold. "Get in touch if you think of anything. And if you hear from Lyda Case, let me know."

As I passed through the reception area, I did a detour to the right. This was the office where the engineers had their drafting tables. John Salkowitz glanced up at me from the rough diagram he was working on. "Can I help you?"

"Is Ava Daugherty here someplace?"

"She just left. She had some errands to run, but she should be right back."

I took out my business card and placed it on her desk. "Have her get in touch with me, if you would."

"Will do."

I was home again by 3:00, feeling hot and grimy from crawling the perimeter of Lance's office, peering under things. I let myself into my apartment and tossed my handbag on the couch. A piercing shriek started up and I jumped a foot, grabbing up my bag. I snatched the debugger out of the outside compartment and flipped the switch off. Jesus Christ, I'd scared myself to death! The silence was wonderful. I stood there, heart pounding, enjoying the air-conditioning the sudden sweat had generated. I patted myself on the chest and blew out a big breath. I shook my head and moved into the kitchenette. I felt dry, longing for a beer. The apartment was as close and muggy as a sauna. I checked the refrigerator. I didn't even have a can of Diet Pepsi.

And then I paused, my head swiveling slowly toward the room behind me. I closed the refrigerator door and moved back to the couch. I picked up the debugger and flipped it on again, sweeping the room. The high-pitched squeal cut through the silence like a burglar alarm.

I crossed to the corner and stood there, looking down. I hunkered on my heels, running a hand carefully into the sound hole in Daniel's guitar. The tiny transmitter, no bigger than a matchbox, was affixed to the body of the instrument with tape. A chill started at the base of my spine and raced up my body. Daniel was somehow connected to the case.

21

It took me nearly two hours to find the voice-activated tape recorder which turned out to be hidden on the sun porch that formerly connected my converted garage apartment to the main house. I wasn't sure how Daniel had gotten in. Perhaps he'd picked the lock, as I would have in his place. The tape was new, which meant he must have been there fairly recently, pulling out the old tape, inserting this one. I couldn't even remember what was going on when he had first appeared. It was appalling now to think of all the telephone conversations he must have picked up in the last few days. Even messages coming in on my answering machine would have been recorded and passed on, not to mention the lengthy discussion I'd had with him about the case itself. He'd been so interested, so astute in the questions he asked. I'd felt so gratified by his attention. Looking back, I could see that in his own way he'd tried to warn me. All that talk about what a liar he was. Had every word he said to me been false? I sat on my back step, turning the situation over in my mind. Who had put Daniel up to it? Lyda Case perhaps, or maybe Ebony. One or the other of them might have run into Daniel, the amoral, the promiscuous, bored and at loose ends, restless and sick of life. What difference would it make to him who he betrayed? He'd done me in before. One more time couldn't matter in the grand scheme of things. It was staggering to think of all the information that must have been passed down the line, just by listening in, just by assembling my end of telephone conversations. Maybe that's how Andy Motycka had figured out Darcy and I were onto him. *Something* had caused him to cut and run. Olive's death hadn't hit the papers until the day *after* he disappeared. Had he known what was going to happen? I had to find Daniel.

I gathered up his guitar, the transmitter, and the tape recorder, shoving everything in the back seat of the car, and then I started cruising the neighborhood, looking for his Rent-A-Ruin. I live one block from the beach in an area made up of motels and vintage California bungalows. I started at Cabana Boulevard and circled each block, checking the cars at every motel, scanning the restaurant parking lots along the beach. There was no sign of him. He'd probably lied about where he was staying, along with everything else.

At 5:00, I finally gave up and went home. As usual, I was forced to park several doors away. The intense heat of day was yielding to balminess and it felt like we were in for a warm night ahead. The sun had begun to drop and the combination of January twilight and the summery temperature was disconcerting and set my teeth on edge. I was turning in at my gate when I picked up the smell. Dead dog, I thought. Something fetid and rotten. I looked back at the street, thinking I'd spot some poor flattened creature on the pavement. Instead my attention was caught by the vehicle shrouded by the blue cotton car cover right out in front. I hesitated for a moment and then retraced my steps. The smell was stronger. Saliva began to collect involuntarily on the floor of my mouth. I swallowed, tears welling briefly, a fear reaction of mine. Gingerly, I lifted the car cover, pulling it up off the hood so that I could peer in through the windshield.

I jerked my hand away, making one of those sounds that has no translation in human speech.

Leaning against the window on the passenger side was the bloated face of Lyda Case, eyes bulging, tongue as fat and round and dark as a parakeet's, protruding slightly beyond puffy darkened lips. A scarf gaily printed with a surfing motif was nearly buried in the swollen flesh of her neck. I pulled the cover back over the windshield and went straight to my phone where I dialed 911 and reported the body. My voice sounded low and emotionless, but my hands were shaking badly. The sight of Lyda's face still danced in the air, a vision of death, wed to the smell of putrescence. The dispatcher assured me someone was on the way.

I went back out to the street. I sat on the curb to wait for the cops, guarding Lyda's body like some old loyal pooch. I don't think four minutes had passed before the black-and-white came barreling around the corner. I got up and moved to the street, holding an arm up like a crossing guard.

The two uniformed police who emerged were familiar, Pettigrew and Gutierrez, male and female. I knew they'd seen worse than Lyda Case . . . what beat cop hasn't? . . . but there was something repellent about the spectacle of this death. It looked like she'd been positioned so as to maximize the horror. The message was for me . . . mockery and macabre arrogance, an escalation of the terms between this killer and me. I hadn't taken Olive's death personally. I'd felt the loss, but I didn't believe I'd been targeted in any way. My presence there when the bomb went off was purely circumstantial. This was different. This was aimed at me. Someone knew where I lived.

Someone had made very special arrangements to get her here.

The next two hours were filled with police routine, comforting procedures, as formalized as a dance. All of the responsibility belonged to someone else. Lieutenant Dolan appeared. I answered questions. The car turned out to be another rental, Hertz this time instead of Rent-A-Ruin. I'd first seen it this morning, as nearly as I could remember. No, I'd never seen it before. No, I hadn't seen any strangers in the area. Yes, I knew who she was, but she hadn't been in touch. No, I had no idea when or why she'd come to town except that she'd told Terry Kohler she had information for him. Dolan had waited with us at the bird refuge so he knew she hadn't showed up. She was probably already dead by then, her flesh beginning to bake in the toaster oven of the locked car.

Out of the corner of my eye, I watched the medical examiner do his preliminary examination of the body. The car doors were hanging open, the neighborhood perfumed by the stink of the corpse. By that time it was fully dark and neighbors were giving the crime scene a wide berth, watching from porches all up and down the street. Some were still in work clothes. Many held handkerchiefs to their faces, filtering the smell. The police personnel working directly with the body wore protective masks. Lights had been set up and the fingerprint technicians were going over every inch of the dark-blue car with white powder and brushes. Door handles, windows, dash, steering wheel, steering column, plastic seat covers. Since the rental car was probably cleaned up between uses, there was a good chance that any prints lifted would be significant. Easy to match, at any rate.

Pettigrew had gone into my apartment to contact the Hertz manager by phone.

Lyda was zipped into a body bag. The gases that had collected under her skin made her look like she'd suddenly gained fifty pounds, and for a moment, grotesquely, I worried she would burst. I got up abruptly and went inside. I poured myself a glass of wine and chugged it down like water. Officer Pettigrew finished his conversation and hung up the phone.

"I'm going in to take a shower if no one objects." I didn't wait for an answer. I grabbed a plastic garbage bag from the kitchen, closed myself into the bathroom and stripped, dropping every article of clothing, including my shoes, into the bag. I tied it shut and set it outside the bathroom door. I showered. I shampooed my hair. When I was done, I wrapped myself in a towel, searching my face in the mirror for reassurance. I couldn't shake the images. Lyda's features seemed to be superimposed on my own, the stench of her competing with the scent of shampoo and soap. Never had my own mortality seemed so immediate. My ego recoiled, incapable of contemplating its own surcease. There's nothing so astonishing or insulting to a soul as the suggestion that a day might come when it would not "be." Thus springs religion with comforts I couldn't accept.

By 9:00 the neighborhood had cleared again. Several prints, including a partial palm, had been lifted from the car, which had then been towed to the impound lot. The Hertz manager had appeared on the scene and the fingerprint technician had taken a set of his prints, as well as mine, for comparison. The crime-scene investigators would dust and vacuum the car like a crew of charwomen and then they'd begin the painstaking business of analyzing trace evidence.

In the meantime, I was too restless to stay at home. Any sense of refuge and safety I felt had been obliterated by the angle of Lyda's face, tilted so she seemed to be watching my gate. I hunched myself into a windbreaker and grabbed my handbag, depositing the sackful of fouled clothes in Henry's trash can on my way out. I cruised the neighborhood again, looking for Daniel's car, covering the same restaurant parking lots, the same motels. I still had his guitar in the back seat and I didn't think he'd skip out of town without retrieving it.

I hit pay dirt at the Beach View, which in fact only had a view of the backside of the adjacent motel.

Daniel's ratty rented vehicle was parked in front of room 16, ground floor, rear. Parked beside it was a little red Alfa-Romeo convertible. Uneasily I turned to stare at it as I pulled in. I locked my car, pausing to check the glove compartment in the Alfa for the owner registration slip. Not surprisingly, the car belonged to Ashley Wood. My, my, my.

I knocked on Daniel's door. I could see that the lights were on, but there was a long wait. I was beginning to think they might have gone off somewhere on foot when the door opened and Daniel peered out. He was barefoot and shirtless, but he'd pulled on a pair of faded jeans. He looked slim-hipped and bronzed, his blond hair tousled as if he'd been asleep. His cheeks were flushed and the lines had been eased from around his eyes. He looked ten years younger, the haggard cast to his face magically erased. If he was surprised to see me, he gave no indication of it.

"Mind if I come in?" I asked.

He hesitated slightly and then stepped aside. I moved into the room, noting with grim amusement that the bathroom door was shut. The musky smell of sex still hung in the air like ozone after a rainstorm.

"I have your guitar in my car."

"You didn't have to do that. I told you I'd pick it up."

"It's no problem. I wanted to talk to you again, anyway." I strolled around the room, noting the roach clip, the darkened stub of a joint in the ashtray. "God, you got right to it, didn't you?" I remarked.

His gaze was watchful. He knew me well enough to realize I was in a mean mood. He said, "What's on your mind? I'm kind of tied up right now."

I smiled, wondering if he meant that literally. Bondage had never been part of his sexual repertoire, but who knew how Ash's taste ran? "I found the transmitter. The tape recorder's in the car along with the guitar. I thought I might dump it all off the pier, but I'm too nice. I give you credit for balls, Daniel. It took a lot of fuckin' nerve to come waltzing back in my life and betray me again."

His expression altered, but at least he had the decency not to deny anything.

I moved to the bathroom door and opened it.

Bass was standing there. Something like pain shot through me, followed by the cessation of all feeling. Even rage was washed away in that moment of recognition. I thought about the last time I'd seen them together . . . Bass's twenty-first birthday party at the country club. Daniel's jazz combo had played for the occasion and I'd been invited, too, since I knew Ash. Two weeks later, Daniel was gone, without so much as a by-your-leave. I was looking at the reason. Who, I wondered, had seduced whom. Daniel was older than Bass by thirteen years, but that wasn't necessarily relevant. Not that it mattered anyway. Passion had ionized all the air in the room. I felt nearly giddy as I drank it in.

Bass had a towel wrapped around his waist. I found myself checking out the body Daniel found preferable to mine. Bass was pale, narrow through the chest, but he carried himself with perfect composure as he brushed by me.

"Hello, Kinsey." He paused at the ashtray and picked up the roach. He tilted his head, lighting it with a disposable Bic. He took a hit and held it out to Daniel, who declined with a slight shake of his head. The two men locked eyes, exchanging a look so filled with tenderness I had to drop my gaze.

Bass glanced over at me. "What brings you here?"

"Lyda Case is dead."

"Who?"

"Come on, Bass. Don't give me that shit. She was married to Hugh Case, who worked for Wood/Warren. Surely, you haven't forgotten him so soon."

Bass set the roach aside and moved to the bed. He stretched out, crossing his arms behind his head. The hair in his armpits was silky and black and I could see bite marks in the crook of his neck. When he spoke, his tone was mild and relaxed. "No need to get ugly. I haven't been around for years. This has nothing to do with me," he said. "You're the one."

"*I* am? That's bullshit! I got backed into this business because of California Fidelity."

"So I heard. The D.A.'s office got in touch with Mother. You're being charged with insurance fraud."

"And you believe that," I said flatly.

"Hey, I can understand it. Lance got his tit in a wringer and needed some cash. Burning the warehouse was better than a bank loan. All he needed was a little help from you."

"Oh, really? You seem well informed for someone who's been gone. Who fills you in?"

"What's it to you?"

"You can't believe everything you hear, Bass. Sometimes you can't even believe your eyes. There's something going on here, and none of us has been smart enough to figure out what it is."

"I'm sure you'll come up with something. I understand you're very good at what you do."

I looked at Daniel. "How did you get sucked into this, or is that a bad choice of words?"

Daniel seemed uncertain how to reply so Bass answered for him. "We had to know what was going on. Obviously, you weren't going to tell us so we had to take steps." He paused to shrug. "We'll be turning the tapes over to the D.A., of course."

"Oh shit, yes. Of course. We who?"

"I'd rather not discuss that, in case you're inclined to retaliate," Bass said. "The point is, I knew Daniel and he knew you and it seemed like the logical way to gather information."

"And Andy Motycka? How does he fit in?"

"I don't know all the details on that. Why don't you tell me?"

"Well, I don't know the details either, Bass. My guess is that somebody pressured Andy into it. Maybe he got nervous when he found out that Darcy and I were onto him. Or maybe he got wind of Olive's death and felt like it was more than he had bargained for. Anyway, it looks like he's left town unless he's been murdered, too. Doesn't it bother you that Lyda Case died?"

"Why should it? I never knew the lady personally. Sure, I'm sorry she died, but I didn't have anything to do with it."

"How do you know you aren't next, Bass? Or maybe Daniel here? If you're not concerned about Olive, at least give some thought to your own vulnerability. You're dealing with someone who has less and less to lose."

"What makes you think he knows who it is?" Daniel said.

"What makes you think he doesn't?" I snapped.

22

When I got home, I turned on all of Henry's exterior lights, flooding his yard like a prison compound. I checked locks on all his doors and windows first and then secured my own. I cleaned and checked my little semiautomatic, loading eight cartridges into the magazine. It worried me that the sights were off. A gun is no protection if you can't control what it does. I stuck it in my handbag. I was going to have to leave it at a gun shop in the morning. Grimly I wondered if a gunsmith supplied loaners.

I brushed my teeth and washed my face, then surveyed my various burns, bruises, and minor cuts. I felt like shit, but I decided it was better to bypass the pain medication. I was afraid of sleeping deeply on the off-chance that someone might have a go at me. I was afraid, too, that Lyda Case might appear in my dreams unannounced.

I watched the digital clock flick its way through the night. Outside, the wind was hot and dry, teasing the palm fronds into rattling conspiracies. The air in my apartment seemed stifling, sounds muffled by the heat. Twice I got up and moved silently into the bathroom where I stood in the shadows of the bathtub, peering out of the window. The tree branches bucked in the wind. Leaves scuttled along the street. Dust was funneled up out of nowhere into whirling spirals. Once a car passed slowly, its headlights fanning up against my ceiling. I pictured Daniel sheltered in the protective curve of Bass's body and I envied them their security. In the dead of night, personal safety seems more important than propriety.

I slept, finally, as the darkness was lifting to the soft gray of dawn. The wind had died and the ensuing silence was just as unsettling as the erratic creak of the live oak in my neighbor's yard. I woke at 8:15 with a start, disoriented by the sense of the day gone all wrong. I wanted to talk to Ava at Wood/Warren as soon as the plant opened, which meant I'd have to skip my run. I was going to have to live with the brooding dread that was circulating through my bones. Exercise sweeps that away as nothing else can. Without the jog, I suspected the anxiety would accumulate. I dragged myself into the shower, then dressed and made a quick pot of coffee, double-strength, which I poured into a thermos and sipped as I drove the ten miles to Colgate.

Lance wasn't expected until after 10:00, and Terry was on a leave of absence, but Ava was at her desk, looking dark and sour. She'd had her cracked nail repaired and the color had shifted from harsh red to a mauve, with a chevron of dark maroon painted on each fingertip. Her outfit was purple jersey with a cross-chest bandolier of red, altogether dazzling, I thought.

"I left my business card yesterday. I was hoping you'd call," I said, taking a seat in the metal chair beside her desk.

"I'm sorry. We were swamped with work." She focused a look on me. All the flint was gone and worry had taken its place. The lady was in a mood to talk. She said, "I heard about Lyda Case on the radio this morning. I don't understand what's going on."

"Did you know Lyda?"

"Not really. I'd only talked to her a couple of times on the phone, but I was married to a man who killed himself. I know how devastating that can be."

"Especially when there was no way to have it verified," I said. "You did know all his lab work disappeared within days."

"Well, I heard that, but I wasn't sure it was true. Suicide is sometimes hard to accept. People make things up without even meaning to. What happened to Lyda? The radio didn't say much except that her body'd been found. I can't tell you how shocked I was. It's horrible."

I told her the details, sparing little. Ordinarily I'd downplay the particulars, not wanting to pander to the public appetite for the gruesome specifics of violent death. With Ava, I felt the reality of the situation might loosen her tongue. She listened to me with distaste, her dark eyes filling with anxiety.

"Do you mind if I smoke?" she said.

"Not at all. Go ahead."

She opened the bottom drawer of her desk and pulled out her handbag. Her hands were trembling as she shook a Winston from the pack and lit it. "I've been trying to quit, but I just can't help myself. I stopped at the drugstore and picked up a pack on the way to work. I smoked two in the car." She took a deep drag. One of the engineers peered around from his drafting table as the smoke drifted toward him. She had her back turned so she missed the look of annoyance that crossed his face.

"Let's go back to Hugh's death," I said.

"I can't help you much with that. I'd only been with the company a few weeks before he died, so I hardly knew the man."

"Was there an office manager before you?"

Ava shook her head. "I was the first, which meant the office was a mess. Nobody did a thing. Filing alone was piled up to here. There was just one secretary. Heather was the receptionist, but all the day-to-day business was handled by Woody himself, or one of the engineers. It took me six months to get things squared away. Engineers may be obsessive, but not when it comes to paperwork." She took another drag, then tapped the small accumulation of ash from the end of her cigarette.

"What was the atmosphere like at the time? Was it tense? Was anybody caught up in an office dispute? A feud of any kind?"

"Not that I ever heard. Woody bid on a government contract and we were trying to get organized for that...."

"Which entailed what?"

"Routine office procedure. Forms to be filled out, clearances, that kind of thing."

"What happened to the bid?"

"Nothing. The whole thing fell through. Woody had a heart attack, and after he died, Lance let the matter drop."

"What was it they were bidding on? I wonder if that ties in."

"I don't remember what it was. Hold on. I'll ask." Ava turned and scanned the room. John Salkowitz was passing through, blueprint in hand, apparently on his way to the rear of the plant. "John? Could I ask you about something over here?"

He detoured toward us, his expression clouding with concern when he caught sight of me. "What's the story on Lyda Case? My wife just called and said she heard about her on the news."

I gave him the shorthand version, putting it together with the question at hand. "I'm still trying to figure out how it ties into this business with Lance. There's gotta be a connection somewhere."

"He's not seriously being accused of insurance fraud, is he?"

"Looks that way. Along with me, I might add."

"Appalling," he said. "Well. I don't see how it could have any bearing on the contract we bid on, but I'll fill you in. We get a little trade paper called *Commerce Daily*, published by the government. It was Hugh's job to check it for any contract available for bid that might apply to us. He found one under heating equipment, requesting bids on a furnace for processing beryllium, which is used in the making of nuclear bombs and rocket fuel. It's hazardous work. We'd have had to build in a whole new venting system to accommodate CAL-OSHA, but if we got it, we'd have been in a position to bid on future contracts. Woody felt it was worth the expense of retooling. Not all of us agreed with him, but he was a shrewd man and you had to trust his instincts. Anyway, that's what we were going after."

"What would it have been worth to the company?"

"Quarter million bucks. Half a million maybe. More, of course, in the long run, if we bid on future work."

"What was the status of the bid when Hugh died?"

"I don't know. I guess we were gearing up. I know he'd gone down to the Federal Building in Los Angeles to pick up all the paperwork. Since it was the Department of Defense, we were going to need a company clearance, plus individual clearances. Hugh's death really didn't have much effect, but when Woody died on top of that, we lost heart."

"Could the company have handled the work with both men gone?"

"Probably, but of course Lance was just taking over, getting his feet wet. I guess we dropped the ball, but that's all it amounted to. We weren't out anything. We might not have been low bidder anyway, so it's all speculative."

"What about bids since?"

"That's an aspect of the business we haven't paid much attention to. We're on overload half the time as it is."

I looked at him, truly stumped. "And you don't think it's relevant?"

"If it is, I don't see how."

"Thanks for your time, at any rate. I may need to get back to you."

"Sure thing," he said.

Ava and I chatted a while longer, but the conversation seemed unproductive, except for one minor point. She mentioned, in passing, that Ebony had attended the memorial services for Hugh Case.

"I thought she was in Europe, married to some playboy named Julian."

"She was, but they came back to the States to visit every six months or so."

"How long had she been in town? Do you have any idea?"

Her look was blank. "Can't help you there. I was too new myself to sort out what was normal in that family."

"Maybe I can check it out," I said. "Thanks for your help."

Driving back into town, I was kicking myself. I'd falsely assumed that neither Ebony nor Bass could have been tied in to Hugh's death as both of them were out of the picture at the time—Ebony in Europe, Bass in New York. Now I wasn't sure. I stopped at a public phone booth and called the Woods' house. The maid answered. I was willing to talk to just about any member of the family, but that turned out to be problematic. Mrs. Wood was resting and had asked not to be disturbed. Ebony and Ashley had gone to the Santa Teresa Monument Company to look at memorial tablets for Miss Olive's gravesite. Bass was due back at any minute. Did I care to leave my name and number? I decided to hold off on that. I said I'd call again later and hung up without identifying myself. I hauled more change from my handbag and tried Darcy at the office. She had nothing new to report. I brought her up-to-date and we commiserated briefly on the blanks we were drawing. She said she'd leave word on my answering machine if anything developed. Fat chance, I thought.

I returned to my car and sat there at the curb. I poured the rest of the hot coffee into the thermos lid, sipping it with care. I was getting closer to the truth. I could feel it in my bones. I felt like I was circling, the orbits getting tighter as I approached the central point. Sometimes all it took was one tiny nudge and everything fell into place. But the balance was delicate, and if I pushed too hard, I might barge right past the obvious.

I didn't have that many trees to shake. I screwed the lid on the thermos and tossed it in the back seat. I started up the car and drove back into town again. Maybe Andy's mistress had heard from him. That might help. Fifteen minutes later, I was standing at her door, knocking politely. I wasn't sure if she worked or not. She was home, but when she opened the door, she didn't seem that thrilled to see me.

"Hi," said I. "I'm still looking for Andy and I wondered if you'd heard from him."

She shook her head. Some people think they can lie

to me that way, without forming the actual falsehood with their lips. It's apparently part of an inner conviction that if they don't speak the lie aloud, they won't burn in hell.

"He never checked in to let you know he was okay?"

"I just said that, didn't I?"

"Seems odd to me," I remarked. "I half expected him to drop you a note, or make a quick phone call."

"Sorry," she said.

There was a tiny silence wherein she was hoping to close the door and be done with me.

"How'd he get that account anyway?" I asked.

"What account?"

"Wood/Warren. Did he know Lance pretty well or was it someone else in the family?"

"I have no idea. Anyway, he's the claims manager. I don't know that he sold the policy in the first place."

"Oh. Somehow I thought he did. I thought I saw that somewhere on one of the forms we processed. Maybe it was his account before he got promoted to claims manager."

"Are you through asking questions?" she said snappishly.

"Uh, well, actually I'm not. Did Andy know any of the Woods personally? I don't think you told me that."

"How do I know who he knew?"

"Just thought I'd take a flyer," I said. "It puzzles me that you're not worried about him. The man's been gone, what, four days? I'd be frantic."

"I guess that's the difference between us," she said.

"Maybe I'll check out at his place again. You never know. He might have stopped back at the apartment to pick up his clothes and his mail."

She just stared at me. There didn't seem a lot left to say.

"Well, off I go," I said, cheerfully. "You've really been a peach."

Her goodbye was brief. Two words, one of which started with the letter "F." Her mama apparently hadn't taught her to be ladylike any more than mine had taught me. I decided to drive back out to Andy's place because, frankly, I couldn't think what else to do.

23

I headed out to the condominium complex where Andy lived, thrilled that I wasn't going to have to type up a report on the day's events. The truth was, I had no plan afoot, no strategy whatever for wrapping this business up. I didn't have a clue to what was going on. I was driving randomly from one side of the city to the other, hoping that I could shake something loose. I was also avoiding my apartment, picturing the gendarmes at my door with a warrant for my arrest. Andy represented one of the missing links. Someone had designed an elaborate scheme to discredit Lance and eliminate two key engineers at Wood/Warren. Andy had facilitated the frame-up, but once Olive was blown to kingdom come, he must have decided to blow town himself. If I could pinpoint the connection between Andy Motycka and the person who'd suckered him into it, then maybe I could figure out what the payoff was.

The electronic gates at The Copse stood open, and I passed through without attracting armed guards or vicious dogs. A tall, fair-haired woman in a jumpsuit was walking an apricot poodle, but she scarcely looked at me. I parked my car in the slot Andy had left in the wake of his departure. I trotted up to the second-floor landing and let myself in with the front-door key, which I knew from past experience he kept hidden on the cornice above the front door. I confess I sniffed the air apprehensively as I let myself in, mindful that Andy might have ended up in the same state as Lyda Case. The apartment smelled benign and the dust that had settled on the empty book-shelves attested to the fact that no one had been here for days.

I did a quick pass through the apartment to make sure it was unoccupied. I opened the rear sliding-glass door, peered into each bedroom, then returned to the living room, where I drew the front drapes. I moved through the daylight gloom with curiosity. Andy lived on such spartan terms that his place had looked abandoned even when he was in residence. Now, however, the emptiness had the aura of a vacant lot, the wall-to-wall carpeting littered with paper scraps. In situations like this, I always long for the obvious—cryptic messages, motel receipts, annotated itineraries indicating where the missing might have gone. The various bits of paper on Andy's floor were none of the above and I was no wiser for having crawled around on my hands and knees reading them. The business of private investigation is fraught with indignities.

The medicine cabinet in his bathroom had been cleared out. Shampoo, deodorant, and shaving gear were gone. Wherever he was, he'd be clean-shaven and smell good. In his bedroom, all of the dirty clothes were gone and the blue plastic crates had been emptied of their contents. One tatty pair of boxer shorts remained, wild with fuchsia exclamation marks. I'm always amazed by men's underwear. Who could guess such things by looking at their sober three-piece suits? He'd left behind his bicycle, rowing machine, and the remaining moving cartons. There were still a few poorly folded sheets in the linen closet, one package of pizza rolls in the freezer. He'd taken the bottle of aquavit and the Milky Way bars, perhaps anticipating his life on the road as an endless round of sugar and alcohol abuse.

The card table was still in place, the answering machine on top, aluminum lawn chairs pulled up as if he'd had dinner guests for a banquet of Lean Cuisine. I sat down, propped my feet up on the adjacent chair and surveyed Andy's makeshift office. There were still some pencils, a scratch pad, gummy white-out, unpaid bills. His answering machine turned out to be a duplicate of mine. I reached over and flipped open the side panel where the "oft-dialed" numbers were penned in. Of the sixteen spaces allotted, only six were filled. Andy was real imaginative. Fire, Police, California Fidelity, his ex-wife, a liquor store, and a pizza joint with free delivery.

I stared at the display on the answering machine, thinking about the features on this model. Carefully I pressed the asterisk button to the left of 0. On my machine, the redials the last number called. With a flurry of notes up and down the scale, the machine redialed, the number displayed in green. It was vaguely familiar and I made a note of it. The line began to ring. Three times. Four.

Someone picked up. There was a whir and a pause as a machine on the far end of the line came to life.

"Hello. This is Olive Kohler at 555-3282. Sorry we're not here to take your call. I'm out at the supermarket at the moment, but I should be home at four-thirty or so. If you'll leave your number and a message, I'll get back to you as soon as I return. If you're calling with confirmations for the New Year's Party, just leave your name and we'll see you this evening. 'Bye for now."

I could feel my heart thump. No one had changed the message since Olive's death, and there she was again, perpetually hung up in New Year's Eve day, leaving a verbal note before she went off to shop for the party that would never take place.

Perversely, I pressed the asterisk again. Four rings, and Olive picked up, her voice sounding hollow, but full of life. She was still going out to shop for the New Year's party, still requesting the caller's name, telephone number, and a message. " 'Bye for now," she said. I knew if I called a hundred times, she'd still be saying " 'Bye for now" without ever knowing how final that farewell would be.

Andy's last phone call had been to her, but what did it mean? A tiny jolt of memory shot through me. I saw Olive unlock the front door, her arms loaded with groceries, the package bomb, addressed to Terry, resting on top. As the door swung open, the telephone had rung and that's why she'd tossed the package in such haste. Maybe Andy knew the package was waiting on the doorstep and had called to warn them off.

I closed up Andy's apartment, got in my car, and headed back to town, detouring en route to wolf down a fast-food lunch. The Kohlers' house was the next logical stop, but as I turned into the lane, I noticed a whisper of anxiety. I had not, of course, been to the house since the bomb went off and I was not eager to live through the trauma again. I parked in front and gingerly stepped through the gap in the hedge where the gate had been. Only the posts remained now, the hardware twisted where the force of the bomb had wrenched the heavy wooden gate from its hinges. In places the blast had left the shrubbery completely bald.

I approached the house. Plywood sheets and two-by-fours had been nailed across the yawning opening where the front door had been. One of the columns supporting the porch roof had been snapped in two and a clumsy six-by-six had been rigged up in its place. The walkway was scorched, grass sparse and blackened. Sawhorses and warning signs cautioned folks to use the rear. I could still detect the faint briny smell of the cocktail onions that had littered the yard like pearls.

I felt my gaze drawn irresistibly to the spot where Olive had lain in a tumbled, bloody heap. I remembered then how I'd offered to carry the package for her since her arms were loaded with grocery bags. Her casual refusal had saved me. Death sometimes passes us by that way, with a wink, a nod, and an impish promise to return for us at another time. I wondered if Terry felt the same guilt I did that she'd died in our stead.

I was holding my breath, and I shook my arms out like a runner in the middle of a race, moving then toward the rear of the house. I knocked at the back door, cupping my hand against the glass to see if

Terry or the housekeeper was home. There was no sign of anyone. I waited, then knocked again. In the lower right-hand corner of the kitchen window there was an alarm-company decal that said "Armed Response" across the bottom. I stepped back so I could scan the area. There was a red light showing on the alarm panel to the right, indicating that the system was armed. If the light was green, any burglar would know it was safe to start work. I took a business card from my handbag and sketched a quick note, asking Terry to call me when he got home. I got in my car again and drove to the Woods'. For all I knew, he was still there.

Early-afternoon sunlight poured down on the house with its dazzling white facade. The grass was newly cut, as short and densely green as wool-pile carpeting. Beyond the bluffs, the ocean was an intense navy blue, the surface feathered with whitecaps that suggested a strong wind coming off the water. The hot desert wind was blowing at my back, and the palms tossed restlessly where the two met. Ash's little red sports car was parked in the circular driveway, along with a BMW. There was no sign of Terry's Mercedes. I walked around the house to the long, low brick porch on the seaward side and rang the bell.

The maid let me in and left me in the foyer while she went to fetch Miss Ebony. I had asked for Ash, but I was willing to take pot luck. I wished fervently that I had a theory, but this was still a fishing expedition. I couldn't be far from understanding the truth, but I had no clear concept what the revelation might be. Under the circumstances, all I knew to do is persist, plowing through. Bass was the only member of the family I was hoping to avoid. Not that it made any difference at that point, but pride is pride. Who wants to make small talk with your ex-spouse's lover? I had to be careful that my sense of injury didn't get in the way of spotting his role in this.

"Hello, Kinsey."

Ebony was standing at the bottom of the stairs, her pale oval face as smooth as an egg, expressionless, composed. She was wearing a shirtwaist dress of black silk that emphasized her wide shoulders and slim hips, the long shapely legs. Her red spike heels must have added five inches to her height. Her hair was skinned back from the taut bones of her face. A swath of blusher on each cheek suggested high stress instead of the good health it was meant to convey. In the family mythology, she was the thrill-seeker, addicted to the sort of treacherous hobbies that can spell early death: sky-diving, helicopter skiing, climbing the sheer faces of impossible cliffs. In the family dynamic, maybe she'd been designated to live recklessly, just as Bass lived with vanity, idleness, and self-indulgence.

I said, "I thought we should talk."

"About what?"

"Olive's death. Lyda Case is dead, too."

"Bass told me that."

My smile had a bitter feeling to it. "Ah. Bass. How did he get involved? Somehow I get the feeling you might have put a call through to him in New York."

"That's right."

"Dirty pool, Ebony."

She shrugged, undismayed. "It's your own damn fault."

"*My* fault?"

"I asked you what was going on and you wouldn't say. It's my family, Kinsey. I have a right to know."

"I see. And who thought about bringing Daniel into it?"

"I did, but Bass was the one who tracked him down. He and Daniel had an affair years ago, until Bass broke it off. There was unfinished business between them. Daniel was more than happy to accommodate him in the hopes of rekindling the fires."

"Selling me out in the process," I said.

She smiled slightly, but her gaze was intent. "You didn't have to agree, you know. You must have had some unfinished business of your own or you wouldn't have been suckered in so easily."

"True," I said. "That was smart. God, he nicked right in there and gave you everything, didn't he?"

"Not quite."

"Oh? Something missing? Some little piece of the scheme incomplete?"

"We still don't know who killed Olive."

"Or Lyda Case," I said, "though the motive was probably not the same. I suspect she somehow figured out what was going on. Maybe she went back through Hugh's papers and came up with something significant."

"Like what?"

"Hey, if I knew that, I'd probably know who killed her, wouldn't I?"

Ebony stirred restlessly. "I have things to do. Why don't you tell me what you want."

"Well, let's see. Just in rambling around town, it occurred to me that it might help to find out who inherits Olive's stock."

"Stock?"

"Her ten voting shares. Surely, those wouldn't be left to someone outside the family. So who'd she leave 'em to?"

For the first time she was genuinely flustered and the color in her cheeks seemed real. "What difference does it make? The bomb was meant for Terry. Olive died by mistake, didn't she?"

"I don't know. Did she?" I snapped back. "Who stands to benefit? You? Lance?"

"Ash," came the voice. "Olive left all her stock to

her sister Ashley." Mrs. Wood had appeared in the upstairs hall. I looked up to see her clinging to the rail, the walker close by, her whole body trembling with exertion.

"Mother, you don't have to concern yourself with this."

"I think I do. Come to my room, Kinsey." Mrs. Wood disappeared.

I glanced at Ebony and then pushed past her and went up the stairs.

24

We sat in her room near French doors that opened onto a balcony facing the sea. Sheer curtains were pulled across the doorway, billowing lazily in a wind that smelled of salt. The bedroom suite was dark and old, a clumsy assortment of pieces she and Woody must have salvaged from their early married years: a dresser with chipped veneer, matching misshapen lamps with dark-red silk shades. I was reminded of thrift-store windows filled with other people's junk. Nothing in the room would qualify as "collectible," much less antique.

She sat in a rocker upholstered in horsehair, frayed and shiny, picking at the fabric on the arms of the chair. She looked awful. The skin on her face had been blanched by Olive's death and her cheeks were mottled with liver spots and threaded with visible capillaries. She looked as though she'd lost weight in the last few days, the flesh hanging in pleats along her upper arms, her bones rising to the surface like a living lesson in anatomy. Even her gums had shrunk away from her teeth, the aging process suddenly as visible as in time-lapse photography. She seemed weighed down with some as yet unidentified emotion that left her eyes red-rimmed and lusterless. I didn't think she'd survive it, whatever it was.

She had clumped her way back to her room with the aid of her walker, which she kept close to her, holding on to it with one trembling hand.

I sat in a hard-backed chair near hers, my voice low. "You know what's going on, don't you?" I said.

"I think so. I should have spoken up sooner, but I so hoped my suspicions were groundless. I thought we'd buried the past. I thought we'd moved on, but we haven't. There's so much shame in the world as it is. Why add to it?" Her voice quavered and her lips trembled as she spoke. She paused, struggling with some inner admonition. "I promised Woody I wouldn't speak of it again."

"You have to, Helen. People are dying."

For a moment, her dark eyes sparked to life. "I know that," she snapped. The energy was short-lived, a match flaring out. "You do the best you can," she went on. "You try to do what's right. Things happen and you salvage what's left."

"Nobody's blaming you."

"I blame myself. It's my fault. I should have said something the minute things began to go wrong. I knew the connection, but I didn't want to believe it, fool that I am."

"Is this related to Woody?"

She shook her head.

"Who then?"

"Lance," she whispered. "It started with him."

"Lance?" I said, disconcerted. It was the last name I expected to hear.

"You'd think the past could be diffused . . . that it wouldn't have the power to affect us so long after the fact."

"How far back does this go?"

"Seventeen years, almost to the day." She clamped her mouth shut, then shook her head again. "Lance was a hellion in his teens, rebellious and secretive. He and Woody clashed incessantly, but boys do that. Lance was at an age when *of course* he had to assert himself."

"Ash says he had a couple of scrapes with the law back then."

She stirred impatiently. "He was constantly in trouble. 'Acting out' they call it now, but I didn't think he was a bad boy. I still don't. He had a troubled adolescence. . . ." She broke off, taking a deep breath. "I don't mean to belabor the point. What's done is done. Woody finally sent him off to military school, and after that he went into the army. We hardly saw him until he came home that Christmas on leave. He seemed fine by then. Grown up. Mature. Calm and pleasant and civil to us both. He became interested in the company. He talked about settling down and learning the business. Woody was thrilled." She fumbled in her pocket for a handkerchief, which she pressed to her lips, blotting the film of perspiration that had formed like dew.

So far she wasn't telling me a thing I didn't already know. "What happened?"

"That year . . . when Lance came home and things were going so well . . . that year . . . it was New Year's Day. I remember how happy I was things were off to such a good start. Then Bass came to us with the most preposterous tale. Somehow, in my heart, I suppose I've always blamed him. He spoiled everything. I've never really forgiven him, though it was hardly his fault. Bass was thirteen then. Sly. He knew about wickedness even at that age and he enjoyed it all so very much."

Still does, I thought. "What did he tell you?"

"He said he'd walked in on Lance. He came straight to us with that sneaky look in his eyes, pretending to be so upset when he knew exactly what he was about. At first, Woody didn't believe a word of it."

"He walked in on Lance doing what?"

There was a silence and then she pushed on, her

voice dropping so low I was forced to lean closer. "With Olive," she whispered. "Lance and Olive. In her room on the bed. She was sixteen and so beautiful. I thought I'd die of the shame and embarrassment, the loathing at what was going on. Woody was crazed. He was in a towering rage. Lance swore it was innocent, that Bass misunderstood, but that was nonsense. Absurd to think we'd believe any such thing. Woody beat Lance to within an inch of his life. A fearful beating. I thought he'd kill him. Lance swore it only happened once. He swore he'd never lay another hand on her and he honored that. I know he did."

"That's when Olive was sent away to boarding school," I said.

Helen nodded.

"Who else knew about the incident?"

"No one. Just the five of us. Lance and Olive, Bass and Woody and me. Ebony was off in Europe. Ash knew something dreadful had happened, but she never knew what it was."

There was a silence. Helen smoothed the frayed fabric on the arm of the rocker where she'd picked strands loose. She glanced at me. Her expression seemed tinged with guilt, like an old dog that's piddled somewhere you haven't discovered yet. There was more, something she didn't want to own up to.

"What's the rest?" I asked. "What else?"

She shook her head, her cheeks turning pink in patches.

"Just tell me, Helen. It can't matter now."

"Yes, it does," she whispered. She'd begun to weep. I could see her clamp down, forcing her feelings back into the box she'd kept them in all these years.

I waited so long that I didn't think she meant to finish. Her hands began to shake in a separate dance of their own, a jitterbug of anxiety.

Finally she spoke. "Lance was lying about the two of them. It had gone on for years. Woody never knew, but I suspected as much."

"You suspected Lance was abusing her and you never interfered?"

"What could I say? I had no proof. I kept them away from each other whenever I could. He'd go off to summer camp. She'd stay with friends of ours in Maine. I never left them alone in the house. I hoped it was a phase, something that would disappear of its own accord. I thought if I called attention to it . . . I don't know what I thought. It was so unspeakable. A mother doesn't sit a boy down and discuss such things. I didn't want to pry, and Olive denied the slightest suggestion that anything was amiss. If she'd come to me, I'd have stepped in. Of course I would, but she never said a word. She might have been the one who initiated the contact for all I knew."

"How long did this go on?" I was having a hard

time keeping the judgment out of my voice, afraid if she sensed the full range of my outrage, she'd clam up.

"Lance was obsessed with her almost from infancy. He was five when she was born and I was so relieved, you see, that he didn't resent her. It was just him and Ebony until Olive came along. He'd been the baby so I was delighted he seemed taken with her. It must have started as childish curiosity and advanced to something else. It did end once they were discovered. They could hardly tolerate each other's company these past few years, but by then the damage had been done. She had terrible problems."

"Sexual problems, I'd assume."

Helen nodded, cheeks coloring. "She also suffered deep depressions that would go on for months. All she did was run, run, run. Anything to escape the feelings. Play and spend. Spend and play. That's how she lived."

Rapidly I sorted through all the things I'd been told, processing the trivia I'd picked up in passing. "Olive said she and Bass had a falling-out when he was home for Thanksgiving. What was that about?"

"Something silly. I don't even remember now what the subject matter was. One of those ridiculous spats people get into when they've drunk too much. Bass was furious and wanted to get back at her, but it wasn't *about* anything. Petty temper, that's all."

I watched her carefully, making my mind a blank, trying to let the sense of this filter in. It had started with Lance, with Wood/Warren, talk of a takeover, evidence of insurance fraud. Someone had set Lance up and I'd been caught in the same trap. When Olive died, I'd assumed it was business-related, an accident. It was meant to look like that, but it wasn't. I felt the answer leap at me, so obvious once I knew what had gone on. "Oh shit," I said. "Bass told Terry, didn't he?"

"I think so," she said, almost inaudibly. "I don't think Terry's like the rest of us. He's not a well man. He doesn't seem right to me. Even when they met, he seemed 'off' somehow, but he was crazy about Olive. . . ."

" 'Obsessed' is the word I've heard applied," I broke in. "That he worshiped the ground she walked on."

"Oh, he adored her, there's no doubt of that. It was just what she needed and I thought it would all work out. She had such a low opinion of herself all her life. She couldn't seem to sustain a relationship until Terry came along. I thought she deserved a little happiness."

"You mean because she was 'damaged goods,' don't you? Tainted by what Lance had done."

"Well, she *was* tainted. Who knows what bestial appetites Lance had wakened in her?"

"That was hardly *her* fault."

"Of course not, but what nice boy was ever going

to look at her if the truth came out? Terry seemed like a godsend."

"So the two of you decided not to say anything to him."

"We never spoke of it between us," she said tartly, "so we could hardly speak of it to him. Why stir up trouble when everything was going so well?"

I got up abruptly and went to the phone, dialing Lieutenant Dolan's number at the Santa Teresa PD. The clerk said she'd put me through and I waited for Dolan's line to ring. Helen was right. What was done was done. There wasn't any point in blaming Bass. If anything, the blame lay with Helen and Woody. Olive died because Helen was too bloody polite to deal with the truth.

"Where's Terry now?" I said to Helen over my shoulder.

She was weeping openly. It seemed a little late for tears, but I didn't say so. "He was here a short while ago. He's on his way home."

When Dolan answered, I identified myself and laid it out for him, chapter and verse.

"I'll have him picked up for questioning," Dolan said. "We'll get a warrant so we can search the premises. He put that bomb together somewhere."

"He might have assembled it at work."

"We'll check that," he said. "Hang on." He put his hand across the mouth of the receiver and I could hear him issue an order to someone else in the room. He came back on the line. "Let me tell you what we have on this end. We got a match on the prints we lifted from the rental car Lyda Case was found in. They belong to a fellow named Chris Emms, who was charged with the murder of his foster mother twenty years ago. Blew her up with a package bomb he sent through the mail. The jury brought in a verdict of temporary insanity."

"Oh geez, I get it. No prison for him."

"Right. He was committed to the state hospital at Camarillo and escaped after eighteen months."

"And he was never picked up?"

"He's been free as a bird. I just talked to one of the staff docs and they're hunting up the old records to see what else they have on him."

"Was he really nuts or faking it?"

"Anybody who does what he did is nuts."

"Will you let the family know as soon as he's in custody?"

"Will do. I'll send somebody over in the meantime just in case he decides to come back."

"You better beef up security at Wood/Warren, too. He may make a try for Lance."

"Right," Dolan said. He broke off the connection.

I left Helen huddled in the rocker. I went downstairs, looking for Ebony, and told her what was going on. When I let myself out, she was on her way upstairs to see her mother. I couldn't imagine what they'd talk about. I had a flash of Olive sailing through the air, flying to oblivion. I just couldn't shake the image. I drove home feeling low, my perpetual state these days. I get tired of digging around in other people's dirty laundry. I'm sick of knowing more about them than I should. The past is never nice. The secrets never have to do with acts of benevolence or good deeds suddenly coming to light. Nothing's ever resolved with a handshake or a heart-to-heart talk. So often, humankind just seems tacky to me, and I don't know what the rest of us are supposed to do in response.

Under the bandages, my burns were chafed and fiery hot, throbbing dully. I glanced at myself in the rearview mirror. With my hair singed across the front and my eyebrows gone, I looked startled somehow, as if unprepared for the sudden conclusion to the case at this point. Quite true. I hadn't had time to process events. I thought about Daniel and Bass. Mentally I had to close the door on them, but it felt like unfinished business, and I didn't like that. I wanted closure, surcease. I wanted peace of mind again.

I pushed through the gate, pulling mail out of the box as I passed. I let myself into my place, and slung my handbag on the couch. I felt a desperate need to take a bath, symbolic as it was. It was only 4:00 in the afternoon, but I was going to scrub up and then go pound on Rosie's door. It was Tuesday and she was bound to be back in business by now. My neighborhood tavern usually opens at 5:00, but maybe I could sweet-talk her into letting me in early. I needed a heavy Hungarian dinner, a glass of white wine, and someone to fuss at me like a mother.

I paused at my desk and checked my answering machine. There were no messages. The mail was dull. Belatedly, I registered the fact that my bathroom door was closed. I hadn't left it that way. I never do. My apartment is small and the light from the bathroom window helps illuminate the place. I turned my head and I could feel the hair rise on the back of my neck. The knob rotated and the door swung open. That portion of the room was in shadow at that hour of day, but I could see him standing there. My spinal column turned to ice, the chill radiating outward to my limbs, which I couldn't will to move. Terry emerged from the bathroom and circled the couch. In his right hand he had a gun pointed right at my gut. I felt my hands rise automatically, palms up, the classic posture of submission guns seem to inspire.

Terry said, "Oops, you caught me. I expected to be gone by the time you got home."

"What are you doing here?"

"I brought you a present." He made a gesture toward the kitchenette.

Trancelike, I turned to see what he was pointing to.

On the counter was a shoe box wrapped in Christmas paper, white HO HO HO's emblazoned on a dark-green background with a cartoon Santa swinging from each O. A preformed red satin bow was stuck to the lid. Surprise, surprise. Terry Kohler wanted me to have a box of death.

"Nice," I managed, though my mouth was dry.

"Aren't you going to open it?"

I shook my head. "I think I'll just leave it where it is. I'd hate to give it a bump."

"This one's on a timer."

I managed to loosen my jaw, but I couldn't form any words. Where had I put my gun? My mind was washed absolutely blank. I reached for the edge of my desk, supporting myself with my fingertips. Bombs are loud. The end is quick. I cleared my throat. "Sorry to interrupt you," I said. "Don't stick around on my account."

"I can stay for a minute. We could have a little chat."

"Why kill me?"

"It seemed like a good idea," he said mildly. "I thought you might like to go out with a bang, as opposed to a you-know-what."

"I'm surprised you didn't try for Lance."

"I have a package just like it in the car for him."

Probably in the bottom of my handbag, I thought. I'd meant to take it to the gun shop. Had I stuck it in the briefcase in the back seat of my car? If so, it was still out there and my ass was grass. "Do you mind if I sit?"

He did a quick survey of the area, making sure there weren't any rifles, bullwhips, or butcher knives within range. "Go ahead."

I moved to the couch and sank down without taking my eyes off him. He pulled my desk chair closer and sat down, crossing his legs. He was a nice-looking man, dark and lean, on the slight side. There was nothing in his manner to indicate how nuts he was. How nuts is he? I thought. How far gone? How amenable to reasoning? Would I trade my life for bizarre sexual favors if he asked? Oh sure, why not?

I was having trouble appraising the situation. I was home where I should have been safe. It wasn't even dark out. I really needed to pee, but it sounded like a ploy. And honest to god, I was embarrassed to make the request. It seemed advisable to try opening a dialogue, one of those conversations designed to ingratiate. "What's the timetable here?"

He glanced at his watch. "Ten minutes, more or less. The bomb should go off at four-thirty. I was worried you wouldn't get home in time," he said. "I can reset it, but I don't want to mess the wrapping paper up."

"I can understand that," I said. I checked the clock on my desk. 4:22. I could feel my adrenal gland squirt some juice into my veins. Terry didn't seem concerned. "You seem calm enough," I remarked.

He smiled. "I'm not going to be around when the damn thing goes off. They're dangerous."

"How can you keep me here? You'll have to shoot me first."

"I'll tie you up. I have some rope." I could see then that he had a coil of clothesline he'd tossed on the kitchen floor.

"You think of everything," I said. I wanted him to talk. I didn't want him to tie me up because then I'd be dead for sure. There wasn't going to be any way to hump and thump my way out. No broken glass by which I could saw through my ropes. No knives, no tricks, no miracles. "What if it goes off prematurely?"

"Too bad," he said with mockery, "but you know what Dylan Thomas said. 'After the first death, there is no other.'"

"How does Hugh Case fit in? Do you mind if I ask? I just want to know for the sake of it."

"I don't mind. We don't have anything else to talk about. Hugh was made the security officer after Woody bid on a government contract. We were all going to have to have clearances, but the guy went overboard. Forms, interviews, all these questions. He really took himself seriously. At first I thought it was all a game, but gradually I realized he was coming up with too many penetrating questions. He knew. Of course, he wanted my fingerprints. I stalled as long as possible, but I couldn't refuse. I had to kill him before he told Woody all the sordid details."

"About your mother."

"Foster mother," he corrected.

"Wouldn't somebody else have come up with the same information?"

"I'd figured a way around it, but I needed him out of the way for it to work."

"But you don't know that he was actually onto you."

"Oh, but I do and he was. I destroyed the file he kept at work, but he had a duplicate at home. Talk about a breach of security," he said. "That came to light just recently."

"Lyda found it."

"Now that was your fault. After you flew to Texas, she went through the papers she'd packed up and came across all the data on Chris Emms. She had no idea who he was, but she figured it was someone at the plant. She called me from Dallas and said she had some information Hugh had unearthed. I told her I'd be happy to take a look at it and help her figure out what to do with it. She made me promise not to mention it to Lance since she was so suspicious of him anyway."

"Nice," I said. "And the threat from her . . . you just made that up?"

"Yep."

"And the day we waited at the bird refuge, she was already dead out in front?"

"Righty-o," he said.

"How'd you kill Hugh?"

Terry shrugged indifferently. "Chloral hydrate. Then I strolled in and stole his blood and urine samples so it couldn't be traced."

"Takes nerve," I said.

"It had to be done and I knew I was right. I couldn't have him upsetting my life. What made me so mad afterwards, of course, is it was all for nothing. Olive had a past just as bad as mine. I didn't need to protect myself at all. I could have traded her, tit for tat, if she'd leveled with me."

"You must feel better now that she's gone. She's been paid in full, hasn't she?"

His face clouded. "I should have killed Lance and left her alive. I could have made her life miserable."

"I thought you'd already done that."

"Well, yes, but she didn't suffer nearly enough. And now she's off the hook."

"She did love you," I said.

"So what?"

"So nothing. I guess love doesn't count for much with you." I felt my eyes stray to the clock. 4:25.

"Not when it's based on lies and deceit," he said piously. "She should have told me the truth. She never shared the facts. She let me go right on believing our sex life was all my fault. She made me think I was inadequate when all the time it was her. Sometimes I think about him with his mouth all over her, feeding like a leech, sucking at her everywhere. Disgusting," he said.

"That was a long time ago."

"Not long enough."

"What about Andy Motycka? How'd you persuade him to help?"

"Money and threats. The carrot and the stick. Janice was hosing him for every cent he had. I paid him ten grand. Every time he got nervous, I reminded him that I'd be happy to tell Janice about Lorraine if he tried to back out."

"How'd you find out about her?"

"We've all known each other for years. The four of us went to UCST together before he and Janice got married. This was after I conjured up my new identity, of course. Once I settled on the frame-up, it didn't take much to figure out he was in the perfect position to assist me."

"Did you kill him, too?"

"I wish I had. He ducked out on me, but I'll find a way to lure him back. He's not very smart."

Even with the tinnitus I suffer, I could have sworn I could hear the package bomb ticking merrily. I wet my lips. "Is there really a clock in there? Is that how it works?"

He glanced over at the kitchen counter. "It's not a complicated device. The one for Olive was more elaborate, but I had to make sure it would detonate on impact."

"It's amazing I wasn't killed then."

"Might have simplified things," he said.

I remembered then how he'd bent to recoil the hose lying on the walk. Any excuse to hang back out of range. I was beginning to feel strangely free. The time left was brief, but it was beginning to stretch and sag like a long strand of chewing gum. It seemed absurd to think I'd spend the last minutes of my life discussing trivial points with the man who was going to do me in. Oh hell, why not, you know? I flashed again to my brief flight off the front of Olive's porch while she soared beyond me like a bird. A death like that barely registers. What scared me was surviving, maimed and burned, living long enough to feel the loss of self. Time to make a move, I thought, regardless of the consequences. Once your life is threatened, what else do you have to lose?

I reached for my handbag. "I've got some tranqs in my bag. Do you mind?"

He seemed startled, waving his gun at me. "Leave it where it is."

"I'm a wreck, Terry. I really need a Valium. Then you can tie me up."

"No," he said peevishly. "Don't touch it. I mean it!"

"Come on. Indulge me. It's a small request."

I pulled the bag over and unzipped the top, rooting through the contents until I located the crosshatched ivory handle of my beloved .32 and eased the safety off. He couldn't believe I'd disobey him, but he couldn't seem to think what to do.

As he rose to his feet, I fired through the bottom of the handbag at a range of ten feet without any visible effect. He did jump as if I'd tossed hot gravy on his pants, but I didn't see blood and he didn't topple to the floor as I'd sincerely prayed he would. Instead, he roared to life, coming at me like a mad dog. I pulled the gun out of my purse to fire again, but he was on me, taking me with him to the floor. I saw his fist come at me, and I jerked to the right. The blow landed on my left ear, which rang with pain. I scrambled up, grabbing at the couch for support. I had no idea where my gun had gone, but he was aiming his at me. I snatched up my handbag and swung it. I caught him in the head. The momentum knocked him sideways.

He was blocking my passage to the front door, so I veered the other way, and raced into the bathroom. I slammed the door after me, turned the lock, and hit the floor. He fired twice, bullets zinging through the door like bees. There was no way out. The bathroom window was right in the line of fire and I couldn't see anything to defend myself with. He started kicking at the door, savage blows that splintered the wood on impact. I saw his foot come through the panel and he kicked again. His hand shot through the hole and he fumbled for the lock. I jerked the lid off the toilet tank and cracked him a blow. I heard him yelp and he snatched his hand back through the hole. He fired again, screaming obscenities. Suddenly his face appeared in the gap, eyes roving wildly as he searched for my location. The nose of the gun peered at me. All I could think to do was to protect myself with the tank lid, holding it in front of me like a shield. The bullet slammed into it with a clang, the impact fierce enough to jolt the lid right out of my hands, breaking it in two. Terry started kicking at the door again, but the blows were losing force.

On the other side, I heard him fall heavily. I froze, astonished, gasping for breath. There wasn't time to wait to see if he was faking it. I flipped the lock, shoving at the door, which I couldn't budge. I dropped to my knees and peered at him through the panel. He was flat on his back, his shirt front drenched in red. Apparently I'd wounded him the first time I fired, but it had taken him this long to go down. Blood seeped from him like a slow leak from a worn tire. His chest was still heaving. Above his stertorous breathing I could hear the package ticking like a grandfather clock.

"Get out of the doorway! Terry, move!"

He was unresponsive. The clock on my desk said 4:29.

I shoved as hard as I could, but there was no budging him. I had to get out of there. Frantically I glanced around the room and then grabbed up one half of the broken toilet tank. I smashed at the window. Glass showered out into the front yard, leaving fangs of glass in the frame. I grabbed a towel and wedged it over the glass-ragged sill as I boosted myself up.

The boom from the explosion propelled me through the window, like Superman in full flight. I landed on the grass with a whunk that knocked the wind right out of me. For a moment, I felt the panic of paralysis, wondering if I'd ever breathe again. Debris was raining down around me. I saw a hunk of the roof hover briefly above me, like a UFO. Then it began to tumble and bounce down through the intervening branches of a tree. A cloud of white smoke drifted into view and began to disperse. I angled my gaze up to the wall behind me, which seemed to be intact. My sofa bed was sitting in the driveway with the cushions askew. Perched on the arm was my perky green air fern looking like it had hopped up there by itself. I knew the whole front wall of my apartment would be gone, the interior a shambles, all my possessions destroyed. Lucky I don't have much in this world, I thought.

I was temporarily deaf again, but I was getting used to it. Eventually, with effort, I roused myself and went back inside to see if there was anything of Terry left.

Epilogue

Henry Pitts came home to find a crater where his rental unit had been. He was more distressed about my troubles in his absence than any damage to his property, which was covered by insurance. He has big plans now about building a new studio for me and he's already conferring with an architect. I managed to salvage a few articles of clothing, among them my all-purpose dress and my favorite vest. What could I complain about? As soon as I was on my feet again, I went back to work. Mac arranged for California Fidelity to refurbish my office as a way of making amends for my temporary suspension. Andy Motycka was fired and criminal charges were filed against him. The D.A.'s office probably whited my name out and typed his in its place. Within two days of the explosion, Daniel left with Bass. I can't say I felt much. After all I'd been through, his betrayal seemed beside the point.

In surveying the situation, there was only one other matter that needed cleaning up. I conferred with Lieutenant Dolan in private about the five thousand dollars Terry'd deposited to my account. He advised me to keep my mouth shut, which I did.

—Respectfully submitted,
Kinsey Millhone

About the Author

SUE GRAFTON has written novels, articles, short fiction, a screenplay, and numerous teleplays. She has also lectured on writing at colleges and conferences in Southern California and the Midwest. Her first mystery, *A Is for Alibi*, won an award from the Cloak and Clue Society of Wisconsin and was recently named one of the one hundred favorite mysteries of the century by The Independent Mystery Booksellers Association. *B Is for Burglar* won both the Anthony and the Shamus awards for best novel of 1985, and *C Is for Corpse* won the Anthony Award for Best Novel in 1986. "The Parker Shotgun" won a Macavity Award from the Mystery Readers of America and an Anthony for Best Short Story of 1986. Grafton, who was born in Louisville, Kentucky, now lives in Southern California with her husband, Steven Humphrey.